THE SURVIVAL GAME

For Tom Burke

Who first told me I might need to go to Scotland with a gun

1

MAN AND BOY

I hear them before I see them. Of course. You don't travel ten thousand kilometres without being aware of what's behind you as well as what is ahead.

It's not a large noise. Just the small snap of a twig. Two twigs. And there are lots of twigs here. A thousand twigs, a thousand broken branches, a whole hillside of storm-uprooted trees. And yet I hear those two small snaps. Or rather, I hear the pause that follows them.

The silence of it.

It's the sound of somebody listening to their own footfalls. Their own breathing. Hearing the sudden yelp of air in their chests. I know this, because I too have listened to my own footfalls and held that shout of breath in my chest.

I turn around.

I've learnt this too. It is always better to face whatever it is. Most things can be dealt with. If they can't be dealt with, you can put them in Castle.

There are two of them and they are not soldiers. Not soldiers! Just a man and a boy. Standing quite still. Not trying to hide.

1

Maybe they are too exhausted to hide? I scan them quickly. Life and death these days is often about speed. The boy is young, maybe five years old. I could kill him with my bare hands if necessary, so I turn my attention to the man.

The man is old and thin – though that means nothing, everyone is thin these days. He is dressed in rags. Clothes which, like mine, were probably once brightly coloured but which now have the dirt of travel on them. Travel dirt gets between the fibres of cloth and stays there even if you go to the river to wash. The man and his clothes are now the same colour. The colour of mud.

The man stoops, as if he's carrying an invisible weight on his shoulders. I note his veined hands, his bare legs, his shoeless feet. People who want to live need to take very good care of their shoes. But although the man's head is bowed, his eyes are not. From beneath his mud lids he is looking straight at me.

I take the gun from my belt and point it at him. The gun is a revolver. I got it in the riot at Heathrow DC, five hundred kilometres and twenty-one days ago.

I am much too close to home to be stopped now.

Home.

The gun has no bullets in it. I know this, but the man and the boy do not know this. They would be wise to assume the gun does have bullets. I always assume this about people with guns.

'Halt,' I say.

Halt is a good word. An excellent word. Many more nationalities understand the word 'halt' than understand the word 'stop'. Probably because it's the word the soldiers use. Halt. Halt. Halt. HALT. Put your hands up.

2

The man halts. He puts his hands up. Or rather he puts just one hand up because his other hand is holding on to the child.

I flick the gun muzzle in the direction of the child. My eyes follow the eye of the gun. I allow myself to look at the boy now. He is also thin and dark, perhaps darker than the man, and his eyes are like cups.

Eyes like cups.

The phrase ambushes me, coming as it does in my father's voice. A phrase from one of the Sudanese folk tales he used to read to me when we lived in Khartoum. In the days before the desert, before the soldiers, before

CASTLE.

Remember, Papa said, *whatever happens, the world is beautiful.*

Yes, Papa.

This boy is beautiful: his hunger plumped out by the still-soft skin of the very young. His head is almond-shaped and he has a dark rose-petal mouth. There is a smudge of sunlight on his nose. His deep-as-cups eyes give nothing away.

'Let go of the boy,' I say.

The man loosens his grip immediately, puts a second hand in the air. This is good. It means that the man understands English. Things are always trickier if you have to conduct negotiations like these in sign language. It's also good because I'm a girl and some people think they can take advantage of girls.

'Move apart.' I twitch the gun left and right, indicating the space I want to see between them. The man moves a pace or so from the boy but the boy remains where he is. Not moving

3

himself but not seeking to close the gap either. Just as he did not move when I made the old man let go of his hand, did not grab for the man, or cry out or make any sound at all.

'Good,' I say. 'Good.' And then I add: 'Papers.'

2

PAPERS

Everyone has papers.

Passport. Passeport! Passaporto. Baasaboorka. جواز سفر Pass. Halt. Pass. Halt. HALT. Visa. Fisa! Viza. Visum. Visa. Visa. تأشيرة

My papers are marked 'Global Citizen'.

Global citizen, Papa said, *such a beautiful idea.*

If a little impractical, said Grandmother.

There are many pages in the passport of a Global Citizen. Some are more frightening than others.

The opening pages are factual and – in my case – truthful.

Name: Mhairi Anne Bain.

M.A.B. Mab to my friends. Only I don't have any friends any more. Friends belong to Before.

There is a picture of me. Just my head, of course. My skin is pale and washed, my dark hair brushed, and my blue eyes shine. This picture also belongs to Before. I do not really know what I look like now, but I do know it is not like this.

Age: 14.

This is important. You are safe when you're fourteen. That's why many people – especially people at borders – dispute my age.

'You don't look fourteen,' they say.

This is possible. When you walk a thousand kilometres, your body changes. Your face changes. You change.

'We believe you're fifteen,' they say. 'Or even sixteen.'

Fifteen is the age of consent. At fifteen you can gift bits of your life to other people. One year, two years, ten years. You can give them away. You can promise to die. Check out early, before they kill you anyway at seventy-four. Now I know there are too many people on the planet, I'm not stupid, and I know that the earth is too hot and people are moving. Moving, moving. Moving north. And I know the north can't cope. But here's the thing: I want to live.

My mother said: *Mhairi, you have to stay alive. Promise me. Whatever happens, you have to stay alive.*

Yes, Muma.

'Nobody's forcing you,' the officials say. 'It's a choice. In Equator Central, the planet chooses. She kills with heat, with drought, with famine, with war. But here in the north – we choose. This is civilisation.'

Place of Birth: The Isle of Arran, Scotland.

I wasn't supposed to have been born on the Isle of Arran. I was supposed to have been born in Glasgow, where my parents lived at the time. But every year they visited my grandmother-to-be on the island and I came early. I weighed just 1.7 kilograms. I wasn't strong at all. That was also Before.

The next four pages in my passport are titled: 'Global Citizen: Credits'. There is nothing on these pages yet. But between now and the time I turn fifteen, I have to file something, something that proves what sort of person I am and what I can offer my community. These things (if they can be stamped and verified) may save my life.

The final pages are reserved for 'Global Citizen: Debits'. There are six of these pages. These will also be filled up, but not by me. They are stamped 'Official Use Only'. If I filled them up I would probably have to write:

1: Murderer.

And then I might have to add:

2: Murderer.

For that is – to date – the number of times I have killed.

3

FALL

When I say 'Papers', this is what happens: the man falls.

Before that he sways. Because he has his arms in the air it looks like a dance. He sways a little to the right and then a little to the left, his body making a soft 'S' shape. And then, all at once, his hands begin to flap as if he has suddenly realised things are going wrong and he needs to do something about it. So, he flaps and he jerks for a moment before his legs finally give way, and then, quite quietly and without fuss, he crumples to the ground.

I am still pointing the gun.

But there are no bullets in the gun so this death – if it is a death – is not to do with me. If it's just a faint this is not to do with me either. People faint from hunger. They faint from exhaustion. They do not faint because they are asked for papers. If people fainted when they were asked for papers the roads and the checkpoints and the borders would be strewn with bodies.

Still, I need to be careful. It could be a trick. That would be unsurprising. I observe the boy. He has not – and is not – reacting. Perhaps he has seen this trick before? The man is quite still now;

the only thing about him that moves is the torn flap of his jacket, lifting a little in the wind.

'Kick him,' I say to the boy.

The boy stares at me.

His eyes are like cups.

'Kick him!' I shout and I make a kicking motion with my right foot.

The boy kicks the man, but only lightly, on the shin.

'Harder!'

The boy kicks him harder, quite a vicious little kick.

There must be, I think, quite a few things in that boy's Castle.

4

CASTLE

There is only one way to keep things safe.

In Castle.

Castle has many gates and many walls and many gardens. The walls and the gardens are laid out in concentric circles. Twenty-seven concentric circles to be precise. Twenty-seven is a lucky number. Some of the gardens are very beautiful. They have flowers.

Papa says: *Take time with flowers, look at them closely, flowers are quite remarkable, they are mathematics in colour.*

This is one of the reasons it takes a very long time to go from the outmost garden to the inmost garden, because of the stopping to look at the flowers. Some of the most beautiful flowers have thorns; for instance, the gorse in garden sixteen. The flowers of the gorse are a gaudy, giddy yellow and they smell of coconuts. I always stop to look at these flowers. I think of them as the flowers of my childhood, note how the yellow petals are always just that little bit shorter than the green thorn spikes which surround them.

Headway is also slow because of the gates. The gates are all at different compass points in the circular walls and they shift constantly. You will never find a gate in precisely the same place as you found it the last time. This means a great deal of searching, although, to be fair, you can just follow the wall round. And then there are the locks. The gate locks are not controlled by iris scan or voice recognition, not even by fingerprint or pass code or card key. No. These locks have real keys made of iron. The sort of keys which come from Before, from out of Papa's storybooks. But progress is still slow because you may not have these keys. You may have lost them. So, sometimes you start off intending to get to Castle but you never arrive. This is usually a good thing.

If you do arrive at Castle, you'll find it's actually a tower. A very tall tower made of stone. There isn't much garden around it at all. It's bleak and dark. The tower has just one door and it's secured with three additional old-fashioned locks. There are three very particular iron keys for these locks and only two of them really work. The third and final key is quite a fiddle. It's extremely difficult to turn and it screams if you try, which makes you want to stop trying. It also reminds you that, if you do get the door open, the screaming will become very much louder.

These are all the obstacles to visiting things which are locked in Castle. Depositing things in Castle is very much simpler. You just say: *CASTLE!* And then the impossible thing that was in your mind flies out and plops straight into the tower like a stone plopping into a still pond. And the concentric rings of water immediately become walls of stone and the screaming stops.

At least for a while.

5

TWO DEATHS

When the boy does his vicious kick, the man's leg moves back and forth and the material of his trousers catches on a spike of broken tree branch. The spike holds the material taut for a moment and then there's a tiny tear as the weight of the man's (unsupported) leg drags downwards. The leg comes to rest. The man makes no attempt to disentangle his trouser leg from the branch.

I've begun to notice the small things as well as the big things in life. The small things can be useful. Today they are telling me that this falling is not a trick after all.

I advance, still pointing the gun (caution always remains advisable) until I'm close enough to see the man's eyes. They have rolled upwards into the sockets. And, close to, the dirt on the breast of his jacket looks as though it might actually be dried blood.

I put my gun away.

The boy – who hasn't once taken his eyes from me – sits down then. Squats down beside the man as a dog might do beside his master. A loyal dog who thinks, given time, the master will revive and the walk will continue again. Maybe this is what has happened before.

It is not going to happen today.

I bend down and begin to search the man's pockets. I search his trouser pockets and then his outside jacket pockets. Nothing. I try to flip open his jacket to search the inside pockets. The job is made more difficult because of the blood. The blood that sticks the man's chest to his shirt and his shirt to the lining of his jacket. Dried blood but not so dry that it doesn't release the smell of metal as I prise the layers apart. Some people have money or jewels sewn into their clothes. Not this man. This man has almost nothing.

This is what he does not have:

He does not have a water container.

He does not have any food.

He does not have a knife.

He does not have a fire flint.

And he does not have papers.

Perhaps he got the chest wound from trying to defend his papers. There are always people who will take your papers. Because all papers, any papers – even fake papers – are better than no papers at all. A person without papers is pretty much dead anyway.

This is what the man does have:

A phone.

It is not a magnetic induction phone, it is not even a solar phone, it's an old-fashioned smart phone. The sort that needs cables to plug into a fixed source of power. The sort that is not worth stealing. The first thing you learn when you travel is not to carry anything inessential. Inessential things just weigh you down. But this not the first old man I've known to refuse to let go of his smart phone. Old people seem to believe that, one day, they will be able to power their smart phones and retrieve images of the people they love.

Or loved.

'He's dead,' I say to the boy. 'He's not getting up.'

The boy stares at me.

Which is when I realise that, actually, this is not one death but two. Because the boy cannot come with me. No. He cannot. Ten-year-old Muhammad made that mistake and it did not end well. It ended in

CASTLE.

However, travelling alone, the boy is unlikely to survive more than a few days.

6

BURIAL

There remains the problem of the dead man.

It is not a good use of my energy to bury him but nor can I leave him exactly where he's fallen, lying here on the hillside where I have chosen to stop for the night. This hillside is a good place. The storm-uprooted trees provide a windbreak and there is a beck with fresh water at the bottom of the hill. I plan on sheltering beneath the highest fallen tree, so I will have a commanding view of the rest of the slope, be able to see – but not be seen. This is important because I heard drones last night. The noise they make is quite distinct. In the Sudan, we called them 'mohars' – mosquitoes – because of the constant low buzzing. Perhaps I should be grateful that, so far, I have only heard spy drones, not the ones which carry guns – or bombs. These are bigger and they don't sound like mosquitoes. They whine and scream like metal being cut with a circular saw. Sometimes I wonder what it would be like to kill someone remotely, sitting safely in a comfy chair in your control centre. Just a quick press on a button like in a video game in Before. I do not think it would feel the same as killing someone with your own hands.

You wouldn't hear the screams, the struggle.

You wouldn't hear that last gurgle for breath.

And you wouldn't have a body to bury.

Only human beings bury their dead, Papa said.

Why do we do that, Papa? I don't remember you explaining. Why not let Nature do the job?

In the desert, when you sat down to rest, the vultures would come and sit with you. This proves vultures are intelligent birds. They got used to finding corpses in the sand and knew it was only a matter of time before you would be one too. And, although they were incorrect about me, they were not incorrect about

CASTLE.

I don't think vultures have come to the north of England but there are certainly crows. And also wild dogs. Papa says: *Every year we lose more animals from the planet.* This does not seem to apply to wild dogs. Wild dogs are on the increase. And, like everyone else, dogs get hungry. The last thing you want on a hillside is a pack of hungry dogs.

One solution would be to consume the man myself. Even now the thought of cooking meat on a little fire makes water spring in my mouth. I have a knife as well as a gun and it would be an easy thing to cut small enough chunks to cook. And it can be of no interest to the man whether he returns to earth through me or a dog or a crow. Or indeed the boy. Although the boy might not wish to eat the flesh of his companion, but that would be his choice. Everyone has to make their own choices now.

But a fire may not be wise tonight. Smoke from a fire gives you away, not just to the drones but also to other people who might like your food – or your papers. Besides, I still have some of the cheese I stole two days ago, and a nub of bread. Better to use the body as decoy. Put it downwind of my shelter so any dogs that come this way will choose the corpse rather than me.

I cannot simply roll the man down the hillside because he will get stuck among the fallen trees. He will have to be lifted and dragged. I test the wind direction with a moistened finger and then I unhitch his trouser leg from the branch spike and grab him under both armpits.

I pull and I drag the man, bump him over branches. Even though I watch where I'm going he gets stuck again. This time the branch spike rips his trousers from knee to ankle. The boy watches the bumpy, spiky progress of his companion from his vantage point at the top of the hill. He doesn't follow us, either to help or hinder.

And he doesn't cry.

Papa says: *Only human beings cry.*

In the desert you get so thirsty you cannot cry. Your body dries up. You have no saliva in your mouth and no tears in your eyes.

Maybe this boy left something of himself in the desert.

I certainly did.

7
MUTE

I leave the body near to the stream, but not so near that it might roll in and contaminate the water. Clean water is precious. This side of the border a stream is called a beck. The other side of the border it is called a burn. This is another apparently small thing which is not small at all. When I come to my first burn, I will be in Scotland.

I refill my water bottle. It's a tin bottle with a screw cap which I have learnt to guard with my life. I routinely fill it whenever I'm near water. The water in this part of England often runs off peat hills and so it looks brown. But when you cup it in your hands it is pure, translucent, cold and delicious. I do not think I will ever get over the miracle of water. I drink some palm-cupped water – even though I am not thirsty.

Thirst is not something you forget.

Then I make my way back up the hillside. The boy sits watching me from the triangle of space beneath the trunk of the largest uprooted tree on the slope. My tree. The storm-uprooted tree under which I propose to spend the night. Storms are one of the penalties the north pays for the increase in global temperatures.

But storms pass. Unlike the heat in Equator Central. The storm that uprooted this huge tree must have been particularly violent. The tree lies on the hillside like a gigantic mushroom, the trunk its stalk and its gills the giant circle of earth and roots torn from the ground.

When I get closer I see that the boy has cleared the earth beneath the tree trunk: moved branches, pushed away twigs, swept it flat. Clearly, it is not the first time he has had to seek shelter where there is none. He has even, I think (although I cannot be sure), removed some stones.

My space now appears to be his space.

Only smaller. A one-person boy-sized space.

In Before, I would have laughed.

I get down on my knees and begin to clear a slightly larger space. He watches me as I push branches further out, twig-sweep the earth and then check for stones. If you want to sleep, you clear the stones, even the small ones. Small stones seem to increase in size as the night wears on.

So.

It seems we will spend the night together. There is no harm in that. Neither of us can stop tomorrow coming. And then I will walk.

Faster than him.

Eventually, I sit down and unknot my food cloth. This piece of cloth used to be white but now it is grey. The cheese, which has crumbled slightly against the small heel of bread, smells slightly rancid. This surprises me until I realise that it is not the cheese that smells but the boy. I sniff. The boy smells sour, unwashed, a mix of fish and urine and sweat and mould. It's possible, I think, that I smell like this too.

The boy looks at my bread.

He looks at my cheese.

This boy is not my responsibility. Tomorrow I will leave him behind. He will not be able to keep up and, even if he did keep up, he won't make it across the border. He won't get to safety. It is stupid to share resources with people who aren't going to make it.

I eat a bit of bread. A very small bit. I eat a bit of cheese.

The boy watches my mouth. He watches me chew.

But he does not speak.

'What's your name?' I ask.

Silence.

There are other questions I could ask:

Where are you going?

Where have you come from?

What have you seen?

These are not useful questions. Everyone is travelling north, everyone has come from Equator Central. Everyone has seen hardship. When we started on the road, everyone asked these questions, not any more. It's enough to bear one's own hardships, live one's own story.

'My name's Mhairi,' I say. I point at myself. 'Mhairi,' I repeat. I'm surprised to be introducing myself. If you introduce yourself, it implies you are going to have a relationship with the other person and I am not going to have a relationship with this boy. I made this mistake with Muhammad. Although, to be fair, I was never actually introduced to Muhammad. He was just there, the son of my parents' driver. There seems such a short bridge between knowing someone and taking responsibility for them. As I had to do with Muhammad. Just because I was older: fourteen to his ten. It is not a mistake I plan to repeat.

Meanwhile, this boy continues to say nothing.

His eyes betray nothing.

Something occurs to me.

'Open your mouth,' I say.

He opens his mouth. I see his tongue, small and pale pink. 'Stick it out, I say, 'your tongue.'

He sticks it out.

'OK. Enough.' In the desert, they told us that the soldiers sometimes cut out the tongues of children. I've not seen it myself so I don't know if it's true. What is true, is that the boy's silence is not a physical thing, he could obviously speak if he wanted to. So he must be choosing not to speak.

The boy's tongue is still out.

I put a minuscule piece of cheese on it.

Then I knot the rest of the food away.

8

DREAMS

The boy does not chew his cheese, he sucks at it. His mouth and his jaws and his cheeks all move as he sucks, as if the piece of cheese is very much bigger than I know it to be. As if he's having some trouble swallowing it, it's so big. When he's finished, he puts his hand in the pocket of his shorts and extracts a pebble. The pebble is round and grey and about half the size of my thumb. The sort of pebble worn smooth by water. The boy pops the pebble in his mouth as if it was a sweet, looks at me one last time, lies down, curls up (with his back to me) and falls asleep.

Just like that.

I used to think, if you were exhausted enough, you could sleep anywhere. I didn't know then about cold and hunger and dreams.

I believed cold was an outside thing. I didn't know how cold can find its way inside your teeth or make your kidneys shudder. I didn't know how wind can whip your neck or blow so hard beneath your fingernails you think it's actually got beneath your skin. I learnt this in the desert at night. I learnt that, even if you curl up tight with your hands in your armpits, you still can't sleep. Not for any length of time anyway. And there's a difference to a pain that you know will not go away. Cannot go away. At least, not until the morning. Of course, tonight is not such a bitter night. It's just an ordinary north of England, May-time night. Cold with a little damp. Moisture that comes up from the earth as well as down from the sky. Damp is something you get used to.

As for hunger, at first it's only your belly which hurts, it flutters and pangs. Then, as time passes, the gnawing becomes continual and the pain sharpens as the hunger hollows you out as if with knives. EMPTY. EMPTY! Your belly screams, which is when your brain gets involved and then your brain begins to hurt too. But tonight, I am not hungry. This is partly because my stomach has shrunk and partly because I still have food in my food cloth. Having food in my food cloth feeds my brain, keeps it quiet, reminds me that today at least, I cannot starve.

But dreams.

Oh dreams.

Dreams come without warning.

Dreams shout through the locks in Castle.

Dreams vault over stone walls.

Dreams find the perfect key for the final lock in the tower.

Every night I wrestle with dreams. Sometimes dreams stop me having the bravery even to try and sleep.

Of course, I have strategies.

One of them is Concentration. This is what I will use tonight. I focus on the boy, lean over and scrutinise his face.

Oh, Papa!

23

The boy is even more beautiful asleep. In the dusk light, his face is soft, peaceful, and there is a trace of a smile around those rose-petal dark lips. His head has been recently shaved and I can see the strong yet fragile form of his skull. No one shaves a child's head when they travel. Not unless they keep a razor for other reasons. The old man must have loved the boy, I think. Or cared for him anyway, until whatever happened happened. I watch the boy's cheeks suck a little as he breathes around the stone in his mouth. He's not exactly African, but not Arab either. Perhaps he is a Berber. Papa says you find Berber people scattered across all of north Africa; you find them in Morocco, Algeria, Tunisia, Libya, Egypt, Mali, Niger, Mauretania.

'I-Mazigh-en', Papa said, *that's what the Berbers call themselves. It means noble men, free people. It was the Romans who first called them 'Berbers', from 'barbarus' – Barbarians.*

It was last year when Papa said that.

Muma said: *Why don't you tell your daughter useful things?*

Who knows what's useful nowadays? Papa answered.

I see my mind is drifting. It's drifting away from the boy and on to Muma and Papa. But it's night and Muma and Papa often visit at night.

Grandmother Arran (who is Papa's mother) said: *I don't know why your parents got together. They are very unalike.*

This is true. Muma is an engineer and Papa, Papa is – Papa. It is also untrue. For they are both searchers, though they search in different places.

We went to Khartoum because of Muma.

Muma said: *All that sun. All that energy! We have the know-how and they have the raw material. The desert could power the whole world!*

That was Muma's dream. Dreams are slidy things.

Grandmother said: *Hah! And do you think, Catriona, that when you've made the desert bloom, the Sudanese people will thank you and share with the world?*

And Muma said: *We are climate debtors, they are climate creditors. It's only fair.*

Papa said, *You have to believe in the goodness of people, Mother.*

Hmm, said Grandmother. *Good luck with that.* And then, looking hard at her son, she added: *And what are you going to do while your wife harnesses the power of the desert for the benefit of all mankind?*

Papa replied: *I'm going to bring up my daughter.*

And? said Grandmother.

Isn't that enough? Papa said.

Grandmother waited.

So Papa added: *And I'm going to look.*

Look? repeated Grandmother. *At what?*

At everything I can, said Papa. *I'm going to grab the world in all its magnificence.*

These are the things that I bring to my sleeping tonight. The familiar rugs I tuck around myself to ease my fear. When you lie to sleep, you shut your eyes. But your ears, your ears never sleep. Your ears do not have off-buttons. Your ears are always awake. Awake for the dogs and the crows, the twigs and the drones, but also for the voices of the people you love. The voices don't need a power cable to come. The voices come anyway.

I lie on the earth with my eyes shut and my ears open. As well as the voices, I hear the soft rush of the water in the beck, the wind as it catches the dry leaves in the dead trees and also the sound of the boy breathing. The low in-out, the occasional muted suck.

And of course, I cannot not remember the last two people who lay on the ground so close to me. The first, ten-year-old Muhammad. I didn't know him well. Not at first. He was just the son of my mother's driver. I didn't have to know him. But once we found ourselves in the desert together – oh yes. He was a talkative boy, a babbler. Talked when there was nothing to talk about, talked even when it was an effort to talk. Except at night. Lay beside me (it was safer to lie close), quiet and solid as a plank.

The second person was the man. The stranger. The nameless stranger who chose to insert his life into mine that night in the desert at Meroe.

The man who came into the tomb where Muhammad and I were sheltering, breathing his tobacco and his madness. The man who didn't lie like a plank. That's when I learnt that it is not only countries which have borders.

People have borders too.

9

BRICK

You can change things by looking, Papa said.

He showed me this with a coin.

Look at it this way, Papa said, showing me the round, flat side of the coin, the one with the king's head on. *Easy to see immediately what this thing is. It's a coin! No doubt about it. But look at it this way*, and he moved the coin end-on, so it seemed a thin strip of grooved silver. *Not so easy now, is it? Remember, Mhairi, things don't always come with labels on.*

I remember.

I remember the brick I found in the ancient tomb where Muhammad and I sheltered that night in the desert at Meroe.

The night when the stranger came.

It was an adobe brick. Unlike the bricks in this country, adobe bricks are made of mud and baked in the sun. They are beautiful things, with the hand of man still on them. I made an adobe brick once. Knelt in the dirt with some friends of Muhammad's father, men who laughed as they worked. They showed me how to make a small box shape with three bits of skirting board and an old camping sign. They showed me how to mix the mud with straw

27

and moisten it with water from a battered brass kettle. They helped me tamp it down with a ball end of a bed leg. It was a good brick. Strong.

The brick in the tomb in the desert was strong too. In the morning, when it was light again, I looked a lot at that brick. It was a rough, gorgeous thing. Fretted and pitted like the surface of some tiny red planet. Jagged with small stones but smooth where the pieces of straw had been. And there was a thumbprint in it. Right at the corner where the man who made it must have pushed away the wooden supports before he left it to dry in the sun.

Yes, I spent a long time that morning looking at this brick, studying it, concentrating on it. I paid special attention to the slightly darker red-brown tinge it had at that thumbprint corner. The colour of dried blood. But it still didn't look like a murder weapon.

No. Not at all.

It looked like a brick. And that's what I hold in my memory tonight.

Not a murder weapon covered in wet blood.

Of course not.

Just a beautiful dried red adobe brick.

So I sleep.

At last, I sleep.

And – tonight – all the doors in Castle remain locked.

10

TEARS

Often, I wake at sunrise. Today I wake late. I'm stiff and damp. I pull myself to sitting to find the boy is already up. He's sitting cross-legged and drinking from my water bottle.

Nobody drinks from my water bottle without permission.

Nobody.

I grab for the bottle, even though I have yet to wipe my eyes, adjust to the light, see properly. The tin of the bottle rattles against the boy's teeth – but he holds on, holds my blurry gaze over the metal rim.

'Give it me,' I say. 'Now.'

He releases his grip, but too fast and – before I have full possession of the bottle – it jerks between us and an arc of water spews from its throat. The water makes a dark splash on the earth and soaks in immediately.

The water is gone.

At once I'm on my feet. He's only small and I tower over him.

'Don't you ever,' I shout, 'do that again.'

And I hit him full in the face, smack his head.

The boy puts a hand to his burning cheek. Looks up, astonished.

'What sort of idiot are you?' I shout. 'Don't you know anything!'

I am bouncing, bouncing with fury, with spite. I can feel it jagged in my veins. Only it's not about taking the bottle without permission, no, of course not. It's about the water. The water draining away into the earth. The water being –

GONE.

And there I am back in the desert, back on the day when I squatted over the sand trying to produce and then collect just one drip of my own urine. Because that's all there was to drink. My own bitter urine.

'The water,' I scream, 'go and get more water!' And I thrust the bottle back at the boy and I point to the stream, where there are

gallons

and gallons

and gallons of fresh water.

The boy gets up – silently, humbly – and he makes his way down the hillside towards the stream. I watch him go, how he picks his way across and around the bigger branches.

I observe him kneel at the edge of the beck and lower the bottle into the water, taking his time, making sure to fill the bottle completely. I see the twist of his wrist as he screws the bottle top on securely.

My heart begins to slow a little.

Then the boy stands up and he's about to ascend the hill again, when his eye is drawn to the body of his companion and, with a quick glance up at me, he changes direction.

He walks away from me, towards the body. It's only a couple of metres. He stops still, looks a little and drops to his knees.

I start down the hillside then.

I walk fast. I've always walked fast.

The boy is still kneeling when I arrive. Close to the man's head.

The man has eyes like cups.

Red cups.

The dogs haven't come but the crows have. The overnight crows have eaten his eyes.

And the boy is kneeling by the old man's face, pouring clean water into his empty eye sockets. So much water that it's running out, over.

So, although the child is not crying, the man is.

The man is crying a river of red tears.

I take the bottle from the boy's hand – and then I take his hand.

'Come,' I say, pulling him to his feet. 'It's time to walk.'

11

PEOPLE

I head up the hill, but not before I've refilled the water bottle. The boy stumbles behind me, barks his shin on a fallen tree. But he still keeps coming.

I only pause when I get to the top. The day is laid out in front of us. Forty kilometres of undulating landscape under a leaden sky. Few dwellings, no animals, only one road. There are many fewer towns in this northern part of England. This is good. People in towns defend what they have:

- Their food
- Their safety
- Their nanonets
- Their functioning lives

It's not so surprising.

The road is to our left, the west, and on that road, far ahead, small as ants are a hundred people. Maybe two hundred. Maybe three. They crawl north in huddled groups. I've walked in groups like that. Met companionship. Met danger. Left such groups and rejoined later, meeting people I thought I'd never see again and greeting them like brothers because they were known. But now is not a good time to be in a group. We are too close to the border. Even from here I can hear the surveillance drones. Our chances are better if we proceed alone.

Or rather, my chances.

I look at the boy. He looks at the ants. It's possible that some of those ants are known to him. Not just people he's met on the way, but people from wherever he originally came from. Real friends. Real family members.

'You could catch them up,' I say.

This is not true. Even if he could find his way, they are too far ahead.

'I'm going this way.' I point north-east.

The boy looks at the ants and then upturns his face to mine. And he smiles. Or rather he grins, an impish, glittering grin. As if I've made a joke.

It is a very long time since anyone smiled at me. I can see his teeth. One of the front ones is chipped.

'Are you soft in the head?' I ask.

That's what they used to ask about me. Or rather whisper about me behind my back on Arran. People of the village speaking to Grandmother.

Are you sure she's all right, your granddaughter? You know . . . not soft in the head?

Hard in the head more like, said Grandmother.

Papa said: *Sometimes people call you soft in the head when they mean you don't think the things they think or behave the way they behave.*

I cannot know what is inside this boy's head. It's difficult enough to know what is inside my own. I only know what I can see. I can see the boy's teeth. I am interested in his teeth because I have a chipped front tooth too. Though mine is a grown-up tooth and his is a baby one.

I grin back. Or perhaps it's a grimace. My smile muscles haven't been exercised for a long time.

He points at my tooth. Points at his own. And then he laughs. Hahahahahaha.

It's a very strange sound but infectious. So I laugh too.

'How did you do it?' I laugh. 'Your tooth?'

He takes his sucking stone from his pocket. Mimes chewing on it. Biting it.

Hahahahaha.

'I did mine when I bashed someone's head in with a brick in the desert,' I laugh.

Hahahaha.

12

DIRECTION OF TRAVEL

We laugh for quite a long time and then I say: 'Now, shut up. I need to concentrate.'

The boy shuts up immediately. I can't help thinking of Muhammad then. Muhammad the son of my parents' driver. Muhammad who never shut up. Muhammad with his donkey jokes and his boasts about watermelon pip-spitting. Maybe Muhammad knew he didn't have that long. That he only had a short time to do and say everything he needed to.

In the silence, I begin my map-making. I survey the landscape, memorise the shape of the hills, note any distinctive crags. I make patterns from the trees, tracing lines in my head from the copses to the single trees to the patches of denser forest. I log the angles and judge distances, trying to set a picture in my mind that I can refer to when the landscape changes, which it will do, the minute I begin to walk. I did this even when I was walking in the desert dunes, which was stupid. Dunes change shape with each breath of wind.

I need to memorise the landscape because I'm not going to follow the road from here. If you have papers which are in order, you ought to be able to walk up to a border, show those papers and pass through unhindered.

I have found this not always to be the case. At Heathrow, I was detained for four months for 'Verification'. I did not enjoy this experience. This is why I am not going to follow the road. Roads lead to checkpoints, delays, questions, disbelief.

And also soldiers.

Which is why I am going to try and cross the border through the hills and fields. If I am not caught, I will be home quicker. If I am caught . . . Well, Papa, I'll still have my gun, my knife and my brain.

To avoid the road, I will now need to track north-east, instead of due north.

Papa said: *When you walk north, the planet is on your side. She's always pointing the way.* This is one of the things he found out by looking.

Look, Mhairi, he said at noontime. *Look at the shadows. Noon is when the shortest shadows are. If you plant a stick in the earth at noon the tip of the stick shadow always points north. Its base is south.* He showed me this on the Isle of Arran when I was six and then again when we were in Khartoum.

Look, Mhairi, Papa said of the lichen on trees, *this particular sort of rust-coloured lichen doesn't like light. It only grows on the north side of trees. If it isn't sunny and you're near trees, look for the rust-coloured lichen.* He showed me this in the wood behind Grandmother's house in Corrie when we returned to Arran the summer I was twelve.

Look, Mhairi, Papa said at night, *look at the stars. Find the Plough, the group of seven stars that look like a saucepan. The stars opposite the handle of the 'pan' point directly toward Polaris, the Pole star. The Pole star is always north.* I don't remember whether he showed me this in Scotland or the Sudan, or both. Both probably because I remember him adding: *Sudan and Scotland seem a long way apart but they both sit under the same Northern Hemisphere sky. And share the same stars.*

But now I am going north-east, so the planet will not be on my side. And, if I make it over the border, I'll have to track back west again. Or rather north-west. North-west is where the Isle of Arran is. Where Grandmother is.

Grandmother said: *Come home. Come home now!*

That was over a year ago.

Grandmother said: *There are too many people coming north. They're shutting all the borders. I wouldn't be surprised if they shut the border between England and Scotland.*

Muma said: *Don't be ridiculous, we're Scots. We were born there. Even if they do shut the border we can come back any time.*

Don't bet your life on it, said Grandmother. *The rules are changing all the time. Come now.*

But we didn't.

Muma still had work to do. She and her Sudanese colleagues were so close to pushing the button on the power of the desert sun.

Don't you see? said Muma. *This is what it's all about. Not just the power of the sun but power over one's own life. No one leaves their homeland if life at home is good.*

37

You took my son from his homeland, said Grandmother.

Oh, Aileen, said Muma.

And then the Arctic ice cap melted. Or rather, the ice simply didn't form. The first year in the history of the planet when there was no summer Arctic ice. Some people said: *It doesn't matter, we still have ice at the Antarctic.*

Other people panicked.

In Khartoum soldiers took over the energy plant and stationed guards at every entrance. They told the workers that the energy would be staying in Sudan and the foreign engineers would be going home. Muma cleared her desk.

And then they shut the airport. Military use only.

Drive to Cairo, said Grandmother. *Cairo's still open. Get out now.*

And that's where we were going when Muma and Papa CASTLE.

I am alive, Muma.

Papa, the world is beautiful.

Except not today. At least, the sky is not beautiful today, Papa. The sky is a uniform grey. There is no sun to make shadows with, and the trees on the hill are all dead. This is the sort of day, if you want to make progress, you'd be better off with a compass. I used to have a compass, it was on my phone. The solar phone that was stolen from me the week before I got the gun. I do not blame the person who stole my phone compass. There are many reasons for stealing. Some of them quite good. Besides, if I still had my phone I would have to ring Grandmother, and she'd say: *Where are you?*

38

And I'd say: *Still the wrong side of the border, but quite close now. Three or four days' walk maximum. If things go well.*

And then she'd ask the other question, the difficult question, the Muma and Papa one which I do not know how I will ever be able to answer.

13

OTHER WORLDS

All the time I have been map-making, the boy has been squatting, staring intently into the grass at his feet. I sometimes do this too, I call it Other Worlds. It's a way of stopping being yourself for a moment. You look as closely at the grass as you might do at an adobe brick. You see (as I see following his gaze) that there's a beetle in the grass. And you go down small and you imagine that you're that beetle climbing that huge blade of grass. You cling and climb, climb a thousand kilometres of grass blade. As you climb higher and the blade begins taper, you concern yourself about whether it can continue to bear your weight although experience suggests it will bear your weight.

Next you see a droplet of water. The droplet is a giant silver dome, three or four times bigger than you are, a mirror to the sky. What if the droplet should spill? Because there are still terrors in Other Worlds, just not the ones you normally have to face. What if it should pour a thousand litres of water on your head? The droplet wobbles as you move up towards the very tip of the blade of grass. The tip is split, which is why it's holding the drop of water. One more step and that's the tipping point. There's always a tipping point. The droplet cannot hold. It bursts. The water avalanches towards you but you stand your ground and it just washes over and around you. Harmlessly.

There are reasons why beetles have those hard shells round them.

Muma says there are more beetles in the world now. Beetles do not mind rising temperatures. *If we're not careful*, Muma says, *it'll be beetles that inherit the earth.*

I watch the boy scan his tiny world. He's holding himself quite still and then, suddenly, his hand shoots out and I think he's going to grab the beetle but then I realise he's seen something deeper in the grass, a thin filament of mushroom with a grey-yellow cap, and he's pulling it up and along with it some grass and he's stuffing that grass and that mushroom right into his mouth. He hasn't been doing Other Worlds at all. He's been looking for food.

'What do you think you are, a cow?' I shout.

The last time I saw a cow it was just a skull and empty skin dried in the shape of a cow by the side road where the soldiers stopped us at the edge of the desert. I sat down beside that dried-up carcass and sucked at the stiff skin. Sucked at it because it was too hard to break a piece off and chew. Sucked at what would have been its soft belly before the vultures ate its innards and the sun baked it rigid. It tasted of dust and hair. Three hundred kilometres further north I was eating grass. But at least I boiled the grass. Boiled desert grass gives you no nutrition and itches your throat. But mushrooms. Mushrooms! Even Papa couldn't always tell which mushrooms were poisonous.

'Spit it out,' I shout.

I pull strands of wet green out of his mouth but the pale mushroom doesn't come. The mushroom has gone down his throat. The boy looks up at me. He is not smiling.

'If you're going to die,' I say, 'at least don't die of stupidity. Didn't your papa teach you anything?' I get out my water bottle. 'Wash your mouth out.'

He drinks, rolls the water around in his mouth, spits, never once taking his eyes off me.

'For the record,' I say, 'you can last at least three weeks without food, but not without water.'

Then I screw the lid on my water bottle and walk away.

14

WALKING

The boy follows me.

I walk fast, even though I'm walking downhill and the ground is far from even. There are no trees this side of the hill but there are clumps of spiky grass and low-lying thistles.

I hear the boy scrambling behind me. He doesn't whine. He doesn't moan. Even when he trips and falls the cry he makes is very brief. Just a single shout of pain and then he's on his feet again. But, of course, he cannot keep up with me. This is because his legs are short.

I do not wait and I do not look back.

I keep my eyes on the horizon.

15

HORIZON

Behind Grandmother's house on the Isle of Arran is a hill. Not a hill some distance away but a hill that rises right out of her back garden. Each summer of my childhood I climbed that hill: up through the gate past the row-boat on the trailer, across the boggy bit of field and up again on to the beginning of the woodland path. Then past the line of moss-covered boulders until I reached the wood itself. It's here that the Leuchram Burn cascades down off the mountains. In time, I learnt to negotiate that burn – crossing where it pools wide and shallow for a moment – and then travelling higher still, up to the 'horse', the tree trunk which leans giddily over the rushing water. I often sat astride here to rest because I knew what was still to come, the top of the hill that wasn't. The deceptive horizons. So I'd climb – and climb (always with the promise of the top in sight) and yet I'd never arrive. As each horizon reached turned out to be just the bottom of some new incline.

Muma said: *Our family aren't quitters, Mhairi. Once we set our heart on something – we go for it. And keep on going. No matter how tough it gets.*

So I kept going.

I was seven when I first got to the top of that hill. It was so high. The wood suddenly opening out right into the sky. To the west, I could see all the way to the jagged peak of Goat Fell and, to the east, right across the glittering sea to the mainland. I could also see – still see – the chimney of Grandmother's house. I knew where I was.

I try to remember this as I walk hour after hour in these northern English hills which are not my hills. As I climb the unknown ridges, sweat the false ups, the tripping downs, negotiate the slow, deceptive horizons. As I walk and never arrive, never seem any nearer. Never get to the top. Mile after mile of broken promises among hills I cannot name.

There has never been a moment of this journey when I haven't been thinking of home. My home. Being home. Home among the hills of my childhood. Scotland. Today I wonder if this is what home is: walking somewhere where you don't need a map.

Where the landscape is laid in your heart.

16

WILD GARLIC

I walk until my legs ache, my belly aches. I do not unknot my food cloth. I drink water. I fill my water bottle from the beck I've been tracking most of the day. I watch the clouds. They loom darker by the hour but they can look like this for days and it still be all right. And this has been a good day. These are some of the things that could have interfered with my walking and didn't:

    – a storm

    – a town

    – a person with a gun

    – a river

    – an injury

    – a wall

    – rain

    – barbed wire

    – the boy

At dusk, I look for shelter. On the hill ahead, I see what I think my grandmother would call a 'byre', an old abandoned cowshed from the time when these hills had cows. A place of shelter in a landscape which is otherwise a couple of copses and miles and miles of open moor. If I was still in the desert, I'd say it was too good to be true. I'd say it was a mirage.

I quicken my pace, as if it might all just melt away, and then, just as I reach the edge of the wood a new vision appears, lays itself out like a carpet beneath my feet. Garlic.

Oh Papa!

There's an ocean of wild garlic at the edge of the wood!

A mass of white flowers and broad green leaves. I'm treading on it, among it, the smell of it leaps in the air. And under the earth, I know, there will be bulbs. Small bulbs probably. But astringent, pungent, mouth-watering tiny bursts of flavour.

Papa, Papa, Papa! This beautiful world!

My head swims. But I know not to be greedy, not to thrust the edible leaves into my mouth like the boy did with the grass and the mushroom, not to eat too much, too fast, to pace myself. To smell first, to lick, to chew very slowly, not to gulp, let my stomach catch up. That's another thing I learnt in the desert. When you haven't eaten, a single mouthful can make you feel instantly bloated and then your stomach cramps with pain.

So I go slowly. I pull up the plants and take time brushing the earth from the white bulbs. I suck the leaves before chewing. I smell the garlicky scent of all the meals I used to have. Meals my grandmother cooked when I was young and food was plentiful: tomato and garlic pasta, roast lamb with slithers of garlic in the flesh, prawns in garlic butter, garlic-stuffed chicken breast. I hallucinate the smells, the food, lay it out in my imagination as I suck on the white flowers.

Who knows how long I lie in this garlicky meadow? Perhaps I even sleep. Perhaps I actually lie down and roll around and lose consciousness for a while.

And when I wake. There he is.

The boy.

17

MAGICIAN

'Are you some sort of magician?' I say.

He does not look like a magician. He looks small and exhausted. His face is streaked with dirt, his knees are bloody and his right shoe is flapping open.

And yet he's here. This boy who is younger than I was when I first crossed the Leuchram Burn. This boy who has eaten a mushroom and not been poisoned. Nature is good at weeding out the weak. Maybe his papa taught him something after all.

'Sit,' I say.

He sits, or rather he just sinks downwards. I sit beside him, pick a garlic bulb from the dark earth. I rub off the dirt and then divide the tiny bulb with my thumbnail.

'Eat,' I say, offering him half.

He sniffs the bulb.

'Good thinking,' I say. 'You're learning. But it's OK. It's wild garlic.'

He puts the half-bulb in his mouth and crunches. Slowly.

I give him a drink from my canister before giving him the second half of the bulb. Then I tear a leaf into thin strips and feed them to him one by one. I give him flowers.

As he eats, I gather garlic leaves and put them in my pockets for later. Then I point at the sky. The grey clouds are massing blacker and there's the beginning of a headachy heaviness in the air.

'We need to go, not far.' I point at the byre. 'OK?'

The boy nods. And his lips part a little and I see that tiny chipped tooth again. This reminds me that everyone I have ever travelled with has died.

Perhaps it will be different this time.

18

STORM

The byre is not as close as it, at first, appears. We walk slowly with the boy's shoe flap, flap, flapping against the sole of his foot. Twigs get in that shoe, stones get in that shoe, spears of grass.

Then there's a flash of lightning and a rumble of thunder. Sometimes nowadays the clouds can hang black for days and there be no storm, the lowering gloom burning away, burning out, giving way to sudden, bright sunshine. But it can work the other way too. A storm coming unpredictably, viciously. There's a second flash of lightning and, almost immediately, the thunder comes with a spit of rain. Then the heavens just open and we are the beetles below. A dome of water cascades over us, a deluge, a flood.

And we don't have hard shells.

'Run!' I cry.

Only the boy cannot run. Not with his flap, flap, flappy shoe.

'Don't think I'm going to carry you!' These are the last words I utter before the rain shuts my mouth. Or rather my nose. The rain pours so hard and so fast down my face that I have trouble breathing. My ears block, my nose runs snot and I have to open my mouth to get air. I try to wipe my nose on my sleeve but it's gusting so hard now I need to concentrate more on my balance than my sleeve. I cannot run. I can barely stand.

The wind squalls at the boy, harries him, but he's lower to the ground than I am and he's holding his own. And then his shoe goes, whipped high into the air by the wind, and he flails for it, a little mill of arms and that's all before the ice starts.

Hailstones of random sizes, myriad blows to my face. I raise my arms for protection, forearms to forehead, and still the ice keeps coming. Balls and bullets of ice on the top of my head, on my back. On the boy's back. He's been knocked to the ground now. I find myself between him and the wind, try to pull him upright. Just as I think I have him, the wind changes direction and there's another vicious swirl of ice.

And I'm just thinking I don't know how we'll make it to the byre when the clouds part and there is a sudden, unlooked for burst of sun. At once the ice stones melt, melt on contact, with clothes, with skin. We are soaked again – our flesh running water, our clothes drenched through. But, as suddenly as it arose, the wind drops. We can move.

'Run,' I say. And I run and, with his one bare foot, the boy hobbles.

'Foot down!' I shout. And he puts his bare foot down on the harsh, spiky ground.

We run towards that cowshed. As we get closer I see it is just a shack with a missing door, its sides fallen in or bashed in. But it has a roof, a corrugated tin roof. It is a shelter.

I arrive.

The boy arrives.

We stand dripping on the soft earth inside. Stand as the rain pelts and pelts on the tin roof. We shake our heads, shake the hair out of our eyes, press at our ears like you do in an aircraft, swallow, to try and thaw them, clear them.

Finally, our ears do clear, our jaws move again. And, for a moment, there we are with our wind-whipped faces. Safe. Warm.

And then the shivering starts.

19

FIRE

'Take your clothes off,' I yell against the roof-drumming rain.

I've already got my jerkin off and I'm pulling at my sweatshirt. But the boy isn't moving. He's just standing in a daze. His whole body flapping like his shoe was only ten minutes ago. Flap, flap, flap go his hands and his head is shaking like it's on a stick and his teeth are chattering and there are more sounds coming out of his mouth than ever before. A stream of sounds but all the same, bubbling through his trembling lips.

b-b-b-bbb-bbbb-bb-b-b-b-b-b-b-bbbbb-bbb-b-b-

'Take them off!'

The wind is coming in again now. This shelter is not a shelter after all. Not with its ripped-off door leaving a yawning hole into the outside world. And its kicked-in side wall leaving yet another hole through which I can see – the door!

The door is just lying outside on the ground.

So I go out again. I lift that door, pull and drag it against the wind and the rain until I get it close to the opening. Then, with me on the inside, I try and prop it, wedge it into the gap. And, of course, it doesn't cover the hole, doesn't shut out all the rain, all the wind. But it helps.

The boy is still shaking.

'Off, I said!' I lift his shaking arms and pull his clothes over his head. Or try to. But I'm trying two layers at once and they get stuck a moment and my hands are too cold to help properly, so there he is with his face all wound about with wet cloth. And, then, because he can't breathe, he unlocks, starts pulling at the clothes himself, finally gets them off and there, underneath, he's wearing a vest. A little-boy vest.

The vest is sodden and dirty but I can't stop this sudden thought: someone must have loved him to have given him this vest.

'Trousers,' I say, demonstrating with mine, 'take them off too.'

And soon we are both in underclothes.

'Now rub yourself. Rub your arms. Rub your legs. And stamp. Stamp your feet.'

He does as he's told. He makes fewer bbbbbbbbbs.

'I'm going to make a fire.' Making a fire this close to the border is not sensible. In this bleak moorland landscape, the smoke will be visible for miles. But without a fire tonight we won't get dry. We won't get warm. Plus, fire is protection against wild dogs. Risks and choices. That's how life is nowadays.

The lean-to door makes it slightly darker in the byre but there is still plenty of light coming through the hole in the bashed-in wall.

This is what I see: the ground is dry. Dry soil – at least, where the boy and I haven't dripped. This means the roof must be sound. Three sides of the byre are wooden, the fourth is formed of a makeshift sheet of the corrugated metal. If I can light a fire that end maybe the metal will carry the heat. If. These are the other things inside the byre:

- a coil of barbed wire. Each of the barbs is decorated with sheep's wool. Not a cowshed, then. A sheep shed. It is a long time since I have seen barbed wire used for sheep. All the barbed wire I have seen recently was for humans.
- two dry bones. I do not know what sort of bones, but animal I think.
- some torn pieces of thick plastic probably from agricultural bags.
- a small sapling tree trunk with roots attached.
- the metal hinge of the door.
- some large, flat grey stones.
- some wooden slats which must have come from the bashed-in wall.

I get out my knife. I inspect the roots of the tree. They are still bendy, not dry enough for kindling. Some bark is good for burning, especially birch bark. A man called Phil told me that, after the riot at Heathrow detention. This tree has been stripped of bark. I inspect the bone. I do not know if bone burns. At least I know that it burns because humans burn bodies. But I do not know whether you can start a fire with bone shavings. I look at the sheep's wool. I think sheep's wool singes, I think it burns like human hair. I will have to make shavings from the broken slats.

I rub my arms, I stamp, I jump and then I start with the slats, shaving as finely as I can, but with my hands still slick from the wet, the wood bits are still thicker than matches. To be any good as tinder, they need to be as thin as pencil sharpenings. If my clothes were dry I could scratch tinder fluff from the cloth, but my clothes are not dry.

The rain is easing now, the pounding on the roof less fierce.

I continue stripping wood. One of the cross slats seems particularly flaky. I pass it to the boy.

'Use a stone,' I say. 'Scrape me some wood for the fire. Small bits. Understand?'

The boy works methodically, giving the task his full concentration. He is a good boy. Smart. His papa must have been a good man. Or maybe his grandfather. Perhaps it was his grandfather he was travelling with.

When I have a small pile of dry wood shavings, I turn to the sapling trunk, cut some of the smaller side branches. Then I lift it, to check if there are any small branches the other side. That's when I see the sacking. Just a tiny piece of sacking, half-buried in the soil. Heathrow Phil said: *Anything with fibres that you can separate is good for starting a fire.* I pull at it. It's bigger than I thought. Half a metre of torn hessian. Phil said: *Shredded fibres are gold dust for a fire-maker.* I shake the dirt from the sacking, stick my knife among the fibres and start shredding them. Soon I have a little handful of spun gold.

I lay the fire as Phil taught me. I am good at remembering things. I make the tepee shape, starting with the matchstick pieces and then a few of the boy's shavings and then the slightly bigger sticks from the saplings. I leave air. I leave a little space at the front for where I will set the sacking fibres. *This*, Phil said, *is called a tinder nest.* When my fire is ready I get out my fire flint. Which used to be Phil's fire flint. I'm sorry I stole this flint from Phil when he was asleep but, as I said, there are many good reasons for stealing nowadays. I am only sorry that Phil told me his name. If you don't know someone's name it makes it easier to do with them what you must.

Phil's fire flint – my fire flint – is a cylindrical rod about the length of my first finger and half the width. One end is drilled through for a strip of leather so you can hold it close round your wrist. It's a simple thing to strike the flint with your knife to make a spark. I like seeing the spark. I like the way the fibres catch and burn.

I push my burning tinder nest into the heart of my fire.

20

STORIES

The fire catches, a tiny spark of orange, with a rim of black and yellow, and then a little shower of sparks and the first crackle as a wood shaving flares and burns. I stand and watch until I'm sure the tinder nest has done its work and the fire will hold.

Then I take my sodden clothes and wring them out through the hole in the bashed-in wall. The boy watches me and then picks his own clothes from the soil and tries to copy me.

'Good,' I hear myself saying. 'Good boy.' As though I was his mother.

His mother.

But he doesn't twist the clothes right and his wrists aren't as strong as mine.

'Here.' I take the clothes and do the job for him. Then I look for a place near the fire to hang everything. The corrugated side of the shack has been roughly nailed in place and some of the nails protrude. I use these as hooks, hitching shirts through button holes and trousers from belt loops. My jacket I secure half-in and half-out of the bashed-in wall, hoping the wind will do some of the drying.

There is a more yellow glow to the fire now. Instinctively, the boy squats down and stretches his hands towards the warmth. We have both, I realise, stopped shivering. As I wait for the fire to take among the larger pieces of wood, I begin stripping bits of garlic bulb and leaf into the water of my water bottle. The advantage of a metal canister is that you can set it in a fire.

I place it where the tinder nest was, heating it without the lid, so I can check the temperature by the rise of steam. I know to warm but not boil it, so I can extract it from the fire without scalding myself. Gradually the scent of warming garlic fills the shack. As soon as the open throat of the bottle begins to mist a little, I double up the remaining sacking and use it to help me lift the bottle out of the fire.

'Hot-water bottle,' I say, handing the canister to the boy. 'With bonus garlic tea. But don't drink yet. Too hot.'

We sit awhile, waiting, inhaling.

We are both semi-naked still. My skin is a cold, slick white. But the boy, Papa, he has an edge of firelight to him. Half of his face is in shadow but the other half gleams. And he's sitting so still, he's like a tiny bronze statue, the hand of his maker still hot upon on him.

'*Once upon a time,*' I say, '*when men and animals spoke the same language, and all things understood all things, there lived a boy with eyes like . . .*'

And then I stop.

The boy has turned his whole face towards me now. All of it is lit in the firelight glow. His eyes are huge.

'*With eyes like . . .*'

But I can't go on. I know this story like the back of my hand but I cannot go on. Papa said: *Human beings have always told stories, Mhairi. Way before allconnect and the weave, before snapchat and the internet and film and radio and books, even before books, Mhairi, before words were even written down, human beings told stories. Sat around a fire and shared their understanding of the world.*

But tonight, the story words are stuck in my throat. The words are gagging me. Because this is one of Papa's stories and I want it to be in Papa's voice. I want the story to belong to Before, to the time when Papa sat at the end of my bed and I was tucked in tight.

Because when Papa told stories they all ended well. They were truthful stories but happy stories too. Things always worked out. Whatever the hardships, people overcame them. Good always triumphed over evil. The stories had neatness, resolutions, completeness. They were stories from a world that could be trusted.

Not stories for the world we live in now.

The boy is still staring, ablaze with expectation and hope. As if things can be understood, made better. As if I can make things better. Me! With my stories.

What do you want me to do, Papa?

Lie to him?

21

STICK AND STONES

'Forget it!' Rage volcanoes up my throat. 'Forget this story. Forget all stories! They have nothing to say to us now. They come from Before.'

The boy doesn't move, just keeps on staring up at me with those huge black eyes. Waiting again. And wanting. Wanting something I cannot give.

Why do people always have to look at me this way?

'Who do you think I am?' I yell. 'Your mother? Your father? No! You're on your own. We're all on our own. Do you understand? You don't have papers. You won't make it through the border. There won't be a happy ending.'

All this spewing is because of the boy's eyes. It's because, tonight, when I look in his deep, waiting, wanting eyes, I'm actually staring into Muhammad's eyes. I'm back on the road near Cairo – so very close to Cairo and the safety of the plane – and I'm remembering the chiggers that are eating Muhammad's feet, I'm seeing the open bite wounds on his legs, the oozing pus. And Muhammad isn't talking now. Not with his mouth anyway. But his eyes are talking. Oh yes. His eyes are talking as I walk away that last ever time. His eyes are saying

CASTLE.

'Have you never been in border detention?' I shout at the boy. 'That's when you'll need a story. Not some stupid thing from the past but one for now. One for the soldiers. One for Imgrims. And one for the Psychs and the Socials – if you get that lucky.'

Silence.

'So, you'd better start making something up. A story all of your own. Because don't think you'll be able to keep your mouth shut then. No. They'll make you speak. *Make* you! Do you understand?'

Silence.

'What are you – a stone?' I shout, precisely because that look in his eyes proves he is not a stone. And I find myself bending down and pulling one of those huge, flat grey stones from the soil floor. Find myself lifting it (and it's very much heavier than it looks) high above my head. Holding it there a moment, as if it was an adobe brick in a night-time desert tomb. As if you could crush away a look in the same way that you can crush a human skull.

But you can't.

The look comes after you.

It haunts you.

So, I'm in the shack with the boy and not there at all. Because I'm also in Castle and all the locks are bursting. And I have to fight, fight to remember that this little boy is not Muhammad, NOT MUHAMMAD. And this look, this wanting, needing look, is not about me and my walking away. It's just about a story. Or perhaps about a stone. Yes. Because here is the boy's hand coming at me through a veil, a mist, a sandstorm. His fist unfurling like a flower, palm up, reaching for me, or rather reaching for the stone.

That's all he's asking for.

A stone!

So I give it to him.

Quite gently. Lower my arm and drop the stone – carefully – into his cupped hands. At once he stops being Muhammad and becomes the boy again. And, as the hammering and pain in my heart stop hurting quite so much, I wonder if this is how the storm feels when sunlight suddenly bursts through its thunderous clouds.

I breathe.

Hear myself breathe.

The boy, meanwhile, is scanning the fire. He locates a charred stick, pulls it from the flames, and then he places the stone between his feet, holding the stick as if it's a pencil.

He's going to write.

Oh Papa, I think he's going to write!

His first stroke is experimental, he seems to be checking how thick – or thin – a line he can make with this stick. Then suddenly the stick is moving like a wand, flowing over the stone, leaving a trail of sparks and marks, lines, curves and spirals. Smuts of carbon fall from the end of the stick as he works and he smudges them in, incorporates them. He is totally absorbed in the work and I wait – and wait – for the scribbles to become clear, because it isn't writing after all, it's a picture, or a series of pictures, or maybe a pattern.

Soon the stone is covered with drawings. So he takes another stone, wipes it clear of dirt with his fist, and pulls a second smoking twig from the fire. There is a further furious, concentrated bout of mark making. All of his body is involved in those marks.

After a time – and I do not know how long a time it is – he puts down his stick and pushes the stones towards me.

And I look.

But I have no idea what his symbols mean, Papa. They might as well be jottings from another planet. But I know he believes they make sense and maybe they do. So, I look again and this is what I see: stars and filigrees and flowers, flourishes, twists and turns, all intersecting, overlapping, not beginning, not ending. And I still can't grasp it, perhaps because I'm still looking for something overarching, a grand, overall pattern. I'm always looking for this, I realise then, something which joins the things I know to the things I don't know. But maybe that's the point. Maybe these drawings are the shape of something I can never fully know, the pattern of his mind perhaps. A magic carpet of lands I haven't seen and stories I haven't heard. The outlines of his hopes and dreams. So maybe I don't have to understand. Maybe I just have to trust.

Besides, you couldn't say these pictures weren't beautiful, Papa. Because they are beautiful, even though they are unfinished. Yes. These stories come right to the edge and then they fall off, fall off the stones, fall away. But maybe that's OK as well. Maybe this is as complete as anything gets these days.

Although, perhaps, if there were more stones there would be more story. But there are no more stones. Not here. Not now. There is only this. This moment in a shack. And these drawings which he seems to be offering up as a gift.

So, I just say: *Thank you.*

22

UMBRELLA OF STARS

We sit awhile then.

The boy.

Me.

The charcoaled stones.

We sip the cooled garlic tea. We eat the last rain-sogged crumbs of bread and cheese from the food cloth. The fire is a good fire, smouldering not smoking now. More difficult for a drone to spot. I put the metal door hinge in the ashes to warm. It will keep its heat as the fire dies.

It grows dark. The boy gets up and goes to where his trousers are hanging and takes his sucking stone from the pocket. Then he returns to the fire, and curls up on the earth with his back to me. I hear him sucking. Soon I hear his breath go to sleeping.

I debate whether to cover his nakedness with a torn bit of plastic sacking, but don't in case it catches fire in the night and melts. It would be better for me to be his blanket myself. Lie guarding his back with whatever warmth I have. But even though it would keep me warmer too, I cannot do this. After what happened in the desert, I do not believe I will ever be able to lie skin to skin with another human being.

Yet I cannot help but watch the boy. He lies curled about himself, his hands around his upper arms, as though he is hugging himself. Muhammad never lay like this, he lay straight as a plank. It was almost as if Muhammad fell asleep standing to attention. Because he was the son of my mother's driver, I sometimes wondered if he had been sleeping with his own family rather than with me, the boss's daughter, whether his sleeping would have been more relaxed. But I don't think so. I think sleeping like a plank was natural for Muhammad. We were strange bedfellows, fourteen-year-old me, ten-year-old him, but it worked well enough until that night at Meroe.

Papa said: *When people think of pyramids they think of the Egyptian pyramids, monumental tombs fit for pharaohs. The pyramids at Meroe are on a rather more human scale.*

Papa and I were always going to make a visit to the desert north of Khartoum to see these Sudanese pyramids, but somehow it never happened. I don't know how many days Muhammad and I walked in the desert before we saw those pyramids on the skyline. Muhammad, whose head was swimming from the heat, thought they were a mirage. And I would have done so too, except they looked exactly as Papa had described them: *like a series of triangular boiled eggs that someone's knocked the tops off.*

There was no reason for Muhammad and me to change direction and walk towards those pyramids, but no reason not to either. Perhaps it was the thought of bricks, of solidity, after so many days with only open skies and thorn bushes for company.

We had no idea that we would be able to shelter inside the tombs until we actually got there and saw that some of them had little entrances, with pillars either side, as if they were mini-temples. Of course, I thought if we had found such shelter, other people would have too. But the place was deserted – just a few cigarette butts in the sand to show that people had passed through.

Or so I thought.

Besides, we were exhausted and it seemed like a gift. We had been slogging and dragging for hours. We had sand in our hair, in our eyelashes, in between our toes, in between our teeth. Before I was in the desert I thought of sand as soft. But sand is actually composed of tiny fragments of the hardest rock, the bits that resist to the end, refuse to be crushed. It crunched in our mouths. Our lips were bone-dry and, when we tried to lick them, there was no moisture in our tongues. Even the flies, which when we set out, would crowd round our foreheads to drink from our sweat, had moved on because we were no longer producing sweat.

So, it was something to see Muhammad's grin as he poked his head out from the dark interior of one of those tombs.

'Bed,' was what he said.

It wasn't much of a bed. A narrow doorway, a small rectangle of sand and two large rocks where the pillows should have been. But it was shelter, it was out of the wind.

The entrance was marked with a low line of much more modern adobe bricks. You had to step over those bricks to get inside. So I did.

One of those bricks, I noted, was loose.

Muhammad lay to sleep almost immediately, but I was strangely restless. So I sat in the doorway looking out over the sand. The wind was making snakes in the dust and as snake swirled over snake it made the sound of sweeping, as though someone was wanting to brush the desert away. But that person wasn't me that night, because I was full of gratitude:

Muma – I am alive!

Papa – the world is beautiful!

The sky was an inky blue with a flowing river of stars: bright stars, dense stars, Milky Way stars. I think it had been days since I had the energy to look up. That night I looked up. And, although it was growing cold, I remember stepping out of the tomb and finding the river of stars changing to a dome, a dome which spanned the whole world but also seemed a tiny umbrella held above my head only.

I thought of you then, Papa. And how you should have been stood by me beneath that umbrella of stars.

Perhaps it was a sign, your not being there. Perhaps there are no such things as signs. Only what happens and then what happens next. In any case, I went back inside and lay down alongside Muhammad. The sand was still a little warm from the day. I slept then. At some time during the night Muhammad got up and went outside. Maybe that's what attracted the man to our tomb. I don't know why Muhammad got up. Maybe because of the dirty water the blind girl had shared with him the previous day. Maybe he needed to relieve himself. I think it was about then that he began to have diarrhoea. Anyway – he left the tomb and the stranger came in his place. A man who smelt of tobacco and madness and didn't lie like a plank. At first I thought I was dreaming. Dreaming the hand that was searching out my

CASTLE.

So, no, I do not curl what warmth I have around the boy tonight, human being to human being. No! The boy's nakedness – my nakedness, his skin against my skin – it cannot be borne. Even though he is not the man in the desert. Even though he's only a child. Because dreams don't make these distinctions. Dreams come anyway.

So I push away. Put my back to the metal wall. Stay stark awake.

And – eventually – the sun comes up.

23

SOBBING

I am not rested but I get up anyway, pull on my still-damp clothes and go to the beck for water.

I fill the canister, drink – the water tangs of garlic – refill and screw the lid on tight. Then I make my way back to the byre. As I near the shack I hear of sound of sobbing. It is not a gentle noise. It's a fierce, tormented thing. I increase my pace – a useless, instinctive reaction. Whatever is troubling the boy there won't be anything I can do about it.

He is standing by the embers of the fire wearing his grubby little vest. In his hands are the picture stones, only they're blackened now, swirled with ash. He's swallowed them up with new marks, huge angry spirals, like giant thumbprints or whirlpools of water. And he's crashing those stones together so hard little chunks of rock are splintering off. His eyes are all screwed up and he's sobbing so hard, the tears streak down his face worse than the storm. Clash, clash, clash go the stones as the swirling, swallowing pictures fracture and smash. And part of me wants to say: *Stop it! Stop it at once! Those beautiful stones!* But that's probably the point. And it is not as though we can carry these stones with us. These stones are the past now. So I say nothing.

Finally, with a crescendoing wail, he flings one of the stones at the corrugated tin wall, where it screams and judders. And then he throws the second stone at the metal wall, but the clang of it is lost in his moaning as he drops to the floor, his whole body rocking and gulping with the fury and the tears, and I know he's not aware of me standing there looking at him. He's not aware of anything. Except the grief.

And who am I to know what this grief is?

It could be anything. His own personal desert. His particular whirling whorls, his swallowing sea. His still-damp vest perhaps, the not-enough in his belly, the loss of the old man, the loss of his family, his friends, his homeland. It could be the thought of the day ahead, of the border, of another long walk with those flap, flappy shoes. Or it could just be that unspeakable, nameless thing that occasionally overwhelms the traveller.

If my papa was here, he'd bend down and scoop this child into his arms. My papa would hold this not-my-child, hold him anyway, whisper in his ear, shush him, and, when he calmed a little, my papa would still be holding him, cheek to cheek, skin to skin, and the boy would stop gulping. The boy would hush.

But my papa is not here. And I cannot do this. So I don't speak to the boy. I don't reach for him and I certainly don't hold him. I just let him cry. Cry and cry until he's finished with it.

Sometimes it's good to cry. It means not all your emotions have walked away.

24
WALKING

We set out again.

The boy's shoe does not flap. At least not for the first kilometre or so. I have mended his shoe by threading his shoelace through the remaining hessian and tying the whole around his ankle. It looks ridiculous. It looks like his foot is a potato in a small sack.

I do not walk as fast as I usually do. The sky is overcast and there are no trees, so I have neither sun nor lichen to guide me. I think we are progressing north-east but I cannot be sure and it is always harder to march if you might be marching the wrong way. I am also pausing every so often to check for human habitation. Today is a day we are going to need to find food and that will mean stealing. But every time I see a building, I also see a road. And there are people on those roads. There are also drones. The mosquito sort.

I don't mention the people to the boy. I don't mention the drones.

So we just walk.

And walk.

The boy's sacking foot gets damp, it gets muddy, the hessian works loose and begins to shred. The shoelace remains tight round his ankle but the sacking is useless. It gapes. The shoe gapes. The boy sits down, unpicks the shoelace knot and then hurls the whole thing – shoe and sack – away. He undoes his second shoe – the good shoe – and hurls that away too. Then he gets up. He is not wearing socks. His feet are bare.

Muhammad went barefoot. Muhammad got chiggers.

'If you don't wear shoes,' I shout, 'you'll get chiggers!'

I don't even know if you get chiggers in this part of the world. I'd never heard of chiggers until Muhammad got them. Tiny, dark red things that get in the cracks of your body. Spiders, I think. Or insects anyway. They eat their way into your flesh and itch like crazy. At first Muhammad just had them on his feet, his ankles, then his legs, his penis. I didn't see the bites on his penis but I saw him scratching. Muhammad said when you scratch chiggers they urinate. I do not know if this is true. I do know that if you scratch chigger bites they get infected.

'Sit down!' I shout at the boy.

He sits and I inspect his feet. His soles are dirty, blistered. His left foot, the flappy shoe foot, is also streaked with red. I smear the red, to check if it has legs. I do this even though I know that the legs of chiggers are microscopic. In my dreams, the legs of chiggers are not microscopic. They are huge. As are their jaws. And the yellow pus that spews from them.

The red streak on the boy's foot does not have legs.

The red is not chiggers.

The boy is not Muhammad.

'It's OK.' I say. 'It's only blood. Walk.'

25

WALL

We come to a wall.

It's barely knee-high and it doesn't really look like a wall, more like a crazy-paving path. A giant's crazy-paving path. It's about three metres wide and made of random blocks of grey limestone. The blocks are mortared together with moss, a spongy yellow and green. It's not much of a wall now, but it used to be.

Hadrian's Wall.

I know this because, when we still lived in Scotland, Papa took me to see this wall. *It would have been about six metres high originally*, Papa said, *with forts and towers all along its 120-kilometre length – west from Carlisle all the way east to Newcastle. It was built by the Emperor Hadrian, to separate the Romans from the barbarians.*

Papa was interested in walls and he was interested in barbarians.

In those days, Papa said, *we would have been the barbarians, Mhairi. You and me. People who lived north of the wall. Think of that.*

I didn't think about it much at the time. But I think about it now. And I think about walls.

– The Great Wall of China

- The Berlin Wall
- Israel's Separation Barrier
- Turkey's Razor-Wire Fence
- The Mexican Border Wall

Walls to keep people in or keep people out. Mainly out. Keep out the barbarians, the foreigners, the people who don't speak like us or believe the things which we believe. Those rude, uncultured, primitive, wild, savage people like – Papa!

And me.

And this boy.

Us.

Think of that, Mhairi!

Walls which are, in fact, borders. Borders which divide countries, nations, people. Boundaries devised in the heads of men. Territories marked on a piece of paper. Papa once showed me a map of Africa.

Guess who drew the borders on this map? Papa asked.

The people who lived there? I said.

Wrong, said Papa. *These borders were drawn by a bunch of Europeans who'd never set foot in Africa. They sat in Berlin and divided Africa between them as if it was a pie. That's why these borders disregard mountains, rivers, trade routes. And also tribes.*

Lines drawn on a map. Lines drawn in the sand. You this side. Me the other.

These lines are fictions, Papa said.

It is difficult to feel angry with a wall. Especially long-ago, broken-down Hadrian's Wall. A wall which really no longer marks anything at all. But, all of a sudden, I do feel angry. Perhaps it's because I'm tired, exhausted even. Perhaps it's because bumping into this piece of wall means I must have wandered further east than I'd hoped. Or perhaps it's simply because this wall is here. Still here. A solid reminder of every border, every barrier I've faced in the last twelve months. Every checkpoint. Somebody else's decision about whether my face fits. Whether I belong. Whether I'm allowed. Whether I'm to be in. Or out. To live. Or die.

Well, I'm alive, Muma.

And as for this wall, Papa, this once-wall, this Roman 'Keep-Out' sign which has lasted almost two thousand years, this wall is in for a shock.

Anger can give you energy, adrenaline.

I jump on this wall.

I run across it.

I run back.

And forward.

Back and forward again.

I abuse this wall. I refuse this wall.

'Look,' I shout to the boy. 'I was wrong! Borders are nothing. This wall is nothing. So, cross. Cross the wall!'

And my fellow barbarian does.

26

RIVER

I'm still thinking about borders when we come to a river. A river, I think, is not a man-made thing, it's a real border, a natural border. Like a mountain. Like an ocean. Natural barriers also divide tribes and nations. But Nature never asks to see your Global Passport. Nature simply says: *Here it is. It is what it is. But if you're clever enough, determined enough, if you have the courage and the imagination . . . be my guest.*

I have crossed a desert so I can cross this river.

Which is wide.

And fast-flowing.

Of course, I could find a bridge. A man-made bridge. I know there is a road to the west of us, because all day long, I've heard the rumble of trucks. Since I've been travelling I've noticed that road bridges are often positioned where a river narrows a little. If I can get close to this road – but not too close – perhaps we will find a crossing point.

We track the shoreline westwards. The trees are dense to the water's edge, which gives us cover but makes progress slow. Sometimes there's a little beach of dry limestone pebbles.

Sometimes an inlet of slippery, algae-covered rock. But the water itself is clean and clear. This is good. The water will wash the boy's feet, help cleanse his wounds.

The river curves left and as we follow the bend, I see that, though the water is still nearly ten metres or so across, there are boulders midstream here. The water breaks around them, frothing and bubbling, but they look like possible stepping stones. Something to aim at. Cling to. Rest on. Nature's gift.

'Here,' I say. 'I think we might be able to cross here.'

The rumble of the lorries is almost constant now. This close to the border they are probably army trucks. But we are in some dip, so I cannot see how close we're getting to the road. However, if I can't see the road, then no one on the road will be able to see us. Or so I hope.

I take off my shoes, tie the laces together and suspend them round my neck.

The boy hesitates.

'Don't worry. I don't think it's as deep as it looks. We'll be able to wade. You just have to do the wobble test.' I learnt this crossing the Leuchram Burn. 'Put your foot down and test each stone as you go. If it wobbles, try another one. And remember, the big stones can look safer, but if they shift, they shift big too, so sometimes the smaller ones are actually better. I'll go first. I'm heavier than you. If a stone takes my weight, it'll take yours. Just watch for the slimy ones.'

The first couple of metres are easy. The water is shallow and clear, the stones beneath wide and flat. Then the water deepens and the rocks become more jagged. I'd hold his hand if I thought it would help. But it won't. The water is over my knees and almost up to his waist and we both need our hands to grab on to whatever bits of the rocks are dry. There's a random tree branch sticking out of the water and I test if I can use it to steady myself. It pulls loose immediately and I almost lose my footing, but I hang on.

We're close to the centre of the river now and the pull of the water is stronger and the frothing stops us being able to see our feet. I pause, unsure of how to make it to the next boulder, when suddenly there's a rattle of stones and the boy is ahead of me. I don't know how he's done it but he's shimmying up the central rock, where he stands, grinning his gap-tooth grin.

And then he extends a hand, as though he could hold my weight, pull me up behind him.

Hahahahahaha.

He's actually laughing. Bubbling louder than the river. Louder than the buzzing of the drone I suddenly think I hear overhead. I look up at once, but I don't see anything. The breeze in trees, that can sometimes sound like a drone.

The boy grins some more, waits for me and then he's off again. Testing the stones. Standing, crawling, slipping back, crying out but then pushing on again.

'Good,' I hear myself call out. 'Good! Your papa would be proud of you!'

Soon he's at the other side. First on to the safety of the huge slab of rock that slopes out of the water, lying on the hillside like the faultline of some tectonic plate.

Where the slope gets steeper there are overhanging trees so he's pulling himself up using the branches and the slab gives way to a bank of mud and tree roots which (and I'm closing on him now) look like a set of natural steps. So, we scramble up them, him only slightly ahead now, with a sense of achievement, exhilaration even.

Which is, perhaps, why we miss the point when the natural steps become man-made steps and the man-made steps rise towards a man-made path and at the beginning of that path is a pair of feet. Or rather boots.

The polished black boots of a soldier.

27

SOLDIERS

This is what I know about soldiers: they are all the same. Their countries of origin might differ, or the colour of their skin, or their headgear, or their boots, or the make of their weapons or the emblem blazoned at their breasts – but they all speak with one mouth. It doesn't matter where you meet them or what you are doing at the time, you are always in the wrong. Which is why it's advisable to proceed with caution.

These are some of the things which help:

- Not speaking until you are spoken to.
- Keeping your eyes down.
- Saying 'Yes' a lot. Or 'Yes, sir.' Even if the soldiers are women.
- Not making jokes.
- Not trying to be clever.
- Not waving your knife at them when they have a machine gun.
- Not pointing your (bulletless) revolver at them when they have a machine gun.

So, I avoid direct eye contact, look at this soldier from under lowered lids. It's a man, or rather a young man, not much more than eighteen probably. Young soldiers are particularly dangerous. I learnt this at the fourth checkpoint on the desert road out of Khartoum. Young soldiers can be very unpredictable. I keep very still, even though his uniform is blue and the emblem sewn at his breast a white cross on a blue ground. The Scottish saltire. My jump-for-joy flag.

Flag of my country.

Flag of my homeland.

My shout-out-loud flag!

But I still keep quiet.

Shh shh shh shh shh shh shhh!

Because I can remember Before. When Scotland was part of a United Kingdom. When we didn't have our own soldiers.

He holds his gun – which is a machine gun – loosely at his waist, swings it lazily, as though he isn't really pointing it at me at all. But at this distance, less than two metres, he couldn't possibly miss. Not least because he has a predator pack wound around his neck. These loops of bullets allow a soldier to fire five hundred rounds without having to reload. I know this because Muma mentioned it when we passed through that fourth checkpoint on the road out of Khartoum. *I've never seen a checkpoint soldier with a predator pack before*, Muma said. *They're normally reserved for soldiers in battlefield situations.*

That was one of those small details that turned out not to be small after all.

So, I don't say a thing, I just keep my head bowed and my mouth shut. At least, I do until he speaks.

'Papers,' the soldier says.

Or rather he says, 'Paper*rrrs*.'

And it's so very long since I heard a Scottish voice. The soft rolling 'r's of my childhood. As though he was Miss Campbell, collecting up the end-of-term paper*rrrr*s in my Glasgow primary school. And that is what undoes me, I think. The familiarity, the safety of those rolling 'r's.

'I'm Mhairi,' I blurt out. 'I'm fourteen. I was born on the Isle of Arran.'

Or rather I say: I'm Mhai*rr*i, I'm four*rrr*teen, I was born on the Isle of A*rrrrr*an. Even though I've been away seven years, the Scottish burr's still there. He'll recognise it, recognise me. He'll hear the truth that's embedded in my voice, my accent. He'll know that I belong. I'm the right side of his border. That I have finally arrived.

I'm home.

Really home!

I offer my papers in outstretched hands.

The soldier does not take the papers, he doesn't even look at them. He looks at me, at the shoes strung around my neck, at my soaking trousers.

'Which is why,' he says, flicking the gun muzzle toward the boy, 'you'*rrre* c*rrr*ossing a *rrr*iver with an illegal alien, *rrr*ight?'

And then he laughs.

Hahahahahahar*rrrrrr*.

85

28

LORRY

The laughing makes me want to take out my knife – notwithstanding the machine gun – and thrust it in the soldier's neck. But I don't. Survival is not always about the first thing that comes into your head. Or the most impulsive. Survival is sometimes a longer game.

So I allow myself to be marched over yet another deceptive horizon and there it is: the road. There's a lorry parked up and, beside it, a great many more soldiers in blue uniforms with blue and white saltires sewn at their breasts. They seem relaxed, joking and smoking together. The cigarettes smell like tobacco. In the Sudan, the soldiers might smoke tobacco or they might smoke ganja weed. Or swallow cane juice and gunpowder. Things which made them wild-eyed and trigger-happy. So, tobacco is good.

The tobacco-smoking soldiers unchain the back of the lorry and push the boy and me up the ramp with pointed guns. There are many people in the lorry already, all in cages. Only makeshift, rickety cages nailed together with wood and chicken wire, but cages nonetheless. The cages hold men, women, children, babies.

One of the babies is crying, not a loud, insistent noise but a kind of hopeless whimper, as though the baby knows perfectly well that there is no point to his weeping, no likelihood of comfort, but he can't help himself, the tears just keep coming anyway. Otherwise the lorry is quiet. The hush of the wary, the frightened. Around the inside perimeter of each cage is a low, wooden bench. The people lucky enough to have seats here keep their heads low, as if they are ashamed of taking the opportunity to sit down, to rest for a moment. The men-only cages (and there are many more men than women in this lorry) are more tightly packed. Some men stand, some sit on the floor. No one lies full stretch. There isn't room.

One of the soldiers unlocks a cage of women and children. The women nod a small welcome at us as we enter, but they don't say anything. We find a place on the floor just before the back of the lorry clangs shut again. That's when I realise the lorry doesn't have windows. Outside it didn't seem a particularly hot day but the closed lorry is hot. And dark. And it smells. I doubt if any of the people in this lorry have been able to wash properly for days, weeks. Months even. But it's not that smell. Or not just that smell, the sour one of fish and dried sweat. It's the stench of people who haven't been allowed out of this lorry to relieve themselves. It's the smell of people who have done things in their pants. Their trousers. In the corner of their cage.

It's the smell of shame.

But we are the lucky ones, it seems. The cages are almost full and it's nearly the end of the day. Someone bangs a fist on the tailgate and the lorry engine whirrs into life. We are on our way.

I begin to count. If the journey is particularly long, counting will be useless. If not, I will be able to estimate roughly how far we've travelled. I do it like this: count to sixty, log the number on some part of my body by touching and begin again. My fingers are the first ten minutes (I always start with my right hand) and if it goes to eleven minutes, I move on to my forehead. Twelve and thirteen are my eyebrows, fourteen and fifteen my eyes, and so on through ears, cheeks (always the right first), nose, upper and lower lips, chin. If I get to my neck, it's been twenty-two minutes.

The lorry finally stops at my left breast – twenty-eight minutes. The tailgate clangs open.

We take a collective breath. Gulp at the fresh air. Even the baby stops whimpering for a moment.

'Reception 1,' comes the shout. 'Men!'

This time the soldiers remain on the tarmac and it's three body-armoured guards who come into the lorry. The guards do not have guns. They do have grenade-grip batons and riot helmets. The visors of the helmets are up.

'All men. Out!'

Some of the men who've been sitting get to their feet. Some don't. These are the ones, I imagine, who don't speak the language, don't understand English.

'Up!' screams a guard at one bewildered, unmoving man, as though the problem is simply one of volume. 'GET UP.'

They did this to us in the desert. The soldiers who stopped us that fourth time. When we didn't do what they wanted (because we did not know what they wanted) they screamed.

SCREAMED.

It's a terrifying thing when people scream at you in a language you can't understand. Especially in a language like Arabic where – to the outsider – words can sound harsh even when their meaning is not. Fear escalates when you cannot communicate. Can't reason, explain, plead.

Beg.

At first, we thought these desert soldiers wanted what all the other checkpoint soldiers wanted. Money. It wasn't as though we hadn't been stopped on this Khartoum road before. Stops on this road were routine even before the Emergency. Our driver, Muhammad's father, who did understand the language, knew exactly what to do.

The fine at the first checkpoint was for speeding.

Were we speeding? Muma asked, as Muhammad's father climbed back into the car.

Of course, said Muhammad's father. *You can't not speed on this road*.

Why? What's the limit? Muma asked. Always the scientist.

Muhammad's father laughed. *Depends how much money they think you have*.

The further north we got that day, the more we apparently picked up speed. And the longer the negotiations took. At the fourth checkpoint, Muhammad's father had been out of the car for about twenty minutes when Muma, idly looking out the window, made that fatal remark about predator packs: *I've never seen a checkpoint soldier with a predator pack before. They're normally reserved for soldiers in battlefield situations.*

And I, Papa replied, *have never seen a child with a predator pack before. Look at him – he can't be more than fourteen.*

Fourteen. My age. I took a closer look then. As I've said before, it's not very easy to tell someone's age these days, but he did look young, gangly and uncertain, like a newborn giraffe who'd got to his feet without really knowing how to walk. The men – the real men – had gone inside the flimsy, white wooden kiosk to conduct negotiations. Which left him on his own outside, wandering. Wondering, maybe. Who he was there to protect, guard, kill. There was no swagger in him, just a vague unease. Once, as I watched, he hunched his shoulder, as though the weight of the bullets looped there irked him.

Ten-year-old Muhammad (who'd only hitched a lift that day because the border crossing was near the village where his grandparents lived and he and his dad planned on spending the night there) asked if he could get out and go to the toilet. Or piss in the sand, anyway. Muma said: *Probably be better to wait till after the negotiation.* So he waited. We all waited. It was hot, it was irritating but it wasn't frightening and then there was a raised voice from inside the checkpoint kiosk. That wasn't frightening either. It wasn't even surprising. Just part of the negotiation, we knew, or thought we knew, a tactic. But maybe we didn't hear – or understand – what was actually said. Because the predator boy went straight inside the kiosk with his gun.

I still wasn't worried. In fact, I was busily watching the way a fly was tracking up the window of the car, making tiny footprints in the dust. I often wonder what Muhammad's father said – or didn't say – inside that hot kiosk. I wonder what he did – or refused to do – before the boy opened fire. Ratatatatatatatatatat. I hope it wasn't about the money. Papa would have paid whatever was asked. I hope it wasn't about pride. I also hope it wasn't just a mistake. An accidental finger on a trigger.

The kiosk had windows with no glass so there was nothing to shatter but bullets did spray out on to the sand. And some of the white kiosk paint, which was peeling anyway, shuddered and flapped. Or so I thought. Though it might just have been my brain shuddering and flapping with the gun noise.

Papa jumped out of the car then.

Papa, who could fix anything, jumped out of the car.

And three men jumped out of the kiosk. Or rather two men and the boy. Muhammad's father did not jump out of the kiosk.

And then Papa started saying something. His voice was urgent, I remember, but low and quiet, and his hands were open. I do not know what he said because it was overtaken by the screaming.

The unintelligible SCREAMING.

'OUT!' the saltire guards yell at the men in the hot lorry. 'Out. I SAID OUT!'

Perhaps that's what the desert soldiers shouted at us as they surrounded the car. Something like 'Out'. But it didn't sound like out. And, in any case, Papa was already out.

'OUT. OUT!!'

And now there's a bit of mayhem. In my head and in the lorry. Because some of the lorry men are beginning to shout back. And one man is standing, rattling his cage like he's a mountain gorilla, like he can do something about all this. Just like Papa.

And I want to shout: 'Don't. Don't! Be careful!' But I stay rooted, just like I did in the car, when Muma got out. Muma never liked being pushed around.

So. Muma got out and she started talking too.

The soldiers did not like Muma. I don't know if it was because she was a woman, or because she was just Muma. Muma, who wasn't used to taking 'no' for an answer. Sometimes I think I'm a bit like Muma.

As for me, I did not like the eyes of the predator boy that day. The boy's eyes were not wild like those of the boys who smoked the not-tobacco, but they were frightening. Chilling even. Because they were full of fear. I was looking into the eyes of someone who was terrified. A terrified child. It might have been a mirror.

So I didn't get out of the car.

I didn't get out of the car.

I didn't

'Move. Move move MOVE!'

And the men in the lorry are moving, stumbling. And one of the lorry women cries out, in a language I don't understand so I don't know what she says, but it sounds urgent and soft. And it's directed at the mountain gorilla man. Some last hope perhaps, some entreaty, a word of love.

I wish there'd been a last word of love on that desert road.

Between Papa and Muma.

Between Muma and me.
Between Papa and me.
But there wasn't.
There was just one word: *Run.*

29

JUVES

When all the men are gone the tailgate of the lorry is slammed again and there is a sudden silence.

Silence.

Silence.

Silence.

And then the baby starts sobbing again. There is something very intuitive about babies.

The engine revs a second time. But I only get to the fourth finger of my right hand – four minutes – when we stop again. The door opens to a shout of: 'Juves. Unaccompanied juves!'

'Up,' I say to the boy and we stand.

This time even those who don't speak the language understand the drill. Everyone stands up. Just in case.

'JUVES, I SAID!'

There are about eight of us. Juveniles. A bedraggled band of unaccompanied minors, anyone under fifteen travelling alone.

A male guard unlocks the cage opposite and extracts four children who look about eleven or twelve. Kids who have no grown-up clutching on to them. No grown-up who cries out as they are taken. And of course, there's a little mumbling, whispering, but not too much. The women who are left don't want to make a nuisance of themselves. It's not as if they don't have family members of their own to protect.

The guard who comes to our cage is a woman. A big woman, made bigger by her body armour.

She points at the boy. 'Out.'

I nod at him to go and make to follow him.

'Not you,' she says.

'I'm fourteen,' I say.

'"Course you are,' she says.

'It's in my papers. I was born on the Isle of Arran.'

'Tell it to Immigration,' she says.

The boy looks at me.

'I've already been verified,' I say. 'At Heathrow.'

'Heathrow is in England,' she says. 'You're in Scotland now.'

'If I'm not fourteen,' I say, hearing an unexpected lurch of panic in my voice, 'if you think I'm of age, then he's not an unaccompanied minor. You can't take him. You can't separate us.'

'Us?' she says. 'Are you his mother now?'

Mother.

'No,' I say. And then I add: 'I'm his sister.'

I feel something move against my side. It's the boy – aligning himself.

The guard looks at the pair of us.

She looks at my white, Celtic flesh and my blue eyes. She looks at his bronze, African flesh and his deep-as-cups brown eyes.

'Do you think I was born yesterday?' she says and she jabs her baton so hard and so fast into my chest that I fall. The boy is still holding me – just. She detaches him, pulls him out of the cage and locks the door behind him.

'And, for the record,' she adds, 'I can do anything I like.'

30

BAGGING UP

We travel for another three fingers before the lorry tailgate is opened a final time. There are no shouts and no soldiers on the tarmac this time. So, it is just the guards who escort out the remaining women and children.

Ahead of us is a prefabricated hut saying, 'Reception 3'. I walk slowly, partly because my chest still burns from the baton punch and partly because it's important to remain calm, try to map my surroundings. It's clear immediately that this is not a purpose-built holding facility like the one at the airport. The Heathrow Detention Centre was modern, a construction of concrete and steel which looked like a prison. I've noticed this about major cities, or centres of power anyway, about how, the further you get from them, the more makeshift things become. This place does not look like a prison. It's a haphazard selection of tired brick buildings, some of which were obviously once quite grand. I'd say it probably started life as a school. Many of the windows are – newly – barred, but not all of them. This will give me some options but not many. The perimeter fence is over five metres high and has a roll of razor wire on top.

Once inside the reception hut, I'm separated from those travelling with children. My line seems to consist of lone 'adult' women. I'd say most of them are about my age but it's hard to tell. *Try not to take it personally.* That's what Fire-Flint Phil told me at Heathrow. *There are different rules and regs for juveniles. Juveniles must have access to a social worker, a doctor, a psychiatrist. They can't be kept in solitary confinement. It's just about resources, Mhairi.*

The Imgrim behind the desk at the head of this queue has a nanonet with a holographic keyboard and screen, a 3-D printer and a hand-held iris scanner. All of these things hum. In fact the whole room seems to be humming with low, grumbling techno-noise. It's strange to have forgotten this noise, considering it was once the soundtrack to my life. Now it sounds like my ears malfunctioning.

The Imgrim also has a large pile of see-through plastic bags. Probably made from algae. This useless thought comes with the memory of Muma saying how, if she hadn't been an engineer, she would have liked to study long-chain polymers. As each detainee approaches, the Imgrim simply stretches out her hand (without lifting her eyes from the holoscreen) and if the person in front her has papers she takes them. The papers are then referenced with the screen and the detainee iris-scanned and then given a bag and a 3-D printed wristband. Into the bag go all that woman's (or girl's) possessions. Above the desk is a sign which says: *Following registration, all detainees will be strip-searched. Any person found to have concealed possessions will be sent immediately to the Management Unit.* The sign is in two languages only: English and Gaelic. Gaelic first. It doesn't say what the 'Management Unit' is, but I can guess.

When it's my turn, I hand over my papers. The Imgrim looks at the papers, looks at her screen, runs her fingers over the virtual keyboard, scans me with the iris-wand and looks at her screen again. This is the moment she might discover I'm fourteen.

I wait.

She fingers some more buttons of light. Then she simply files my papers in the same tray as everyone else's, and hands me a bag.

So, I just stand there some more.

And finally – she looks up. She does not have a nice face. Her hair is scraped back into a tight bun and her eyes are too small and too close together.

'Possessions,' she says. 'In the bag.'

I take out my gun.

Her eyes go even smaller.

I consider pointing the gun at her head. I consider smashing it against her skull. But I don't. Using my bullet-less gun against an Imgrim in this heavily guarded hall would be a mistake.

Stay alive, Mhairi. You have to stay alive!

Yes, Muma.

So I just poke my first finger through the trigger guard and hold the gun sideways. If you hold a gun like this, on just one finger, you can spin it. I spin the gun. Just a few revolutions. This is as futile a gesture as Papa jumping out of the car with an open hand or the Mountain Gorilla Man shaking his cage. But there are some things in life, I've realised, that you just cannot not do. Things that define you, make you the person you are. Big things. Small things. Personal acts of hope or defiance. Things which hold you to yourself, even when they might be dangerous. Not even risks and choices. Imperatives.

I smile.

Smiling can also be one of these acts. I drop my gun in the plastic bag. The woman's eyes follow the gun.

Next I put my knife in the bag.

Then my food cloth with no food in it.

And finally, I put in my fire flint.

I do not put my water canister in the bag. The water canister is hanging on a string around my neck. *Remember*, Papa said when he gave me my first metal canister, *water is life*.

The Imgrim lifts her eyes to the canister and then points at the notice above her head. *Any person found to have concealed possessions will be sent immediately to the Management Unit.*

'It's not concealed,' I say.

'I have already been very patient,' the Imgrim says.

'It's only a water bottle,' I say.

'Put it,' she says, 'in the bag. Now.'

I put my water bottle in the bag. It's still half-full, I can hear the water sloshing. I look at my bottle through the plastic and feel immediately thirsty. I feel so thirsty I could drink an entire lake. The woman ties the bag up with a plastic tie, the sort you can also use for handcuffs. Then she picks up the newly made identity tag from the printer tray and fixes it – more tightly than she needs to – about my right wrist.

It's at this moment that I stop being Mhairi Anne Bain and become Ret1787F. The F stands for Female. 1787 is my number. But Ret – I do not know what Ret means. At Heathrow I was Sco5271F. Sco for Scotland.

'What does Ret mean?' I ask.

'It means,' she says, 'you go through that door, there.'

31

MATTRESS

I go through That Door There.

It does not lead to a strip-search area. The notification suggesting it might was probably just one of those things they often have in detention facilities: a lie, a threat, a possibility, something to mess with your head. The door actually leads to some sort of holding room. There are about thirty women here, fifteen chairs (set out in three rows of five) and a table with some plastic cups and a water jug. The water jug is empty. No one tells me what I am waiting for or how long the wait will be. This is also quite normal in detention facilities, I've found.

There is also a toilet. It doesn't smell too bad. Some of the women in the queue talk together. They talk in English. With Scottish accents.

'I don't understand it,' one woman says in a low burr. 'How can they do this to us?'

I remember then what Grandmother said when Muma said: *Don't be ridiculous, we're Scots. We were born there. Even if they do shut the border we can come back any time.*

Grandmother said: *Don't bet your life on it. The rules are changing all the time. Come now.*

I think the rules may have changed.

A small, wiry girl twists her wristband angrily, picks at it. She's about my age and, in Before, we might have fallen into conversation but now she's an irritant, a fly buzzing uselessly against a pane of glass. Besides, I'm busy with my own thoughts.

About the boy.

I don't want to be thinking about him, but he comes unbidden. As does his sucking stone. I wonder whether they've taken his stone from him. I wonder whether they've made him put it in a see-through bag and sealed that bag with a handcuff tie? I wonder if they've moved him into a cell yet? And, if they've moved him to a cell, who they've put him with? Grown-ups or just other children? People who speak his own language – or people who don't? People shouting around him, at him, in languages he doesn't understand? Wondering is not helpful. It doesn't change anything. I turn my attention to the guards. I monitor their comings and goings. Logging the patterns of the guards could change things.

It seems we're waiting to be called. Guards appear every half-hour or so with a list. People go in batches when their names, or rather their numbers, are called. The wiry girl goes, still picking at her identity bracelet. Eventually it's my turn. I'm marched away with five other young women towards what I think must be the main building of the complex. I count steps and calculate distances. How long it would take to run between this building and the reception area? How long between here and the main gate? It's possible my calculations aren't accurate. It's over twelve hours since I had anything to eat.

It's dark now. I hope this building will contain the cells so I will be able to lie down. In Heathrow, the cells were not called cells but 'rooms'. The Heathrow 'rooms' had sparse beds (two or sometimes three), a basin, a lavatory without a seat, bars on the high-up window and a spyhole in the door.

We go up a wide flight of stairs, along a brightly lit corridor. A door is unlocked. The door does not have a spyhole but it does have a panel of what looks like re-enforced glass.

'Ret1787,' announces a guard and ushers me in.

It is not a cell, but nor is it a room exactly. It's a dormitory. There are no beds, but there are mattresses. Twelve of them laid out on the floor in two rows of six. There are bars on the windows (makeshift but strong-looking), no basin, no toilet.

Eleven of the mattresses are already taken. The women lying on the mattresses are wearing nightclothes: pale striped pyjamas, ill-fitting pale pink nightdresses. The same sort of Detention Issue clothing I recognise from Heathrow. People who journey do not have nightclothes. Only people who stay still enough, long enough. I do not like to think how long these women have been in this room.

There's only one spare mattress, here by the door. On it is a folded pair of pyjamas in a colour that might have been pink but which is now grey. I'm just about to take ownership of this space when I hear a voice behind me:

'That one's mine.'

It's the wiry Wristband Girl.

She must have been standing slightly behind me, in the small window alcove to the right of the door. I've never liked being taken by surprise.

So.

One bed.

Two takers.

Her body is crouched and tight. She seems to be asking me to fight her for it.

The night-clothed women sit up a little. Here is the evening entertainment. I've been here before. In any prison situation, there are unwritten rules. There's always a Big Mama in a group like this, the person who says how it's going to be, sets the agenda, decides the punishments. Often you can tell who this person is just by looking: by their body language, how or where they sit or stand in a room. Or by the nervous glances that go their way before anyone acts. But this is all happening too fast. I haven't had time to make a judgement.

But I know what the Wristband Girl is doing. She's staking a claim. She wants to look hard. She wants to show that she's got guts, won't be pushed about, wants to play with the big girls.

Even though she's tiny. A blonde pile of skin and bones held together with nervous energy. You have to admire that energy though. That hope. Unfortunately for her though, she hasn't quite got the confidence to pull it off.

'Be my guest,' I say to her and, with an exaggeratedly open hand, I gesture at the mattress. 'I don't propose to stay here that long.'

And the real Big Mama laughs. A laugh full of cigarette smoke. She's a large, breezy white woman with henna red hair who's wearing – I should have noticed – the only well-fitting nightdress in the room.

Good, I think. Now I know what's what.

The Wristband Girl deflates, sinks into her mattress and tries to change into the nightclothes while everyone else watches. We are all looking for the same thing: chinks, vulnerability. I catch a glimpse of her tiny white breasts.

I select the piece of floor in the alcove. This positions me on a diagonal with Big Mama and with an equally commanding view of the room. Sleeping on a floor is not a hardship. With a floor, you do not have to sweep stones away first. And floorboards are comfortable enough, but not so comfortable that you can forget that your journey isn't over. It's always a mistake to drop your guard just because you're getting close to your destination. I found this out when I got near the airport at Cairo.

I lie full-stretch in my clothes, which are almost dry now.

There are no curtains at the alcove window so I look out at the sky as it grows darker, but never wholly dark. Too many security lights.

I hear the women's breath go to sleep. They do not breathe like the boy. I miss the boy's sucking sleep breaths. But maybe tonight the boy is not making those sucking breaths because he does not have his stone. Maybe, like me, he's lying awake now, looking out into the security-lit dark.

I begin to make plans.

I am still awake when, in the middle of the night, the guards come into the room. They turn on the lights and blow whistles. They shout: 'Up! Everyone up!'

Everyone gets up. Those with mattresses, stand by them.

Numbers are read out. In turn, the women say, 'Yes.'

When my number is read out, I say, 'Yes.'

It's all over in under two minutes. The guards leave and no one says a thing. From this I ascertain they must do this head count every night. This explains why even Big Mama sleeps in nightclothes.

I change my plans.

To escape this place, one clearly needs to do it in daylight.

32

QUEUE

In the morning, there is a queue. I am at the back of it. The queue contains not just the twelve other women in my dormitory but also women from every other room that opens on to this corridor. As soon as the doors are unlocked there is a ferocious scramble and I'm not fast enough. Nobody mentions what the rush is for but, as some of the women have towels, I imagine it's for the washroom. I expect the washroom will only be open for a certain amount of time and, if you don't make it to the front of the queue by then, you will miss your opportunity.

If Heathrow is anything to go by, the certain amount of time might be an hour or an hour and a half. It will feel both longer and shorter.

I used to think time was simple. And also numerical, that it ticked by at a certain rate. I have discovered that this is not true.

33

TIME

In Before I counted time in hours and minutes and seconds. It was 9 a.m. or 11 p.m.; 0800 hours or 22.47 precisely. Clock-time. Accurate and available at the push of a button. Usually my phone button. Then I came on this journey and time changed. It broadened, it became sunrise and sunset. It wasn't maths any more, it was light and dark. The rhythm of this was different. Papa, I thought, would have liked this new time.

But then even this new time began to unravel. It wouldn't stay still, began to spool into many different sorts of time. So I began to have to give them names:

– Slow Time
– Deep Time
– Long Time
– Now Time
– Arrested Time

I was first aware of Slow Time that night in the desert tomb at Meroe. It was to do with the brick. We were struggling for it, the stranger and me. Although, it was me who lifted it first, had my hands around it, because I was angry. Frightened too of course, but more angry than frightened. Which made me strong. But he was strong too, because he was a man and I was just a child. I was lying on my back and he was above me, so he also had the benefit of gravity. Nevertheless, at first, that brick was definitely going upwards, away from me and towards him.

Naturally, he tried to defend himself, grabbed my wrist and pushed the brick away from his own face and back down towards mine.

Very, very slowly.

It took that brick about a hundred years to make that journey from his face to my face. In this Slow Time I both saw the brick in minute, starlit detail (it was a beautiful thing even then, Papa) and also imagined all the things that brick might do when it finally connected with my head. I imagined some blood. I imagined some mess. I imagined probably not being able to talk or walk very well afterwards. What I didn't imagine was what actually happened – the sudden last-minute skewing of my head, so the brick deflected off my mouth, where it chipped a piece from one of my top teeth. I remember tasting tooth and brick dust. And also pain. Though I understood the pain could have been a great deal worse. I shouted out then and the brick went in the sand and the man lost his balance. He was drunk anyway. Drunk or high or both and so not as sharp as me, so it was me who first got my hands on that brick again. And this time, I was climbing, I was clawing my way upwards until I was above him. And the brick was coming down again.

Only on him.

I always wondered how it was for him that moment. Did he experience Slow Time? Did the brick take a thousand years to come crashing down on his skull? Or not? Afterwards, he wasn't in a position to say.

At first, I thought that time-shifts like this must just happen. They couldn't be predicted or controlled. But that's not true either. That's another reason for going in Other Worlds. In Other Worlds, you can manipulate time, even suspend it. You can concentrate so hard on climbing up your single blade of grass that you can make the past disappear, the future disappear, so all that's left is this one present moment. This is Now Time.

In Now Time you cannot be held responsible for the past because there is no past. The past is over your shoulder and all is dark there. Nor can anything you do have consequences for the future, because the future hasn't arrived yet. It's all ahead of you and dark there too. You are just wholly and only contained here, in the brightness of Now Time.

It's like standing on a crack in the universe that someone should have told you about, but nobody did. Even Papa never told me about Now Time.

Nor did he tell me about Deep Time. Deep Time is very useful if you're in a queue. Deep Time reminds you that the universe has been around for billions of years and, if you imagine those billions of years as one straight line and then you try and put your queue-waiting-time on that line, you'll see it's really no time at all. I used to do this at Heathrow, when I waited for meetings with Imgrims about my papers. Once I waited so long I imagined myself right back at the moment when the world began. Papa used to call this 'the beginning of time' which implies that there must once have been a time before this. A time before time. A time when there was no time. It's ideas like this that make my head go fuzzy. When my head goes fuzzy, time seems to lose all meaning anyway. I imagine it's like this when you kiss someone you love. But this has never happened to me.

The Deep Time system always works though. I know this as I am now at the front of the queue.

34

CLOAK OF WATER

There are two showers in the washroom area, each with a half-door that shuts but (I observe) can't be locked. The first to come free is the cubicle to the right. I go in, undress, hang my clothes over the half-door and stand under the shower. I turn on the water.

And water comes out.

The water is not hot, but nor is it cold. It's tepid.

Tepid can be another word for warm. Or warmish.

This water, Papa, is the most beautiful warmish water in the whole of the world.

The flow of it is quite strong and the shower head is angled so that the stream of water lands precisely on the crown of my head. The force of it drives the water down through my hair and over my shoulders where it continues to fall around me like a cloak.

I don't know how long I stand in this cloak of water.

It might be a few minutes, it might be a millennium. This is not Slow Time. This is Arrested Time. Because everything has stopped for a moment. Even my heart has almost stopped. If I had soap I might wash, but I don't have soap. So I just stand still in the warmth.

Twigs fall out of my hair.

35

FOOD

We get food.
  – For breakfast: a roll with butter. Butter.
  – For lunch: soup, made from vegetables. Potatoes, cabbage, carrots – cut in big chunks.
  – For supper: a hunk of bread. Some yellow cheese. Sometimes an apple.

We eat in a hall where the tables and chairs are screwed to the floor. Many children are brought to the hall at mealtimes.

But not the boy.

36

INTERVIEW

I am taken to an interview room. There are four chairs around a rectangular table. Three of the chairs – the ones behind the table – are taken. I stand by the empty chair in front of the table.

The chief Imgrim – the one sitting in the middle – is a woman. She's slim, smartly dressed in purple and smells of clean washing. She is flanked by two men in navy uniforms. All three have nanonets, papers and plastic cups of coffee. The aroma of the coffee makes my heart hop. Open on the desk – at page nine – is my Global Passport. This is not good news. Page nine is Global Citizen Credits, the page you need to start filling in when you're over fifteen.

The woman activates the record facility on her nanonet. 'I am Immigration Officer Jean Shanks,' she says. 'This interview, commencing at,' she pauses, '11.51 is being conducted under the Immigration Scotland and Federated Islands Act in the presence of Homeland Officers Peel and McNally.' Then she holds her hand out towards me and adds: 'Wrist, please.'

She says it as if I could detach my hand from my arm and hand it to her.

'My name is Mhairi Anne Bain,' I say.

'I didn't ask for your name, I asked for your wrist.'

I stretch out my hand and she guides the barcode of my wristband into some beam I can't see.

'Ret1787F,' Scottish Homeland Officer McNally reads off his screen.

'Sit down, please, Ret1787,' says IO Shanks.

But I don't. I stay standing. 'I'm fourteen,' I say. 'I'm a juvenile. I'm Scots. It's all been checked already. I was verified at Heathrow.'

'Heathrow is in England,' says IO Shanks. 'You are now in Scotland.'

'Yes, I know. But . . .'

'Please confine yourself to answering the questions asked of you,' interrupts Officer Shanks. 'So – you were born on the Isle of Arran . . . Is that correct?'

'Yes.'

'And when was it that you left Scotland?'

'When I was about seven.'

'Recorded as exiting the country six years, nine months and four days ago,' McNally reads from the screen.

'An absence of in excess of five years. Which makes you officially a Ret,' says Shanks.

'A Ret?'

'A Returnee,' says Shanks. 'And I think I asked you to sit, Ret1787.'

I don't sit.

There's a short pause. 'As you like,' says Shanks. 'HO Peel?'

Peel clears his throat: 'Pursuant to the Scotland and Federated Island Territories Immigration Act dated November 22nd, 2049, the automatic right of return for citizens who have been permanently out of the country for a period of five years or more is suspended until further notice.'

'Do you understand?' asks Officer Shanks.

'No.'

'It's very simple,' she says. 'Your right to return to Scotland is no longer solely dependent on your place of birth.'

I do sit then. The chair beneath me is hard, solid. 'What is it dependent on?' I ask.

'There are a number of requirements,' IO Shanks says. 'The first being the birthplaces of your grandparents. All four of them need to have been born in Scotland Mainland or Island Territories. If Island Territories you could be eligible for a transit visa to same.'

I do not know what 'Island Territories' means. In Before there was only Scotland. But Arran's an island and Papa's mother was definitely born on the island. And possibly Papa's father too. But I have no idea where my mother's parents were born. I haven't had to know before.

'If your grandparents cannot be independently verified – and we are currently conducting checks –' Shanks continues, 'then your eligibility will additionally depend on your suitability for this country as defined by your Global Credit score.'

'But I don't have a score yet,' I cry out. 'I don't have to have one. I'm fourteen! I told you, I'm still a juvenile!'

'That is something also under investigation,' says Shanks.

'Why? I left Scotland when I was seven. You said I'd been away six years something. Do the maths!'

'I should warn you that being obstructive will not aid your cause.'

'I don't have a cause,' I say. 'This is my country. Scotland. I belong here.'

She taps my papers. 'You are a Global Citizen. If you can't be verified or your GC score is too low, you will be sent back to your last registered domicile country which was . . .'

'The Sudan,' fills in Officer McNally.

'The Sudan?' I say. 'The Sudan is at war!'

'The Sudan,' says IO Shanks, 'is still a signatory to the Global Citizen (Equator North) Charter. As such we would have every confidence in her taking you back. Especially after your seven years in the territory.' She pauses to take a sip of coffee. 'If they refuse to take you back you would become officially stateless and there are other regulations to do with that which don't concern us here. What does concern us, I'm afraid, is the matter of your Global Debits. Charge sheet details, please, HO Peel.'

'In direct contravention of the Scotland and Federated Islands Trafficking Act,' HO Peel reads, 'Ret1787F was detained in the act of illegally crossing into Scotland Mainland with an unidentified alien.'

They're talking about the boy. The boy and his sucking stone.

'Do you deny it?' asks IO Shanks.

'Where is he?' I say then. And now I'm on my feet again. 'Why does he never come to meals? What have you done with him?'

'That is none of your concern,' says Imgrim Shanks.

118

'He's a child,' I shout. 'A child! Or do you think he's fifteen too?'

IO Shanks barks into her nanonet: 'Security, please. Ret1787F will be returning to her room. What you may like to consider,' she adds to me, 'is that the penalty for trafficking a child into Scotland is a minimum of twenty-five years. And I'm not, obviously, talking jail years. I'm talking Life Years. If found guilty, you will be required to take the needle at forty-nine. Of course, anything validated on your Global Credits pages will be taken in mitigation.' She hands me a sheet of paper and a stub of pencil. 'So perhaps you'd like to start thinking seriously about what to put on those pages?'

37

TAKING THE NEEDLE

Taking the needle, Papa says, is an almost rational solution to a difficult problem. The difficult problem of there being too many people in our too hot world. In the south, war and famine kill. But in the cooler north, security depends on an agreed solution.

I was your age, Papa said, *when it was first suggested that no one in the north should be entitled to live beyond a certain age. That age was eighty to begin with. Now seventy-four, of course. It was thought that this was the only fair way of stretching the available resources. The only way of having a hope of feeding ourselves. It took some getting used to, but it's not really so very different from what the Chinese did in the last century when they attempted to limit population with their one-child policy.* Then he paused and added: *Why do you think I try and grab life so hard every day, Mhairi?*

It was ten years after the introduction of this Global Life Limit policy that the idea of gifting life became a reality. Or rather gifting death. It came out of love. The case of Ada and John Mullins. Ada and John had been sweethearts since they were teenagers. They knew they would love one another until death, but John was two years older than Ada. Which meant that when he went – gracefully – to the needle in his seventy-fourth year, Ada would have to live a full two years without him. *What*, Ada asked, *if I was to gift him one of my years? What if I promised to take the needle at seventy-three, so he could live till seventy-five, and then us both go together?*

It went all the way to the Supreme Global Court North. The court ruled that it was a matter of indifference to the planet whether two people checked out at seventy-four or one at seventy-three and one at seventy-five. It amounted to the same in terms of resource consumption. So – with certain safeguards – the Mullins' petition was upheld. The irony was that John Mullins was killed in a car crash the following week. He was just sixty-nine but Ada had already signed the paperwork. Of course, she was entitled to live until seventy-three but she chose (with a big fanfare and live on Global News) to surrender to the needle immediately, so they might be buried together. It was hailed as a win-win for the planet and marked the official beginning of the trade in Life Years.

National governments were quick to extend the idea – notably to the prison population. It was cheaper for countries (and globally more efficient) if non-violent criminals paid their dues in Life Years.

So, if they find me guilty – when they find me guilty – I will be required to sign a piece of paper allowing them to inject me with potassium aged forty-nine. I am fourteen. Forty-nine is not tomorrow. But nor is it in Deep Time.

This means, Muma, that I can either begin making a case for myself on my Global Credits pages, or I can look for the boy.

And also, a weapon.

38
WEAPONS

It is quite easy to make weapons if you have the time and the inclination. In detention, you often have both. When I was in detention at Cairo airport I saw a man make a crossbow. He used:

- six toothbrushes
- a cigarette lighter
- four ballpoint pen casings
- a wire coathanger
- one side of a pair of aluminium cafeteria tongs
- assorted electrical components
- the fingers of some yellow rubber gloves
- a piece of string
- some screws

The bullets were made from packed toilet paper and aluminium foil. The maker – Jamil – said it had a range of ten metres, but I never saw it fired so I do not know if this is true.

In Heathrow, industry was smaller scale but definitely lethal. I saw:

- a knife, made from a shard of glass with a handle of torn bedsheet and gaffer tape.

- an eye gouger, made from a plastic fork with the two inner prongs removed and the two outer ones sharpened.
- a knife made from paper. The man who showed it to me said he'd made it from fifty sheets of magazine paper taken from a library copy of *National Geographic*. The paper was then wetted, rolled and shaped, and then dried with salt. It was surprisingly sharp.

There is no library in this detention centre. So, I volunteer to work in the kitchens. Because, as well as making weapons, you can also steal them. To chop those vegetables for soup there must, I think, be knives. And there are. Small serrated knives with blunt, rounded ends.

But ends can be sharpened.

I make myself a good worker. I work hard and efficiently. I chop and chop and chop. I also look. You would be pleased by how much I am looking these days, Papa.

Through the kitchen windows I see a different view of the detention centre than the one I see from my alcove window. One building stands out. A square-set grey stone building with a slightly comical set of grey turrets. The old headmaster's house perhaps. The windows are mullioned, have that very old-fashioned crisscrossing of lead, so they looked barred. But they aren't.

'What is that building?' I ask. 'The one with the towers?'

'Administration,' says the girl on onions to my left.

This is disappointing news. I am unlikely to be able to conjure a reason to visit administration.

'No,' says a woman slicing cabbage. 'It's where they keep the young ones, isn't it? The under-tens. That's why there aren't any bars. Because the young ones don't usually jump.'

This is better news.

I might appear to be putting chopped potatoes into large pans but actually I'm looking out the window and refining my plan. The boy is under ten. I look to see if I can identify any dormitories in the turreted building, spot children at the windows. But I can't. This is annoying. I need to know, if he's being kept there, where he's being kept. Not just the floor but the actual room. If I get to that building, I won't exactly have the time to ask around. Perhaps they keep the children in the rooms that overlook the back of the building? I note the position of the main door and the side doors. I watch how the larger lorries, the ones which actually have drivers, circle the right-hand side of the building and pull up out of sight around the back. Army trucks but also catering trucks. I keep track of how long the drivers leave the lorries there, which is quite some time. This suggests the car park may also be an electric recharge point. A lorry with a temporarily absent driver is a possible escape opportunity.

I don't just look, Papa, I also listen. During my daily three-hour chop, I learn these things about the fifty-two of us currently on Women's Wing 3:

- Nineteen women are awaiting deportation.
- Twelve (including me) are awaiting court dates.
- Fourteen have had their claim to be juveniles dismissed.
- Four have self-harmed.
- Two are on suicide watch.
- Eight have been put in restraints in the last two weeks.
- There have been four escape attempts in the last six months. Only one successful.

125

The escape ratio is disappointing. My chance of changing this ratio depends on paying attention.

I pay attention.

At the end of each chopping session we are led out one by one and required to drop our washed knives in a wooden knife box. A guard counts us and the knives. If there is a discrepancy all of us are strip-searched.

But here's the thing: those of us who have passed the knife box get to wait in the corridor before being escorted back to the unit. In this corridor is an old-fashioned double radiator from Before, the sort that has a dusty space between the two sides.

This, I think, could be a solution to the weapon problem.

39

THE WRISTBAND GIRL

The Wristband Girl is called Finola. I'm sorry I found this out. She also works in the kitchens. She is not a tidy worker. When she peels potatoes, she often drops the peelings on the floor. This is because of the twitching. Perhaps the twitching is a medical condition but I don't think so. I think it's nerves. The peelings can be slippery. This gives me what Muma would have called an 'opportunity'. *Take your opportunities*, Muma always said, *as and when they arise.*

I stand close to Finola. Today she is on potatoes and I am on carrots. I watch her jerk and twitch. When she drops the first couple of bits of potato skin, I say:

'You should pick those up. Someone could slip on those.'

She picks them up.

The next time she drops some, I tut. Of course, she bends to clean them up again, but not before I have edged one of those peelings under the counter with my foot. I push it far enough under to be hidden but not so far that I couldn't retrieve it again if I wanted to, which I do, in the last minute before the end of our shift. I pull that piece of potato peel out with my foot and, as I take my final colander of chopped carrots towards the pans on the stove, I slip.

I slip on Finola's piece of potato skin.

'What the—' I yell as I fall. The sieve skitters across the floor. It goes quite far (I make sure of that) and the carrot rounds spill even further. Then I reach for the offending piece of potato peel and I shake it at her.

'Sorry,' she says, 'sorry.' And she immediately gets down on her knees and starts collecting up the carrot circles.

I stand up, check my (unhurt) ankle, retrieve the colander, bang it down on the chopping surface (right on top of her small, serrated knife), pick up the colander (and with it the knife), reinspect my ankle (slipping the knife into my sock), and get back down on my knees to help in the clear-up operation. We have things nice and neat just at the time when the escort guards arrive to take us back to the unit.

I wash my knife and put it in the wooden box.

The Wristband Girl cannot find her knife.

'Probably on the floor with everything else you drop,' I say as I exit into the corridor. As the escort guards wait for the Wristband Girl to produce her knife, I slip it unseen into the dusty middle space of the double radiator.

When the knife cannot be found, we are all, of course, taken to be strip-searched. The guards conduct the search in the interests of maximum humiliation. They search in places you should never look. Especially not for a knife. It is difficult for me to control my temper, but I do control it. This is what Muma always called: *Looking at the bigger picture.* You sacrifice something small in order to achieve something big. In this case, a ready-made weapon.

Finola protests her innocence. Finola says she has no idea where her knife is. The guards do not believe her. They march her off to the Management Unit in the hope that it will improve her memory.

I wait three days before retrieving the knife and bringing it back to the dormitory.

I do not conceal the knife from the other women. In fact, I make a point of sharpening the blade on the ragged iron of the bars outside our windows. Everyone knows this is Finola's knife but they do not say anything. Mainly because I am the one with the knife.

Big Mama does say something. She says: 'You and I should talk.'

This is not a threat, it's an invitation. She says it because she sees how the other women are looking at me now: which is with respect. Or maybe fear.

'Yes,' I reply, 'we should.' I do this to keep the peace. But I do not think Big Mama and I will have anything interesting to say to each other. After all, Big Mama is still in this place. Whereas, when the knife is sharp enough, I will be leaving.

The following day, Finola is brought back. She is even thinner than she was before. She is also paler. She is the colour of her very blonde hair. This is because in the Management Unit, we learn, they keep you in solitary confinement and feed you nothing but water. Also, the cells have no windows and therefore there is no sky and no sun.

When night comes, she doesn't fight me for the mattress which I have taken over in her absence. She just lies down quiet as a mouse on the alcove floor. But she doesn't sleep. And nor do I for a while.

'I hope they release you soon,' I hear myself saying to her back.

This is not a lie.

It's not everyone who can play the survival game.

40

PLANNING

I like planning.

I like lists. I'm well-organised, I'm practised at looking and at listening. I listen to what people say and also what they do not say. Sometimes the useful things are to be found in the gaps.

Planning is important, Muma always used to say. *You know me, I'm a great planner. But planning isn't everything. Life is not like a game of chess, where you can always be a step ahead, try to visualise the end-game. No, life often throws you a curved ball. You need to be agile, Mhairi, flexible, be prepared to change your plan, take your opportunities as and when they arise.*

Which is why, when a guard unlocks our door at 4.30 p.m. and unexpectedly shouts my number, it takes me less than ten seconds to gather my jerkin and, with it, Finola's – now very sharp – knife.

41

PSYCH

There is no point asking where I am being taken, so I don't ask.

But it soon becomes clear. I am being taken to the turreted house with the unbarred windows. Marched straight into the place I have spent so much time mapping, thinking about, planning around. An ID check and a flight of stairs later and I'm outside a door marked: 'Dr R. Naik, Psychiatrist'. The guard knocks and I'm called in.

The office is small: another desk, another chair, or rather two chairs. But these are not hard, institutional chairs. They're homey chairs with fabric seats, worn and frayed at the edges. Dr Naik (who is not wearing a white coat) has a nanonet but also a shelf of old-fashioned books and a steaming jug of heart-hopping coffee. I can almost taste that coffee in the back of my throat.

The doctor stands up. He's about thirty with neatly brushed jet black hair. His name is Indian, his face is Indian, but he says: *Mhairi, isn't it?* in a broad Glaswegian accent. He smiles. His smile seems genuine, kind even.

'Mhairi Ann Bain,' I reply. I stop myself from returning the smile but I cannot stop myself from taking his outstretched hand. It's warm and dry.

'I'm Dr Naik. I lead the psychiatric team in this unit,' he says. 'Do sit.'

I sit. But straight-backed, on my guard.

'Would you like coffee?' he asks.

'Yes,' I say. I have not had coffee since I was in Cairo. In Heathrow coffee was considered an offensive weapon. And it can be, if it's hot enough.

Dr Naik pours the coffee and asks if I want milk.

I want milk.

'I expect you want to know why you're here,' he says.

I do want to know. The softness of this room, of this one particular doctor, is breeding an unwanted flicker of hope in me. Hope is a dangerous thing. Hope makes you believe things to be true which are often proved not to be true and then, when you fall, you fall further. I have learnt to guard against hope. And yet, in this Now Time moment, I think perhaps that they have discovered that I am fourteen after all. That they have decided to provide me with a psychiatrist, a social worker, that they will call me by my own name, put me in a room without bars, open the door of that room, let me free . . .

'It's about the boy you came in with,' says Dr Naik. 'He's on hunger strike.'

'Hunger strike!' It's a punch harder than the one I got from the baton guard.

'Yes, I'm afraid so.'

'That's stupid,' I say.

'Stupid?' Dr Naik tips his head with interest.

'Yes.'

133

'Why so?'

'Anyone who has known starvation would eat, given the opportunity,' I say. 'Don't you think?'

Dr Naik makes a note on his nanonet. In fact, he makes two notes. 'We have reason to believe he's making a statement,' he adds.

'About what?'

'You.'

'Me?'

'Yes, you. We believe the boy is missing you.'

'Did he say so?' I ask carefully.

The doctor laughs. 'Not exactly. But he did do this.' Dr Naik unclips a piece of paper from a file and pushes it towards me. It's a drawing. But not the sort of intense drawing the boy did on the stones. No, it's a simple, childish thing. A picture of two people, a girl and a boy. The sort of drawing you might do if you were under instruction: *Can you draw your family for us, do you think?* The girl is taller than the boy. They are holding hands and smiling. Or more grimacing than smiling perhaps, their lips snarled back so that you can see their teeth. Both of them are missing a small triangle of upper front tooth. They look like people who belong together but also like people who might bite you. It makes me want to laugh. But I don't laugh because there's also sadness in the picture. Or rather not in the picture. Because not in the picture are his real family. The family I've failed to think about much before. His parents, his brothers, if he has brothers. His sisters. Siblings older than him. Younger than him even. Wiped from this Now Time picture to make way for this new, born-of-necessity family. And I don't know whether it's what's said or what's unsaid in this picture that gives me a sudden, flooding feeling.

'In fact,' continues Dr Naik, 'he hasn't spoken at all since he's been here. Not one word. Won't even tell us his name.' The doctor pauses. 'I was working on the elective mute principle.'

I first heard the term 'elective mute' at Heathrow. I was never sure about the elective bit. As if you could choose what happens to you and how you react to it.

'Mo,' I say.

'I'm sorry?' Dr Naik says.

'His name – it's Mo.'

'Mo as in Mohammed?' asks the doctor.

'No,' I say. 'Just Mo.'

'And his surname?'

'Bain,' I say. 'The same as mine. He's my brother.' I leave a little pause into which the doctor does not jump. 'Not my real brother, of course. My adopted brother. My parents – they adopted him. In the Sudan.'

The doctor fixes his uniform brown eyes on me.

'No one believes me about this,' I add, 'just as they don't believe I'm fourteen.'

'You're a juvenile?' says the doctor.

'Yes,' I say. 'I was verified at Heathrow, but that doesn't seem to count here.'

The doctor's long fingers move about his keyboard.

'As for why Mo's not talking, I can't explain that.' I add: 'At home, he talks all the time.'

'Ah,' says the doctor, still looking at the screen. 'Got a log on you. But not your brother.'

'His papers, they were stolen,' I say.

'Can you give me the details?'

I give him the details. I spin a very beautiful story. In Before there were Lies and there was also Truth. Now these things slide about a bit.

When I've finished, the doctor says: 'Thank you very much, Mhairi. You've been very helpful. Now, perhaps you'd like to help me with one more thing?'

I tell him I'd be delighted.

42

PLAYROOM

Dr Naik takes me into a side room.

The boy is sitting in the middle of the room on a child's red plastic chair at a red plastic table. He has his back to us and does not turn as we enter. To his right is a shelf with some toys on: a miniature train set, a platoon of soldiers with plastic machine guns, a family of fake-fur wolves. On the floor a brightly coloured playmat is printed with a map of the world (Equator North). The toys are untouched as is the plate of food on the white plastic tray in front of him. The untouched meal is potatoes, carrots and chicken. Yes, chicken. Roast chicken. With thick dark gravy. The gravy is going cold, has a skin on it, but I can still smell the meat juice in it. I do not imagine every child in this unit gets chicken. I imagine they have offered him this chicken to tempt him. Though the way he's sitting makes it look like a punishment. He has not refused his water though, seems to have drunk about half what's in his blue plastic cup.

The other smell in the room is soap. They have washed the boy. They have put new clothes on him. The clothes are green. Green is good. Green is a useful colour for travelling. They have also reshaved his head. It makes me notice how very flat his ears lie to his skull. I don't think I've ever looked at his ears before. They are beautiful, Papa.

'Mo?' Dr Naik says. The boy does not react, which is not surprising as 'Mo' is not his name. So, the boy just continues to sit, staring out through the diamond-paned window. The sky beyond is blue. 'I've brought someone to see you.'

Nothing.

'It's me,' I say.

The boy turns.

But he does not get up, he does not come to greet me. He certainly doesn't make to hug me. In fact, he doesn't do anything the doctor might be expecting.

He just looks at me.

'What do you mean by not eating?' I say. Only I don't say it, I shout it. 'When I said you could survive without eating for three weeks, when I said you had to drink,' I point at his half-drunk water glass, 'could survive on water, it wasn't a challenge. It wasn't an instruction to try. Not eating when you're given food is stupid!' I shout. 'Totally stupid!' I walk straight over and slap him hard on the head.

'Hey – hey!' says Dr Naik. 'Stop it! You can't do that!'

The boy makes no sound, no sound at all. He doesn't touch the red welt on his cheek, doesn't feel to see if his ear is bruised. Which it is. He just looks at the doctor, looks at me and then, very deliberately, he cuts a tiny piece of chicken and forks it into his mouth. Chews, very, very slowly.

'It worked, didn't it?' I say to the doctor. 'It's what you wanted.'

The doctor looks down, writes something on his nanonet. Perhaps he writes *violence*, or *trauma*, or *traumatised*. That's what the doctors at Heathrow used to write anyway.

The boy cuts another minute piece of chicken.

'Good,' I say. 'Good boy.' I'm thinking maybe his mother was a clever mother. I'm thinking maybe she taught him the value of looking at the bigger picture too.

There's a pause while we watch him chew again.

'Dr Naik says you're not talking,' I add, only more quietly. 'That's stupid too. Especially considering how much you chatter at home. With Muma and Papa.'

The boy stares at me. I stare back.

'And it's not your fault your papers were stolen,' I continue. 'If you talk to Dr Naik, he'll be able to help get new papers. As soon as it's verified that you're Papa's adopted son, we'll be able to go. To Grandma's. On the Isle of Arran. Right?

The boy says nothing.

'Come on, Mo. I'm your sister!' I remind him. 'You can talk to me.'

Silence.

'Did they take your sucking stone?' I ask.

There's a pause.

'Did they?'

The boy nods.

'Oh,' I say. 'Right.' I turn to the doctor. 'You took his sucking stone.'

'His what?' says Dr Naik.

I explain.

The doctor writes something on his nanonet. I see what he writes. It's *comfort object*.

I go over to the boy and crouch down so that my eyes are on the same level as his. 'Would it help if it was just you and me?'

Silence – but one in which something passes between us.

'To get out of here, you need to talk. To Dr Naik. He has to fill in forms. If he lets us have just a little time together, just you and me, alone, we could find a way maybe? Because you'd speak if the doctor wasn't here, yes?'

'Mo?' says Dr Naik.

For the first time the boy looks at the doctor.

'You can just nod,' I add emphatically.

The boy nods.

'But you'd have to promise to speak to me directly afterwards,' says Dr Naik.

'You can just nod again,' I say quickly.

The boy transfers his gaze to me, then nods a second time.

'OK.' Dr Naik checks his nanonet. 'I have a meeting in five minutes,' he says. 'I won't be more than an hour. You can have that time. I can't promise about any new papers, of course. And I'll have to lock the door. I know it's absurd, as I'm going to be right next door. But it's the rules.'

'No problem,' I say.

And it won't be a problem, because our exit does not lie through that door.

43

LEDGE

As soon as I hear the key turn in the lock I cross to the window and look out. I'm hoping for a drainpipe. I've always been a good climber. *You climb like a monkey*, Grandma always said. But there is no drainpipe, not one near enough anyway. There are, however, garbage bins. Three of them. Almost (but not quite) directly below the window. One of the bins, the black one, has a domed lid and the other two have flat or at least just very gently sloping lids. Annoyingly, it's the domed bin which is the nearest. There's a large red cross on this bin and a notice which says: *Danger! Do not climb into or sleep in this bin. This could result in serious injury or death.* But I have no intention of sleeping in this bin. Only trying to land on it and not fall off. And trying to do so very quietly.

The window is secured, of course, but only with one of those slim, barrel bolt locks. Naturally, the bolt key is missing but the wood of the window frame around the lock is soft, slightly rotted. I do not think it will pose a problem for my knife. I begin, however, by cutting a small square of fabric from the flimsy grey curtain.

'This is what I want you to do,' I say to the boy. I make my voice quiet and low but all his concentration is on me. 'First, I

141

want you to eat that gravy. Suck it up. Drink as much of it as you can without being sick. Then put the rest of the food in this cloth. This is going to be our new food cloth. OK?' I hand him the piece of cut curtain. 'Then tie it up, so nothing can fall out.'

The boy does as instructed as I begin to gouge the wood around the screw lock. The bolt is longer than I'd hoped but the wood around it is dry and flaky and it scrapes away quite easily. After about five minutes and a bit of wobbling I'm able to extract the bolt shaft. Meanwhile the boy has stopped lapping the gravy and is busy trying to tie the four corners of the food cloth into a knot.

'It was clever of you,' I say then. 'The hunger strike.' I pause. 'And brave.'

Something which might – or might not – be a smile, plays around the boy's mouth. Then he reaches up, touches his ear.

'But also stupid,' I add. 'Don't ever do it again. You have to stay alive. Understand?'

His mouth goes into a tough little line.

It's still daylight outside, so none of the security lights are on yet. This is good, will make things safer. I open the window and secure it on its old-fashioned metal arm, as if I was just a member of staff trying to get a breath of fresh air. Then I stand back and wait. Just in case nobody opens a window here, just in case opening a window triggers some panic, some alarm somewhere.

But it doesn't.

All remains quiet at the back of the building. And it is the back. This window overlooks a car park. Or rather an ecotricity park. Because I was right when I guessed from the kitchen window that this might also be a vehicle charging station. I can now see ten flatwall charging units, each with its coil of bright yellow flex. Seven vehicles are currently plugged in: two cars, two army trucks, two lorries and one small van. One of the lorries is steel-sided, but the other one has canvas curtains as does the van. The curtain sides are secured with ratchet clips. But ratchet clips, I've learnt, can be opened.

'Now listen very carefully,' I say to the boy. 'I'm going to jump out of this window. Then you're going to jump and I'm going to catch you. OK?'

The boy says nothing.

'It's not as high as it seems. Only three metres or so – because we'll be landing on the bins. See?' He comes clutching the food cloth, but he cannot see. The windowsill itself is quite high and he's small enough not to be able to look over the ledge. I fetch the little red plastic chair and he climbs up, peers over.

There's a pause.

'It'll be OK,' I say. 'You have to trust me.' I pause. 'Like I trusted you. With Dr Naik. Right?'

His body looks both fragile and stiff. 'Remember,' I add, 'you did the river. And it's not more difficult than the river. In fact, it's easier.'

He leans back inwards, one hand still holding the food cloth to his chest. It's made a wet mark on his green T-shirt.

'Give me that,' I say and I stow the food inside my jerkin. 'You'll need to have both hands free.' The boy does not have a jerkin. That is a problem I will have to think about later.

143

'OK. Me first.' I open the window fully, pull myself up on the ledge and then sit back down again, my legs hanging out the window. I have a moment of indecision. Perhaps it would be safer to aim slightly right, to the flatter-topped bin? What if I misjudge the dome-shaped bin? What if I slide? Too late. I'm out, I have to jump. I don't want the boy to think I'm hesitating. It's important for him to have total confidence.

I jump.

Or rather I push myself off the ledge and begin to fall. My feet land first, but on the slope and, as I skid downwards, my right knee smashes into the grey metal strip that runs the length of the bin top. From this I learn that I am not such a good jumper as I am a climber. My knee hurts but I don't have time to pay attention to that, because I am still going down. But now this same metal strip becomes my saviour, because it stands proud at the apex of the bin, and I can clamp my sliding fingers to it, cling on. And I do cling on – not least to stop the noise. Which is considerable. The clang of my landing, the reverberating boom as my sliding weight moves the bin to hit the brick of the wall. There is also the sound of my heart smashing into my ribcage, though maybe only I can hear that. So, for a moment I lie sprawled, flush to the bin, gripping my metal bar and not crying out. And no one comes. No one shouts. There is a silence. So, I breathe again, haul myself to a rough sitting position astride the bin and check again. I listen for voices, for footsteps.

And hear only birdsong. A little twitter in the afternoon air.

The bin lid is ridged. To catch the boy, I'll need to stand. I pull myself up, wedge my left foot between the metal strip and the hinge of the rubbish flap and position my right foot against a ridge the other side.

Right. Now it's the boy's turn.

I don't have to tell him what to do. Already he's out on the ledge, his feet dangling. But he just sits there. Sits there as if frozen. I have not, I realise, modelled a good landing.

'Come on,' I hiss. 'Come on!'

And still he sits. And then Slow Time starts as I see the underside of the boy's feet, or rather the underside of his shoes, because they've given him new shoes, trainers with deep, zigzag grips. Shoes for running, running away, as if they knew. And I wonder if the doctor gave him these shoes, though it is never the job of a doctor to dispense shoes. Besides, if the doctor had really known, known that the boy would be running, he'd have given him a jerkin too. And I'm thinking this (and also about whether the doctor has deliberately blocked his ears to the clashing of the bin which, after all, is just outside the window where his meeting is taking place – although that thought is just madness) when the shoes, the zigzags, begin to fall.

The boy has jumped. Flung his little body into the air.

And now the zigzags are coming faster, very much faster, they're hurtling towards my outstretched hands and with them the weight of the boy, and he's very much more dense than I'm expecting, so when I catch him – and I do catch him – it's all I can do to keep steady, hold him.

And perhaps it's the shock but he laughs.

Hahahaha.

'Shut up!' I whisper in his beautiful ear. 'It's not a game.'

He shuts up, grins, wiggles out of my arms and bum-slides down the slope of the bin, landing like a cat on the ground.

Then he holds out his hand to me – just like he did at the river.

44

VAN

I also slide down, land safely. I take the boy's outstretched hand, pull him to the darker side of the bin and make him crouch. I crouch too. The lorries are less than twenty metres away but the open space between feels like a minefield. I do not know how many windows overlook this space but it only takes one person to be looking out. I pause, but just for a moment. We need to keep moving. Dr Naik's hour will not last for ever.

'That lorry there,' I whisper, pointing at the lorry with the canvas sides. 'When I say go, you run, hide behind the big front wheel. OK?' The boy nods.

I check again. The silence is eerie.

'Right – go!'

He goes. And I go too, but to the wall, where the charging units are. I check the time. Twenty-three minutes. That's how long before this lorry is fully charged. Not that it needs to be fully charged before the driver comes again. Keeping myself as flat as I can to the wall, I slide along, check the van time. Forty-two minutes. Too long. Dr Naik is likely to raise the alarm before then, then there will be dogs, guards, batons. It will be all over.

The lorry is a better bet, but seeing the boy so tiny in the shadow of the front wheels makes me realise how high off the ground the lorry is. Would he be able to climb up into the lorry? Would I? The van would be much easier. I'd be able to lift the boy straight in and pull myself up behind. Can I hope for forty minutes?

Footsteps.

I drop down between the van and the wall, make myself as small as I can. It's a man. Not a soldier, not a guard. It's a driver – a driver! At least I think it is, someone without uniform. What if he drives away this van right now and we're not in it? But what if he drives away the lorry? All sixteen wheels of it and the boy underneath, the boy hidden behind one of those crushing wheels?

I want to cry out, warn the boy – but I don't. I keep my mouth clamped shut. Because the man is not heading for the lorry, he's making for a car. I push myself further back into the wall as he disconnects the charger and rehooks it to the unit. A moment later, he's driving away.

I watch him go.

Watch him head out towards the five-metre-high razor wire perimeter fence. I can't see the actual gate from here, but I hear the car slow. But only for a moment and then it's off again. They can only have looked at his papers, wouldn't have had time to search the vehicle. This means escape is possible. We just have to be lucky with the time, the driver. We have to keep our nerve.

Our nerve?

I decide on the van after all. Ratchet clips work on the same principle as seat belts on a plane. You just have to lift the metal buckle bit to loosen the strap. This in turn releases the claw that

148

holds the curtain taut to the underside of the vehicle. It's the work of a moment, but my heart is beating fast enough to make my hand tremble and the claw clang against the metal rim of the van. One clip, two clips, three, and then a length of curtain is flapping free. I put my hand up under the canvas, feeling to see if there is space. And there is. This van must have unloaded here, it's empty.

I call the boy softly and he comes immediately. I lift the edge of the loosened curtain.

'In.'

I help him climb. The gap is only just big enough for him. I'll have to unclip at least one, possibly two, more buckles to get in myself.

And then how will I fix them up again, from the inside?

I unclip the first strap. The second. I don't know why my heart is beating this fast. I have done many more terrible things than unclip metal buckles and my heart has stayed quite still.

The gap is big enough – just. I use the still-taut straps to pull and roll myself in. It's dark in the van, but not too dark. The roof is made of a strange blue Perspex which lets in light. I lean out again, or rather I put my hands out, but attempt to keep my head out of sight as I try to reassemble the buckles. The first two are easy as I have room to manoeuvre, but space gets tighter with each one I clip back in. The last one is impossible. I will just have to hope the driver is not an observant man.

We wait.

Me and the boy in a small van with a strange blue roof. The only things in the van with us are five wooden pallets. This means, if anyone opens the door, they won't even need dogs.

There we'll be – in full view. At Heathrow, there was a great deal of talk about hiding in lorries. What to do and what not to do, because everyone knew someone who'd died in a lorry. Like the men who got locked inside a refrigeration lorry and knocked and knocked on the fridge wall only no one heard them. Or the teenager who got mixed up with a load of twenty thousand *Mother and Baby* magazines. He was so afraid of the dogs that he took the shrink-wrap off the magazines and wrapped it around himself. And it's true that the dogs didn't smell him. At least not until he died from suffocation and the wrap could no longer hold his leaking body.

We wait.

The boy begins to fidget. Sucks in his lower lip, searches out his missing piece of tooth with his tongue.

'Dr Naik showed me your picture,' I say. 'It was a good picture.' I don't mention the sadness. It's not as if he doesn't know.

We wait.

We hear more footsteps, a shout, a door opening. But not our door. Not the driver's door of the van. No, it's a bigger bang than that, the opening and closing of a lorry door. But which lorry? The steel-sided one or the one with curtain sides we might have chosen? Not that it matters, because it's going to drive away without us whichever one it is. But I want to know, have to know, so I take my knife and stab it through the canvas. Draw the knife down and across, making a right-angled slit, an 'L'-shaped flap. A little window on the world.

It's the curtain-sided lorry. I have made the wrong decision. The driver is in the cab, there's the soft whirr of his electric engine.

150

And then he's winding down his window and then there's another shout.

Two shouts. Which means two drivers, of course. Two drivers!

I drop my triangular flap. Hold my breath. And here it is, our driver disconnecting the charger cable, hooking it back up, and then the sound of the door of the van being unlocked. The driver climbing up, in. The vibration, the rock of the van as he slams that door shut and switches on the engine.

We're in motion.

The lorry turning. The van turning.

Reversing, and then heading out towards the perimeter fence.

Where we stop. And wait.

And wait.

Too long. And I can't look out. Can't lift my flap, my window on the world.

And of course, it's not Long Time. Or Deep Time. But it is very much longer than the car waited. And I hear talking. An exchange, but good-natured. Cheerful. And the wait is nothing after all. The wait is just a queue and the fact that we are second in that queue, behind the lorry.

The barrier lifts. The gate is open.

We pass through.

45

MOTORWAY

Behind us, the gate clangs shut.

I think three things simultaneously:

– We are free.

– Dr Naik will get in trouble.

– I don't know where we're going.

Free is good, Dr Naik getting in trouble is not good. Next time he will not be so trusting. *We all need to be able to trust*, Papa says. But perhaps Dr Naik will remember something of his own journey to Scotland and understand? Although – with that Glaswegian accent – perhaps he's always lived here? Perhaps it was his parents who made the journey for him, in Before? Or before Before? Perhaps they never told him what they risked or sacrificed. And then my head begins to spin a little from thinking about a man of Indian descent who belongs here and a Scottish girl who is no longer welcome, so I turn my mind on to where we're going.

Which could be anywhere.

Normally I'm good at thinking ahead, but I realise I haven't got any further than this, all my energy concentrated on simply getting out of the compound.

What now?

I lift my little flap on the world as if I could orientate myself through this triangle of canvas. Ahead are some green fields, some distant buildings. No obvious landmarks, no sun, no lichen, no stars. Nothing to indicate our direction of travel, but it has to be north. If we're going south, we will have to do the border all over again.

Slow down.

One thing at a time.

We just need to put a little distance between us and the detention centre. Be patient for ten minutes, perhaps twenty. And then – whichever way we're facing – we'll have to jump. I'll do the count on my body again, ten to my left hand little finger, twenty to my lower lip. Choose a time between the two, on an eyebrow possibly, when the van draws up at a traffic light, a junction, a crossroad – but not in a town. Towns bring people and problems. We need to jump when we're still in the countryside.

Third finger.

Fourth.

We have to be going north.

The van slows, strains a little, we're going up an incline, climbing a hill. I look out. We're approaching yet another horizon. Finally we reach the brow, and then I see it.

Or rather I smell it.

Scotland.

Not the fringes of my country, not border territory – but the real Scotland. My Scotland. The Scotland of my childhood.

It's laid out like a fantasy before me. Thirty kilometres of moorland and rising hills, a patchwork of green and brown, purple and straw white. But mainly green. Ten different shades of green, twenty, a hundred. The colours I hallucinated in the desert, the impossible freshness of vibrant, living green. All of it misted with that unforgettable (though I have forgotten it) smell: that intoxicating, heart-lurching smell of damp, of peat, of rain in the air and rain on the land, the smell of brackish water, wet stone, sodden moorland vegetation, bracken and heather. And even though I grew up in the city, went to school in the city, it was here I came with Papa. To hills like these. Land like this. Muma was always working, but Papa and I – we walked.

You're a good walker, Mhairi, Papa said. *Some children moan, but not you.* Actually, it wasn't the walking I liked so much as the being with Papa. He showed me things as we walked. Big things. Little things. Especially when we walked (as we did every summer) on the Isle of Arran, walked the paths of his own childhood: Goatfell, Beinn Tarsuinn, Cir Mhor.

Sacred places, Papa said, as he shared their songs. Sang them. Hummed them. Songs of the land. Ancient songs that one of our Arran neighbours – Peter's father – played on his fiddle late at night. Songs that Peter himself, a boy just a few years older than I was then, whistled to himself in the little harbour at Corrie. Songs of belonging. One I remember above all – of hills and mists and leaving. But also returning.

All at once I'm in Arrested Time, breathing deeply, inhaling this landscape, this homeland. This song of steaming green.

'Oh, look,' I cry to the boy. 'Just look!'

He joins me at the canvas window. Stares out into the late afternoon. But only for a moment before retreating back into the relative dark of the van. He sits down on the pallet again. Blankly. Joylessly. And I see what he sees then: hills, just hills, yet more interminable hills, hardship hills, travelling hills.

And also perhaps injustice.

My wet green land, an accident of birth. So different from his own land. His land of sand and dust. Too hot now, too dry to sustain life. But loved anyway. The yellow gold of his own childhood. The yellow gold of his dreams, his own particular hallucinations.

I put down the flap.

There's a pause and then I say: 'We're going to have to jump. As soon as the van comes to a stop, you need to be ready to jump. OK?'

He nods.

We wait.

But the truck does not come to a stop. In fact, far from slowing down, it begins to pick up speed. We leave the snaking rural lanes, begin to follow a straighter, slicker road. A dual carriageway which turns into a three-lane highway, a motorway. Soon we are travelling at what must be seventy miles an hour. We have missed our opportunity. A moment later we pass a sign.

We are heading to Glasgow.

46

CITY

It's dusk when we reach the outskirts of the city.

We flash past the jagged horizons of buildings, fly over them, pass under them, tunnel through them. My childhood memories of Glasgow do not include this motorway which seems to spool straight into the heart of the city, spilling finally, unexpectedly, on to a real street. Yes, look, just up ahead, no distance at all, it's the dark spire of Glasgow cathedral. And now I'm the city child again, the one who walked to school down the nearby streets of Dennistoun, orientating myself by the spire, liking the way it jabbed into the sky like a black spear.

As the van slows, the boy comes to join me at the triangular window but he is not drawn by the cathedral spire. No. He is drawn by the noise. A shouting, tramping noise.

One look out and he's ripping at the window, trying to tear the canvas wider, make the viewing space bigger because of what he is seeing and hearing.

People.

Hundreds of people.

This part of the city – which always seemed emptily spacious to me as a child – is teeming.

Packed. Thronged.

It's as though all the people I've seen on the whole of my journey, the thousands of them, the tens of thousands, have all ended up here, in this one street. Because these are not ordinary people, not city-dwellers going about their ordinary milling business, shopping, chatting, getting on buses. No, these are tramping people, marching people, a ragged mass of young men, old men, families, travellers, barbarians, people like us, the boy and me, all heads down, all tramping on, on, on.

Where are they going?

And how can there be so many? When they've shut the border? But maybe this is why they have shut the border. Or perhaps there aren't more people than we saw snaking across the lowland landscape, only here they're confined, pressed together, funnelled down an increasingly narrow street.

The line of them is broken, but it is a line. Ahead are larger groups, groups big enough to spill on to the pavement and disrupt the traffic. Groups large enough to draw shouts and missiles. People in the houses along this street are shouting from windows. They are throwing objects, pelting the travellers. Glass bottles, tin cans, coathangers, old shoes. One woman empties something out of a bucket from a third-floor window. I do not know what is in the bucket but it reminds of those pictures from history books in Before, when city-dwellers without lavatories threw the contents of chamberpots out on to the streets. The travellers don't even look up. Don't try to shield or protect themselves, they just keep moving as though they have got used to this way of travelling, as though there is no point in expecting things to be different. Occasionally a child goes down under a missile only to be hauled to his or her feet again, dragged on. For still they march. March as if, somewhere ahead, there is a destination.

The van driver begins to honk at those who are forced off the pavement by the mass of people already there. He begins to shout.

The boy is still at the window. The canvas flap is bunched in his fist. He is as focused on this swelling scene as I was on the hills of Scotland. Only mine was a landscape of green and this is a landscape of brown. For half of Africa is here, it seems. People from his golden world. Brown faces. Black faces. He scans them all. Each a potential homeland. He checks their hair, their height, the way they walk. Making individuals from numbers. Looking, searching. His own body is tense, his breathing a pant. He's gone into Now Time. Nothing else exists but this one moment.

And now his tight, bunched hands dive under the canvas, pull at the ratchet clips, snap them open, haul at the curtain.

'What?' I cry. 'What!'

I shout this even though I know it's not a *what* but a *who*. A man? A woman? A family even. His own family. The family missing from his picture who are, perhaps, not missing at all. Or not all missing! A brother? A sister? A cousin? Who has he seen? My heart, which is normally a steady thing, somersaults.

The curtain is still quite tight, but he's already trying to squirm under, feet first.

'No,' I say, even though the van is hardly moving for the crowds. 'No – it's too dangerous!'

And now he's feeling the tension in the curtain, and he's wriggling, forcing himself under and out, but his balance is wrong and I know he's going to fall and he does fall, his wrist somehow caught in one of the straps.

'No!' I shout and grab his hand, try to disentangle him. My reaction is physical, instinctive, he must not be pulled, dragged along the road, against the road!

Even though the van has pretty much slowed to a stop.

I get his wrist free, but I find I'm still holding him. Still grasping him against his wriggle, against his will to be on the street. And it's only gravity that finally takes charge – even though he weighs so little. Gravity that slips him from my hands and brings him to the tarmac of that busy street.

And no one notices.

Except me. I notice that he does not stand and stretch a hand for me as he has done before. He just gets to his feet and, without a backward glance, begins to run.

47

FOREIGNER

Of course, I have no option but to follow.

I'm bigger than the boy, so there's a pause because I have to unclip an extra strap. Two extra straps. They clang against the undercarriage of the van. The driver does not react, the noise lost in the general melee. I'm also taller than the boy. This makes it easier for me to swing my legs out, make what is quite a small jump to the road. I land softly. No one notices.

There are hundreds, thousands, of people in this street, but I have no problem spotting the boy. Because he's running. If you want to disappear in a crowd all you have to do is to walk at exactly the same pace as the crowd. I learnt this in Cairo when I was being chased. So long as you move slowly, so long as you hold your nerve, you cannot be found.

But today the boy is not trying to disappear. He's not, for once, being chased or trying to run away. Today the boy is running towards. So I run too, run after him. People curse as I push past them, but so long as he runs, I run.

It's not very far.

He stops behind a tall woman wearing what must once have

been a brightly patterned robe. This ankle-length garment looks too thin for the climate and is matted with mud at the hem. Her hair is wound up on top of her head and covered with a loose orange scarf. The scarf is fringed with tiny silvery coins which jangle as she walks. The boy cries out. Not with words, but with a kind of wail, pulls at the back of her skirt.

The woman turns.

There is a spindly baby at her breast. She looks too old to have a newborn but the baby is suckling, or trying to. The woman holds the child loosely, like an afterthought, as though she cannot quite see the connection between them. As though she's drained already, has no nourishment to give because she's just the shell of a woman. Someone who moves or walks only because her legs and feet have been doing that for so long, they don't need instruction.

She unhitches the boy's fingers from her skirt. Not roughly, just matter-of-factly, as though the boy was just one more in a long line of impediments with which she has to deal. As though she'd actually just caught her skirt on a twig or a piece of barbed wire. This silent exchange hardly takes a moment, but it's long enough for the woman's male companion to look back over his shoulder, to see what the hold-up's about. When he sees the boy he shouts, but not in any language I know or – from his face – that the boy knows. But it's not that sort of shout anyway – it's more the sort of noise you'd make to deter a scavenging dog. Then they both turn away, walk on.

And it does for the boy. He sinks, collapses, drops to the ground and curls up in a ball on the pavement.

People are annoyed. They have to step around him. He's in the way.

'Get up,' I say.

He does not get up. He stays in a ball. He pummels the ground with his fists. He sobs. Not the raging sobs he cried when he battered his beautiful stones together. He sobs little-boy sobs. Hiccupy, toddler sobs. Sobs that go with the vest his mother probably gave him. A mother who probably wore a scarf of orange fringed with silvery coins.

'Get up,' I say again.

'Yes, get up!' A woman is trying to negotiate her way around us, get to the steps behind us. She's small and stout and has a bag, a purse, a set of keys. Keys to a house. Keys to safety. 'Get up, you little shit.'

'Leave him alone,' I flash at her. 'He'll get up in his own time.'

She flashes something back. A smile.

'Bin's over there,' she says, pointing. 'That's where we put trash in this country.' Then she laughs, marches up the steps, opens the door of the house and slams it shut behind her.

162

48

NECROPOLIS

The boy gets up.

Tears stain his cheeks. There is snot coming from his nose. I wipe his face with the sleeve of my jerkin. He looks small and, now I'm paying attention, weak. Or perhaps crushed. He shivers. I take off the jerkin and wrap it round him. It is far too big for him but it stops the shivering.

'Walk,' I say.

He walks. Walking will keep him warm. Will keep me warm too, stop the goose-bumps I now feel rising on my own arms.

We walk in the same direction as everyone else. There's no point in asking where we're heading because we'll find out soon enough. But I half-hope it will be the cathedral. There would be something full-circle, something comforting about spending the night in that huge, dour building. It's lit now, the cathedral, but still dour. Or *dreich*. Grandmother would use the Scottish word: *dreich*. The soft yellow of solar lamps makes little impression on the darkness of the stone. As though the building had been burnt but refused to yield, a blackened hulk from Before.

The cathedral is not the only thing that has my attention though. I'm also alert for any woman with once-bright clothes and an orange scarf with silvery coins around her head. I listen out for the jangles, take the boy's hand, clasp it in mine.

Just in case. Although I'm not entirely certain whether I'm more afraid for the boy – or for myself.

We walk.

Just when I think, I'm right, it will be the cathedral, the line takes a veer right. And then I see what should have been obvious from the start. We are marching towards the necropolis.

The city of the dead.

I know quite a lot about this graveyard right in the centre of the city. Not all of it useful. I know, for instance:

– that over fifty thousand people are buried here
– that most of them are men
– that the bodies lie in over three and a half thousand tombs and mausoleums

Papa did not tell me these things. They were told me by Miss Sperry. Miss Sperry was a witch. Or that's what all of us in Primary 6 thought. We thought this partly because Miss Sperry dressed only in black, outlined her eyes in thick black kohl and had waist-length black hair, but mainly because – summer and winter – she wore gloves: black lace fingerless gloves. The lace was fine and covered her wrists and the back of her hands like tiny spiders' webs. She wasn't just our teacher, she was also the self-appointed guardian of the necropolis and every year she took a group of us to explore the tombs. She talked a lot about plants and symbols and many people didn't listen but I did. I remember for instance that the aspen tree is the symbol of lamentation and that the garlands carved into many of the tombs represent 'victory over death'.

As a child, looking at all the tombs and knowing how many people were buried there, 'victory over death' didn't seem very credible. But now I see, perhaps, what Miss Sperry meant.

These tombs are crawling with the living.

49

THE TOMB OF COLIN DUNLOP

At the gates of the necropolis is a cherry tree. It's in blossom. Or just out of blossom. It's still beautiful, Papa, even though the wind has scattered most of its pink petals on to the paths. They look white in the dark.

And it is dark now.

The mound looms above us. There are tiered ranks of monuments, the black outlines of obelisks and statues, skylines of towers, domes, minarets (which look more Sudanese than Scottish), as well as crosses and the ridged roofs of mausoleums.

Stick close together now. Miss Sperry's words come down the years. *It's easy to get lost here.*

And it was easy to get lost, even with a map, and Miss Sperry always gave us maps. The paths are winding, seem circular and yet you never seem to end up quite where you began. They snake up and around the hill, surprising you with their curves and switchbacks. I remember how, just when I'd marked a tombstone in my imagination, logged it as a landmark, it would disappear around a bend or drop behind some new horizon. And that was in the daylight because, of course, we only ever came with Miss

Sperry in daylight. Miss Sperry loved this graveyard. I thought it grim and lonely.

It is not lonely now. The darkness is alive with people. They have made the tombs a shelter, strung tarpaulins from the spikes of monuments, hooked them over stone swords and the broken wings of angels. They have battered down the doors of mausoleums, taken positions on tomb roofs. There are some lone figures – their single backs to the backs of single gravestones – but most of the people are huddled, clustered. They are preparing for the night. Some have coverings, blankets, others don't. Who knows how long these people have been in this tented city?

The only light in this dark place is given by the odd solar phone screen and the few sparse fires that burn here or there, giving flickering light to the faces gathered around them and, sometimes, sending the smell of cooking into the air. The smell of meat, though I wouldn't like to say what type of meat. I'm glad then to think of the boy's chicken stowed in the curtain cloth in my jerkin. Tonight at least, we will not have to fight for food.

We follow the line of humanity upwards. We keep going because, on the lower slopes, all of the viable places are already taken. And we learn not to stop, particularly near the fires. Each fire circle has appointed a guard it seems. New arrivals who stop near fires are shouted at. Sometimes in English but just as often not. Though the not is perfectly understandable.

'Keep close to me,' I say to the boy, even though I still have his hand. We continue to wind upwards. It soon becomes clear why the lower slopes are taken. The higher you go, the more exposed it is, the sharper the wind. But we have spent the night outside before and can do it again. When the stream of people finally thins and the path divides, I pull the boy to the right. There are no fires this way which is why, perhaps, the ever-hopeful others turn left.

We pass a few tombs that only have one occupant, but I don't want to share, don't want to take any chances. I'd prefer a tomb just for the two of us.

Although that brings me back to Meroe and the knowledge that a tomb for two does not always remain that way.

Our eyes are accustomed to the dark now. And, of course, it is not wholly dark because, behind us, laid out like another country, is the centre of Glasgow. A thousand, or perhaps a thousand thousand windows are lit here. They are bright with the glow of technology, of lives connected by electricity and machines, plugged into some mains denied me for so long. And I imagine those people in their warm houses where things work at the touch of a button, where there's food in a fridge and water in a tap and their friends (their friends!) are just one click away. Part of me longs for return to this glowing land, feels like the child with her face pressed up against the glass in Papa's storybooks. The excluded child. The winter's night child looking in on the untouchable warmth of the blazing fire. But when I look again, I see this Glasgow fire doesn't burn blazing warm and orange as the graveyard fires burn, as my tinder nest fires burn. Glasgow burns lurid, electric, neon. Strange. I no longer know if I would be able to find comfort there.

Not that I have the choice. My choice is the tomb of Colin Dunlop of Tolcross. This is a good tomb, I think. It's on a triangle of land on one of the switchback paths, so attack (and I have to assume attack) could come from any side. But actually, the right-hand path slopes so steeply downward, that the retaining wall that side is taller than most men. An attacker would have to climb. The plot is also bounded by eight or more low-lying pillars, which seem like natural battlements. Enclosed within these defences is a possible sleeping place, a strange low-lying stone table engraved with the names of other Dunlop dead too small to read in this light. The stone will be cold of course, but not damp like the earth. And it's flat and just about wide enough for two.

'Here,' I say to the boy. 'We'll stop here.'

50

TOWER

We sit on the stone tomb. There is a moment when I wonder whether we should be sitting on Colin Dunlop's tomb, but it is only a moment. Colin and his clan are dead. We are alive. I know this because the cold of the stone comes through my trousers like ice.

'Food cloth,' I say.

The boy unzips my jerkin and extracts the cloth. The cloth is greasy, the food squashed. I divide the meal into two portions. I want to knot one of those portions straight back into the cloth. To conserve it, preserve it, keep something for the morning. But there is not enough for that. I give the boy his half. Or rather more than his half, as there are five carrot rings and I give him three. The carrot rings remind me of Finola, the Wristband Girl. Finola will be eating her supper in the warmth and relative safety of the detention centre. A strange thing to feel jealous of.

'Eat.'

The boy eats. And so do I. There is some meat juice left on the chicken but it mainly tastes of the dust in the curtain cloth. It is still good, Papa.

We scoop water from a puddle at the base of one of the battlement pillars. I go first in case the water is actually urine. But it isn't. As I drink I consider whether I should go on a water-bottle hunt tonight. Or a water-bottle steal. But I decide it will be too dangerous. Not least because it would mean leaving the boy.

The jerkin is more complicated. We only have the one. There are three options:

- I can have it.
- The boy can have it.
- We can open it flat and both try to shelter beneath it.

If we do the latter, the boy and I will have to lie very close together. Almost skin to skin. I decide it is better for him to keep the jacket. Besides, being cold will help me keep awake and I'm not sure it will be safe for me to sleep tonight.

I lift the boy on to the stone table. 'Sleep. More walking tomorrow.'

He lies down but he does not curl up immediately as usual. He lies on his back, his front. He tosses. He turns. I think it's perhaps because of the lack of a pillow, the harsh stone against his face. But then I hear him sucking his teeth. He hasn't got his stone.

'Shush,' I say. 'Shush. Be still.'

And, eventually, he quiets.

I walk around him then, around the grave, patrolling my perimeters as though I'm a guard and this is my castle.

Castle.

It gets darker.

It gets colder.

The lights illuminating the cathedral go out. The lights in the windowed city of Glasgow begin to go too.

I rub my arms with my hands. I rub my legs. I put my hands in my armpits, like I learnt to do in the desert. Your armpits do not lose warmth like the rest of your body.

I do Concentration.

I think about the blossom tree at the entrance to the necropolis. I recreate its pink-white petals in my mind. I wonder why it is in bloom, considering it is not springtime. I say aloud:

The world is beautiful, Papa.

I'm getting tired. I sit on the edge of Colin's tomb. It's uncomfortable to sit up with nothing to lean back on. I lie down a moment, near the carved edge of the table. There is still a lot of noise in the graveyard. People are still moving about. Still arriving probably.

I must not fall asleep.

It's strange lying looking up at the sky here. The sky should be black, but it isn't, it's blue. A very deep blue but blue nonetheless. It's the monuments which are black. They seem to be leaning over me. They fringe my vision. One of them seems almost about to topple on top of me.

It's a tower.

A black tower with a crenellated top. It looks like a giant pepper pot. It also looks like the black tower right in the centre of Castle. As though, somehow, I have broken through all the walls and locks which hold my horrors safe and arrived right here at the centre, the heart of things.

And, as always near the lock of the tower at the centre of Castle, I can hear a soft sort of screaming.

Or perhaps it's just jangling.

The jangling of tiny silvery coins.

And now, as well as the tower looming over me, there are the women. Two of them, five, ten. Tall women with dark skin and scarves of orange: dull orange, burnt orange, bright orange, plain, patterned. All of the scarves are fringed with coins. The silvery sound of the jangling getting louder, more intense as the hands – orange hands now with silver rings – stretch towards me, or rather towards the boy. So many pairs of jangling hands, two, four, six, all of them reaching out for the sleeping boy. Pulling him upwards, pulling him away from me into the blue-black night.

And then there is some screaming.

Real screaming. Not soft.

Only it's not the women screaming.

It's me.

The screaming is coming out of my mouth. Because somehow, I've fallen asleep and now I'm waking up. I'm opening my eyes. And I've dreamt the women and I've dreamt the orange scarves and the silvery coins.

But I haven't dreamt the absence of the boy. There is no one lying on the stone table beside me.

The boy is gone.

51

GHOST

I sit up.

I am not screaming. The screaming was also in the dream. I'm glad about this. Screaming is stupid.

Besides, there is probably an innocent explanation for the boy's absence.

The innocent explanation is that he has got up to relieve himself. Just as Muhammad did that night in the desert. It's not such an unlikely thing.

Only I can't see him.

Although, if you wanted to piss, you'd hide behind a gravestone, wouldn't you? Even at night. He won't have gone far.

I stand up.

'Mo,' I call, 'Mo.' Calling 'Mo' is also stupid. His name is not Mo. But what else should I call? Besides, he will recognise my voice. He will come to me.

'Mo!'

Nothing.

'Mo!'

Nothing.

Where will I look? In the whole of this teeming dark graveyard?

I need to stay put. He will return here. Of course he will. He, after all, knows where to return to. He knows what he's looking for.

Me.

The pepper pot tower.

The tomb of Colin Dunlop of Tolcross.

If he's paid attention. Which he won't have. At least not that sort of attention.

But he cannot have been taken.

No. That is just a nightmare. If he had been taken against his will, he would have called out. I would have heard something, felt something.

So he is not gone.

He cannot be gone.

'MO!'

And maybe I am screaming now. For what if he wasn't taken? What if he left voluntarily, because the right tall woman with the right orange scarf came walking by? Just stretched out her hand and he took it? Quietly. Softly. Walked away without looking back?

No. Not at night. No one comes searching like that in the night. The night is not for finding, it's for losing.

'MO!'

There is movement in the shadows. Someone, some thing coming out of the gloom towards me. It's a small thing, blanketed in white. Like a ghost. A child, the size of the boy, but covered head to foot in white, or rather pink-white, as though all the blossom from the cherry tree had fallen about him. And the figure keeps coming and I don't move, can't move. And Long Time passes and then the pink-white ghost steps into a shaft of moonlight.

It's the boy.

'Where the hell have you been!' I scream.

The ghostly petals are woollen threads. A strange knitted blanket of pink and white. It looks handmade. It looks made of someone's love. He's wrapped about with it. He's smiling.

'And what have you been doing!' I shout.

The boy opens his eyes wide and then his mouth. Out of his mouth he picks a small white stone. Grins his chipped-tooth grin.

'You went looking for a sucking stone?' I shout. 'So, what's with the blanket!'

'I gave him that.' A woman steps out of the dark. I cannot believe that I have been so focused on the boy I have failed to notice her standing in the shadows behind him. And of course, I expect her to have an orange scarf fringed with silvery coins. But she doesn't.

What she does have is a pair of fingerless black lace gloves, which cover her wrists and the back of her hands like tiny spiders' webs.

'He was lost,' says Miss Sperry. 'And I found him.'

52

MISS SPERRY

At least I think it's Miss Sperry. But all I really have to go on is the gloves. And many people could have black lace half-gloves like spiders' webs. But they don't. I have never in my life seen such gloves except on the hands of Miss Sperry. Such gloves do not come from Before. They come from before Before.

But I cannot be totally certain.

'Is that you?' I ask. 'Miss Sperry?'

There is a pause. And then the woman steps forward a pace. In those spider-web hands, she's carrying a black plastic sack with more knitted blankets spilling from its throat, as if she's some latter-day tented city Santa Claus. Her eyes are ringed in black (though that might just be the effect of the light or lack of it) and she has grey hair. Long hair, which falls in untidy knots to her waist. Miss Sperry always had neat hair. Neat black hair. But time has passed. Long Time has passed.

'Who are you?' she says.

This question does not have a quick or simple answer. This is the sort of question they can catch you out with when you have to fill in your Global Passport Credit pages. I'm:

- a Scot
- a Ret
- a child (subject to juve review)
- a fugitive in an illegal immigration case

It's also the sort of question that has different answers depending on who's asking. I'm being asked by a witch in a midnight graveyard.

'I'm Mhairi Anne Bain,' I say. 'You used to teach me, Miss Sperry, in Primary 6.'

The woman shakes her head. 'Teach? No. I think there's some mistake,' she says. 'My name's Corlinda. Corlinda Lee.'

The name rings in my head. A small bell from the past. But I can't place it.

There's a short pause and then she continues: 'Are you also lost, Mhairi?'

This is another question to which there is no simple answer. There are, after all, so many different ways to be lost. For instance:
- when you make your bed on a hillside or in a shack or a tomb
- when you lie or cheat or steal and feel nothing at all
- when you kill with a brick and think mainly about the brick
- when you've forgotten how to cry

And also when you dream that someone takes a small boy from you and you wake more terrified than you have ever been in your life.

'No,' I say. 'I am not lost. I am on my way to my grandmother's. On the Isle of Arran.'

This sounds about as likely as if I'd said: *I'm Little Red Riding Hood, I'm off in my little red cape to visit my grandma in the forest.*

Which is, perhaps, why she replies: 'Then I'll take you. Tomorrow. In my car. Just ask for me. Everyone knows where I live. Corlinda Lee. Queen of the Gypsies.'

And then she's gone. But not before she's given me one of her knitted blankets.

53

CORLINDA LEE

In the morning, I remember something.

I didn't say thank you. Corlinda Lee gave me a warm blanket of purple and white and I didn't say thank you.

I just took it.

Of course, she wasn't exactly waiting for thanks. She just turned on her heels and walked straight into the night. Or, more likely, walked around some other corner or switchback until her bag of blankets was empty. But still.

I wonder then: is a lost person actually someone who has forgotten how to say thank you?

Because I am thankful. Thankful not just for the warmth of this blanket (and that of the boy's blanket) but also because it exists. Still exists.

Now.

In the morning.

If it wasn't for this blanket I would not believe in Corlinda Lee. I would think Corlinda Lee belonged in one of Papa's stories. Or that she came in a midnight dream. A hallucination. A mirage as intense as any I ever saw in the desert.

Which is why I'm sitting here in the early dawn not just wrapped in this blanket but feeling it. Rubbing the wool between my finger and thumb, trying to keep hold of its softness, its newness, its just-made quality. Its made-for-you, made-for-me, given-to-me quality. Given. To me. Unasked for.

Something inside my chest hurts because of this blanket.

But I'm still not going to try and find Corlinda Lee today. I'm not going to ask for her address, search her out, knock on her door and mention a lift to the Isle of Arran. I saw what happened to the boy when he hoped for a mother and found only a wizened breast. Besides, I know exactly how long the car journey from Glasgow to the ferry port for Arran is. One hour and sixteen minutes. One hour and thirteen minutes if you're lucky with the traffic. The offer of a car journey is not the same as the offer of a blanket. Only an insane person would take a couple of strangers on a random car journey to the Isle of Arran.

Corlinda Lee.

Corlinda Lee.

Queen of the Gypsies.

And then I have it. That little bell inside my head. Ding ding ding.

Corlinda Lee is dead.

I know this because Miss Sperry showed us her tomb. *Most of the people buried in this necropolis*, Miss Sperry said, *are men. Robert, William, John, Alexander, Archibald, Charles, Thomas, George. Rich merchants, gentlemen of the Victorian era. But look here, children,* (said Miss Sperry) *look at the tomb of Corlinda Lee, Queen of the Gypsies.* And she made us repeat the inscription, learn it, chant it.

Her love for children was great
And she was charitable to the poor
Wherever she pitched her tent
She was loved and respected by all.

Yes. I think I have that right, though it doesn't seem to rhyme. Perhaps I didn't pay quite enough attention after all. Perhaps I was concentrating on the coins pushed in and around Corlinda Lee's tomb, because her tomb had a number of plinths, was tiered like a stone wedding cake, and people used to push coins between the layers. Tiny little silver coins.

Jangly little silver coins.

Gypsies bring them for remembrance and respect, said Miss Sperry. *And also for wishes. Does anyone here want to make a wish?*

I never made a wish then. Perhaps I didn't have to. Perhaps things then were good enough without wishes.

But now I look at the boy still sleeping on the tomb of Colin Dunlop. Still sleeping not least because of the warm rug of pink and white. I look at his gentle brow, his golden face.

And I make a wish.

It is not a good wish. At least not for the boy. It's about his mother and whether or not he'll ever find her. The sort of wish which, if it was in one of Papa's storybooks, would get you a thunderbolt.

54

BLANKETS

The boy wakes.

'Two days,' I say. 'Just two days more.' And it will be, if he can manage five or six hours' walking a day. And I get my directions right. 'We just need to get a little more food and a water bottle.'

Arran is west of Glasgow. Or rather south-west. Not as easy as travelling north, but this is a journey I've made a hundred times before. Driven (Papa at the wheel) from Glasgow, via Paisley to the ferry port of Ardrossan. This is the road route anyway. There might be a more direct route for a walker, but I don't know it.

As for food, I can steal it:
- from my fellow travellers in this graveyard
- from shops in the city
- from the woman with the garbage bin in which she wished to put foreigners

I am tempted by option three. I imagine returning to the garbage woman's house and (carefully) smashing one of her windows. I imagine posting the boy through on a scavenging expedition. I expect Garbage Woman has a fridge. I expect it's full of food. Or full enough anyway. She might even have a water bottle.

Unfortunately, this is not sensible. Mainly because I don't have papers any more. So, if I get caught, it'll be straight back to the detention centre. The same applies to the shops.

No one, however, on this mound of death would report me for stealing. No one would want to get that close to officialdom. It would be too dangerous. So, if I'm caught here there'll be a fight, that's all. And I'm quick with a knife. Besides, a traveller needs to learn to guard their food. If anyone in this graveyard is not guarding their food then, for them, my stealing will be an education. Teach them an essential survival skill. Later on, they'll thank me.

The boy gets up. Dressing consists of him giving me back my jerkin and me somehow tying the pink and purple blanket about him so as to give him maximum warmth and maximum freedom of movement. It's not a style Muma would approve of. Muma likes things neat.

We both take a drink of puddle water and then we begin our descent. The necropolis looks different in the morning light. Less frightening but more weary. Tarpaulins and bin-bag shelters have come unhitched in the night. A sheet of polythene flaps from the shoulder of an angel. Stone angels with polythene wings. Papa would have made something of that. The fires have burnt out and most people are up already, shuffling muddy and underslept between the tombs. Someone's tied a red scarf around the marble neck of a seated man. In Before it might have been a joke, now it's probably a marker. *You'll find us by the red scarf.* I wonder how

184

long it will last before someone steals it. I'd steal it myself if we didn't have the blankets.

As we wind downhill, I keep my eyes out for any single traveller leaving their single gravestone for a moment. Because people have to get water, they have to pee. I watch for any left-behind bags, rolls of clothes. But they're smart these people. They take what they have with them. It isn't much to carry after all.

I pay attention to the groups. Not the bigger groups who had the fires (and guards) last night, but the smaller groups, the ones that look less established. People, perhaps, who have only just arrived. You can feel safe in such a group, let down your guard.

I make myself walk slowly, try to adapt to the rhythm of this tomb and polythene city. And, as I slow (pretending I'm engaged in talking to the boy), I see something quite extraordinary. And also ordinary. In every group we pass there is a person wearing a blanket. A knitted blanket of sewn-together squares. They have them draped from their shoulders, hooding their heads, clutched to their chests. Some of the blankets are pink and white, but there are many other colours too: blue and blue; blue and black; green and pink; red and bright yellow. Some of the blankets look quite new, but others are limp and dirty. They look as though they were knitted months ago, years ago. Although that might not be true. I don't suppose things in the camp last the way they might in a house. But even the dirty ones rise above the dun of the mound, dot it, are part of the grander patchwork, as if the graveyard were earth and these many blankets its flowers. Little bursts of colour and hope.

Miss Sperry.

185

And I'm probably underslept myself, probably hallucinating, but suddenly all these blankets, all these tokens of Miss Sperry's care, seem like amulets. Woollen spells to keep their owners safe. Magic that means I cannot, must not, cross these people's enchanted thresholds. Or maybe it's something rather simpler, Papa. Maybe it's just that Miss Sperry has made the world a little more beautiful this morning. And I want to leave it that way.

I jam my thieving hands in my pockets.

55

EGG

We pass the blossom tree. Already there's a line of people entering the necropolis from the opposite direction. I wonder if these people have walked all night? Or if they just slept on a pavement? And, if so, whether their blankets last night were coathangers and tin cans flung from upper-floor windows?

We exit the gate. I know where the big road junction is from here. That's where Paisley will be signed. I hope we'll pass some food shops on the way. If I go in without the boy I might get away with it. I turn left. At least, I attempt to turn left, but there is a sudden urgent tug on my hand.

'What?'

The boy points.

But I see nothing. Just the street, some cars. And the line of people.

'No,' I say. 'This way. We need to go this way.'

He tugs again and when I tug back, he simply drops my hand and sprints across the road.

And I scan for a tall woman with hair coiled beneath an orange scarf. Of course I do. But it isn't that at all. It's a car. It's a car filled to the brim with pink and white balls of wool. By the time I've crossed the road, the boy is rapping on the driver-side window.

Miss Sperry, lying cocooned in the wool and as flat as you can in a car seat, wakes up. She winds down her window.

'Good morning,' she says, pulling herself to an upright.

The boy grins.

'Well, get in then,' she says.

This is not possible. The whole of Miss Sperry's life appears to be in this car. If you call a life a thousand balls of wool, some knitting needles and a primus stove. But the boy grabs the back door handle of the car anyway.

'There's loads of room in the boot,' she says, getting out and helping the boy to clear a space on the back seat. She piles things into his arms, as if he's a contestant in some game show from Before. 'It all compresses down. You'll see. Open the boot, Mhairi.'

Mhairi.

It feels strange to willingly do what I am instructed. Recently I've only been doing as instructed when the other person has had a weapon. Maybe Miss Sperry does have a weapon. That very dangerous one. Hope.

Loads of room in the boot is an exaggeration. The boot is jammed with blankets (in various stages of completion) and cardboard boxes. The boxes randomly contain: cutlery, a kettle, books (books!), underwear and more wool – balls of purple, red and brown.

'Stuff it all in,' she says to the boy, who cheerfully begins dumping in load after load.

When they've cleared the back seat, they start on the front seat footwell. And I just stand. Not helping, not joining in. Just watching this blaze of activity.

And the boy smiling.

'Careful of those,' Miss Sperry shouts at him. He's found some knitting needles and is gathering them, clacking them together rather too enthusiastically. 'Can't have too many needles. I used to be terrible at knitting,' she adds, 'but I seem to have the hang of it now.'

They bring their new haul around to the boot and push and poke it in. 'Now slam it,' she says. 'Just slam it.'

I slam it. The hoard disappears.

'See?' she says and then, 'Oh damn, forgot breakfast. You'll have to open it again.'

For breakfast, I would open anything. Not that I saw any breakfast.

Guarding against hope, I open-sesame the boot.

She rummages in the box with the kettle.

'Here we go.' From the kettle's aluminium interior, she extracts her treasure.

Eggs.

It is over six months since I last saw an egg.

'Here,' she says, and she hands them out.

One for me.

One for the boy.

One for herself.

Three whole eggs.

'I boiled them up last night with my tea. Conserves gas. Although egg tea is not my favourite.'

Three eggs for the three people she knew would be at breakfast this morning. Miss Sperry is definitely a witch. She is also Miss Sperry. I'm sure of that now.

'Righto. In you get.'

We get in, the boy in the back.

'Welcome to my humble abode,' she says and then she laughs. Her laugh is not hahahahahaha. It's a kind of sweet, high-pitched sniff. It sounds like 'hymff'.

She looks in the car mirror. The boy is simply staring at his egg.

'Well, go on, crack it,' she says. 'Aren't you hungry?' She bangs her egg on the door frame.

The boy bangs his egg.

I bang my egg and even though I bang it on the car door metal, it doesn't break. I've done it too softly. I bang it again. It breaks.

I peel away the first hard, sharp little piece of shell. I haven't even broken the inner membrane but the smell of egg floods my nose. I still can't help bringing the egg to my face, in order to inhale more deeply.

I breathe egg for a few moments and then I peel a little more. Now the membrane does break and I pull away a piece of it, put it in my mouth. It tastes like paper. Egg paper, only chewy.

Miss Sperry is already halfway through her egg. She's not eating greedily, just matter-of-factly. Like eating eggs is something you do every day.

I have all the shell off now and the egg in my hand. It fits snugly in my palm.

I lick it.

Behind me the boy licks his naked egg too.

A tiny piece of white comes away on my chipped tooth and I gulp to taste it. Then I take a huge deliberate bite, bite the top off that egg. Taste the delicious, slippery white and the rough, dry golden yolk.

I have never, in my life, Papa, tasted such an egg.

I eat it all. Every last bit. I eat it with the confidence of someone who might reasonably expect to get another meal today.

Miss Sperry chucks her eggshell out of the car window.

Miss Sperry! My teacher!

'All biodegradable,' she says as she starts the car engine.

The boy chucks his eggshell out.

I'm about to follow suit but I can't. It's not because Miss Sperry's actions shock me (though they do) but because I still need to hold on to some part of this egg. So I put it in my pocket.

Just in case.

56

LUSH WITH STEAMY RAINFORESTS

Miss Sperry drives.

This is what Miss Sperry does not do: she does not ask questions. For instance, she does not ask:

– where we have come from
– what has happened on the way
– where our parents are
– why I am travelling with the boy

She does not even ask the boy what his name is. This is very restful. What she does do is talk. This is surprisingly restful too. Mainly she talks about the past. Not just things to do with the necropolis (though she certainly talks about that) but things to do with Deep Time. She says things like:

'Of course, that was when Scotland lay at the equator, in the Carboniferous age, over three hundred million years ago. Just think about that! Scotland surrounded by coral reefs and tropical seas. Scotland lush with steamy rainforests. There were trees that grew fifteen metres in just a few years. And then the world stretched. Tectonic plates. The crust of the earth rifted. And Scotland moved. Moved north.'

I do not know if this is true, but Miss Sperry was a teacher so she should know. Besides it sounds true. I don't just mean in the rational, scientific sense, the sort Muma liked. But in the Papa-couldn't-make-it-up story sense. In the sound of the words themselves: in the earth's crust rifting. *Rifting*. And the world stretching and Scotland (safe, wet, cool Scotland) once being at the equator, once being at the place that is now just sand and dust. And I listen like you listen to a story, letting the words all spin around me and seeing how they catch the light. Seeing how, but for rifting, I might have been born at the equator. It might be my land now all sand and dust.

And the boy's land cool and wet.

The words continue to spin and glitter as Miss Sperry kills her fifteen-metre-high trees and lays them down as peat bog. As she squeezes molten rock and crystallises magma into dolerite, into whinstone; into the rocky crag of her beloved necropolis. And all this squeezing, Miss Sperry says, all this cooling and crystallisation was ten million years ago. Before the last ice age. And yet, I think, the boy and I were there just last night – lying on the crag of Deep Time. As if we belonged to a greater whole. Were part of something bigger than ourselves.

And maybe this dreamy, hypnotic thing I feel is actually because of Miss Sperry's voice, the continual, contented, uninterrupted drone of it. Or perhaps it's because of the car itself. The enclosed warmth around us, the soft whirr of the engine and the fact that we are travelling, travelling incredibly fast, while making no effort at all. Just sitting in this warmth and the outside world can't touch us for a moment. Even though it's raining.

Raining!

Not terrifying storm rain, but normal rain. The sort of everyday rain you used to get in Before. Drops of silver running down the windows. Running and sparkling. And Miss Sperry's front windscreen wipers go, swish, swish swish, like some childhood song, while on the window next to me the rain just falls in streams of sparkling silver. And if around us, other vehicles splash and splatter, none of it touches us here in our steamy, tropical, magical warmth.

And the boy is asleep. Sleeping – without the sucking stone in his mouth. Just fallen asleep, crashed into the softness and warmth. And maybe I'm half-asleep too. Maybe I'm rifting, drifting, just like Scotland herself, being moved by forces beyond myself.

And also – just for a moment – letting go.

57

ARDROSSAN

At Ardrossan, Miss Sperry parks up just outside the ferry terminal and gets practical.

She says: 'Do you want to call your grandmother? Tell her you're here?' She rummages among the black layers of her clothing and extracts a phone. 'Yes. Here we are.' It's an old solar phone but one of the reliable sort that springs into life after just a moment or two in the sunlight of the dashboard. 'Sorry,' she adds. 'Should have asked earlier, shouldn't I? Too much talking.'

She hands the phone towards me.

'No,' I say.

'No?' says Miss Sperry.

No. No. A thousand times no. For eleven months, I have avoided all possible opportunities to speak to Grandmother on the phone.

'But how will she know to come and meet you?'

Good point. And it had to come. It always had to come. Grandmother and the question. The Impossible Question. But it's not a question that can be answered on the phone.

'Need to check the time of the crossing first,' I say. 'Don't I?'

'Oh yes, silly me.' There's some more rummaging and then Miss Sperry extracts an embroidered pink silk purse which looks Chinese. She peers inside. 'Should be enough for a couple of tickets. One way anyway.' She presents me with a handful of coins. I hesitate.

A blanket.

An egg.

A lift.

And now money.

Money!

Miss Sperry is making me nervous. In Before people gave you things and asked nothing in return. People who loved you – like Papa. Your family, of course. Your friends. But, often, other people too. Teachers. Neighbours. And sometimes even random people. Strangers. But not any more. Now there is always a price to be paid. What is Miss Sperry's price?

'Come on,' Miss Sperry says. 'Haven't got all day. Need to get back to the knitting.'

Or maybe I'm just confused because it all seems too easy and I've learnt that nothing is easy these days. Nothing. And if you start thinking things are easy, if you think people will give you things without wanting something in return . . .

'Miss Sperry . . .' I say.

'Corlinda,' she corrects.

Perhaps this explains it. Perhaps it's only mad people who give you things these days.

'Corlinda,' I repeat and then I just go dry.

'Yes?' she says.

'I don't know how to say thank you.'

'Get on with you,' she says and then she laughs.

Hymff, hymff, hymff hymff, hymff.

58

TERMINAL

I get out of the car into the rain, put the hood of my jerkin up.

Miss Sperry leans towards the open door: 'I'll stop here with the lad, if you don't mind.'

Whatever else Miss Sperry is, she isn't stupid. This outside rain is not sparkling or silvery. It's the sort of needle rain that makes you very wet, very quickly.

I head for the long, low-lying white hut that serves as the ferry terminal. It's busy, crowded even, a press of people trying to get through the glass entrance doors. But an orderly press – maybe because at either side of the doors is a soldier. A blue-clad soldier with a gun, or rather a pistol. A pistol in a leather holster.

I keep my head down, make myself invisible, just one of the crowd as I go through the door, pretend I'm moving quickly to keep dry, get out of the rain. My bowed head turns out to be at about the level of the left-end soldier's breast. So, I see his emblem. It's the white cross on the blue ground, the Scottish saltire. But not just that. This emblem has something else embroidered at the bottom, a jagged line infilled in black, like a little line of mountains. And I know that shape and I know those mountains.

It's the outline of the Sleeping Warrior, the profile the hills in the north of Arran make which the local people see as a helmeted warrior lying with his hands across his chest. But what is this Arran warrior doing stitched in black at the bottom of the Scottish saltire? Part of me wants to tap the soldier on the shoulder and ask. But of course, I just keep going, head down.

Inside the terminal, the crowd becomes a long, snaking switchback queue. I join the end of it. People are shaking the wet from their coats, pushing back their hoods to reveal their faces.

I try not to stare at the faces but I can't help it. There's something strange about them. But I can't place it. Not at first. Then I realise it's skin-colour. Almost all these faces are white.

Celtic white.

And it was always a bit like this around the island but I realise my own landscape has changed. And the lack of dark faces feels odd. The boy, I think, will stand out here.

Carefully, I map the rest of my surroundings. I note the position of the other soldiers in the terminal. There are six of them: two by the glass hatch of the ticket office and four by the exit which leads out to the dock, to the ferry itself.

Meanwhile, the queue is slow. The man behind me 'tsk's under his breath.

'Oh, come on,' he mutters. 'We'll all be taking the needle before getting tickets at this rate!'

I turn slightly to look at him. He's white too, but the weather-beaten white of men who work outside on the island. He catches my eye, so I have to nod at him. Then I see what he's holding in his hand. His papers.

And suddenly everything makes sense, the number of people, the length of the queue, the delay. People are having to show their papers.

Since when has anyone needed papers to go from one part of Scotland to another?

'I don't get it,' I hear myself say aloud.

'You don't get it!' the muttering man exclaims. 'None of us get it!' He waves his own papers in his fist. 'I mean I'm fine with Independence, I get the point, Arran for the islanders, rise up the Sleeping Warrior and all that, but . . .'

'Independence? What independence?'

'Whoa,' he says. 'Where have you been? The Island Territories. Independence from the mainland. Or rather' – he points out of the terminal window – 'from that.'

I follow his finger, through the glass and across the marina beyond the docks to what used to be an area of barren, reclaimed land to the west of the town. A place of marram grass and silt. It's now a tented city, an ant-like heap of people and bright polythene. The polythene flaps. Flap, flap, flap. In the wind.

'But doing away with multiple tickets,' the muttering man continues, 'making us all queue every time. I mean really. What is the Inter-Generational Council thinking of?'

And I don't say 'what Inter-Generational Council?' because that will give me away for sure. That will tell him that, despite my white Celtic face, I don't belong his side of the border after all. That I'm one of them. People without papers. Me and the boy. That we belong in that tented city.

'Better get my papers then,' I say cheerily. 'Left them in the car.'

'Can't save your place, I'm afraid,' Muttering Man says, though he doesn't sound sad.

'No problem,' I reply. 'I'm not in a hurry.'

I walk out of the terminal building to find it's stopped raining, but I still keep my hood up, right until I reach the car.

'All fixed,' I say as I open the door. 'But I think you were right, Corlinda. I need to make that phone call.'

59

THE QUESTION

I tell Miss Sperry I think phone reception will be better by the terminal building. I walk to the end furthest from the door, furthest from the crowds, the soldiers.

Dial Grandmother's number.

The number is a mobile, so Grandmother could pick up anywhere on the island. But, as I dial, I imagine her in her kitchen. I don't know why I imagine this because Grandmother is not an ordinary grandmother, not a storybook red-and-white-check-cloth kitchen grandmother. Not rosy-cheeked and smiling. No. Grandmother is thin, raw-boned, strong. Muma occasionally used the word 'harsh' about her, but this is probably only because Grandmother is a very definite, decisive person. The sort of person who tells it how it is and likes to be in charge. In this she is actually much more like Muma than her own son. That's why Papa was always a bit of a mystery to her. If Grandmother is in the kitchen she will not be baking, she'll be throwing logs in the wood burner. Logs which she will have chopped herself with an axe.

When Grandma asks questions, she asks them the same way that she chops wood. This is the reason for my eleven months of silence. That and The Question. The answer to which is locked up in Castle. So, if I have to make the call (and I do have to make the call), then there's only one way to do it. In Now Time.

In Now Time the number rings. It rings four times and then she picks up.

'Hello?' says Grandmother. Her voice is sharp, alert: part-suspicion (she doesn't recognise the incoming number) and part-anticipation. When I don't respond immediately she adds: 'Who is this?'

'It's me,' I say. 'Mhairi.'

There's an intake of breath. 'Oh my god,' Grandmother says even though she has never believed in God. 'Where are you, Mhairi?'

'Ardrossan,' I say. 'The ferry terminal.'

'Oh my god,' she repeats. And then she asks The Question.

I don't even pause.

I say: 'No. Papa is not with me.'

My voice is very steady because in Now Time, you cannot be held responsible for the past because there is no past. The past is over your shoulder and it's all dark there. 'And nor is Muma,' I add. 'But it's all right. I'll explain everything later.' In Now Time there is no such thing as 'later'. So this is a lie.

But Grandmother doesn't know this, so she just says: 'Have you got money?'

She moves straight on not just because of *later* but also because of these words: *It's all right.* I'm going to have to think about words. Because maybe words for our time need rethinking just like stories do.

'You could get the 11.05 sailing,' Grandmother continues. 'I'll meet you.'

'No,' I say. 'I don't have money. The last of my money, it was – stolen.'

'Oh.' There's a pause in which I can hear her thinking.

'I'll send Peter,' she says. 'It's Tuesday. He'll be out in his boat. I'll get him to bring you straight to Corrie.'

'Peter?'

'Yes,' she says. 'You remember Peter?'

60

KISS

I return to the car. I tell Miss Sperry that my grandmother is overjoyed to hear from me and that she'll meet us off the ferry at Brodick. Then I give her back the 'change' from the tickets and tell her that, if we don't want to miss the 11.05 sailing, we'd better get going.

The boy gets out of the car. Miss Sperry gets out of the car. The boy pulls at the blankets knotted around him, then wriggles and skinny-bunnies them over his head. Very solemnly, he hands them to Miss Sperry. As if he's thinking about all the people back in the necropolis who are going to need these blankets more than he does now. Because he's safe.

Almost.

'Oh,' Miss Sperry says. 'Thank you. That's very thoughtful of you.' Then she crouches down so that her eyes are at the same level as his. 'But,' she adds, reaching out to touch his bare arm, 'I think you should keep one, for the crossing. Always much blowier at sea than you think.' She unknots my purple and white blanket from the pink and white one she first gave him. 'There,' she says, handing it over, neatly folded. 'Just in case.'

And then, as if it was the most natural thing in the world, she leans forward, folds the boy in her arms and kisses the top of his head.

And he lets her. In fact, he kisses her right back. Just like I used to when Papa kissed me on the head.

Miss Sperry makes the most difficult things look simple.

61

PETER

I do remember Peter.

He was often at Sandstone Quay, the tiny harbour about a hundred metres from Grandmother's house in Corrie. There were only ever four or five boats in the harbour and one of them belonged to Peter's father. Peter and I didn't have that much to do with each other as children, even though we were neighbours, partly because he was a few years older than me but also because he was a boy and I was a girl. Plus, I was more of a thinker and he was more of a do-er. The first time I ever remember seeing him, I think I was sitting astride one of the harbour bollards (which are shaped like sheep) reading a book and he was working with his father on the boat. Taking apart the engine probably. Or coiling ropes or pumping bilges. And also whistling. Peter's father played the fiddle at night and the songs must have seeped into Peter's blood the way they did into Papa's. Scottish jigs and ballads and the one of mists, returning and homeland, the particular one my father sang me among his sacred hills. The thought of that tune, the yearn of it grabs at my throat again, even though I can no longer remember its name.

Peter is obviously old enough to have his own boat now, because it is Peter that Grandmother is sending to pick us up. Or rather to pick me up. Not from the marina next to the ferry port though. Grandmother says the marina is too close to the camp. And there are always people from the camp trying to board vessels for the island. My instruction is go to the jetty:

'The jetty in Saltcoats. The one where we used to land when we wanted to picnic on South Beach. Yes? That will be safer. Peter'll meet you there. Bring you straight to the harbour here at Corrie. Do you understand?'

Do you understand? As if I was still seven years old. As if I hadn't just made my way ten thousand kilometres from Khartoum.

Yes, I understand.

In the car park, we say goodbye to Miss Sperry and she drives away. She doesn't wave and she doesn't look back. I think Miss Sperry has gone into Now Time.

The journey on foot to the jetty will be about forty-five minutes. Before we leave I do two things.

1. I spend some of Miss Sperry's 'ticket' money. Not all of it. Go to the kiosk in the terminal and buy two ham sandwiches (with pickle), two bags of crisps and a bottle of water.

2. I wrap the blanket around the boy's head so it's difficult to see his face.

'Now walk,' I say.

62

TRUST

I eat my crisps. The boy eats his crisps. They are cheese and onion. I do not like cheese and onion crisps but it was all they had at the kiosk. Besides, when you haven't had crisps for about a year they taste good whatever flavour they are. These taste of salt and deliciousness. What is also delicious is not having to conserve them. We just eat. We stuff all the food in. Even though we had breakfast. Even though we had eggs for breakfast. We share water from the bottle. Because soon – there will be more. We are reckless, wasteful, extravagant. My head goes dizzy.

So I'm glad to arrive at the jetty before Peter. Glad to have to sit on the stone jetty wall and wait. I've got good at waiting. We eat more. We eat the ham sandwiches. The pickle zings on my tongue.

Eventually a boat comes across the water. I listen to the sound of the outboard engine closing the gap between me and the island. The boat is small and blue with a plain wooden wheelhouse. The boy at the helm is actually a young man – broad and good-looking. He brings the boat expertly alongside the jetty, throws me a rope. I know not to tie it, just loop it round the railings by the steps and pass it back to him.

When he's sure the boat is secure he turns his attention to me. 'God, you've changed, Mhairi,' he says. 'Wouldn't have recognised you.'

He has also changed. As a child he was not handsome, he was small and solid. 'It's been a long time,' I say.

'Sorry,' he says, then, 'Sorry. I don't know what I was saying.'

The truth probably.

'I should have said, "welcome",' he says. 'Welcome, Mhairi!' and he grins and holds out a hand to help me aboard.

'Take the boy first,' I say.

'Boy?'

It's only then that I notice the boy has not followed me down the steps. He's still at the top, shrouded in the pink and white blanket.

'Come on,' I call. But he doesn't. Possibly because of Peter's face.

'Aileen – your grandmother,' says Peter. 'She didn't mention any boy.'

'No?' I say.

'No,' says Peter.

'Probably the shock,' I say, going back up the steps. 'I'm going to pick you up, lift you,' I say to the boy. 'OK?' I draw the blanket slightly tighter about his face, but not before I see his eyes. His eyes are not like cups. His eyes are terrified.

'What shock?' asks Peter.

I try to lift the boy but he's stiff as a board. 'Relax,' I whisper. 'Relax. It's fine. What's the matter?' We need to get into the boat,

210

we need to get into the boat as casually, as easily and as fast as possible.

'Well,' I call back down to Peter. 'It's not every day you get a new grandson.'

'Oh,' he says. 'Wow. Right. It has been a long time!' And then, as he sees me struggle with the leaden boy, he adds: 'Here. Let me help.'

And he's out of the boat in an instant, bounding up the steps like some cheerful Labrador dog. It's only another moment before the boy is in his strong arms. The blanket flaps open.

'Jesus,' says Peter.

'Adopted brother,' I say. 'Obviously. Adopted grandson. From the Sudan. That's why Papa didn't, you know, want to mention anything in advance.'

The boy looks at Peter. Peter looks at the boy.

'Mhairi,' Peter says. 'No kidding, but . . . this is legit, isn't it?'

'What do you mean legit? He has his papers,' I say. 'If that's what you mean.' Then I take a risk. 'Do you want to see them?' I ask it like a challenge.

'Oh – no. No. Sorry.' Peter begins to walk down the steps. 'Just asking. Only you can't be too careful these days. You know how it is.' And then he adds: 'You all right, mate?' to the boy. 'What's with the trembling? Never been in a boat before?'

And the boy is trembling now. The whole of his body shaking.

'We've been through some bad times,' I say. 'He doesn't trust people,' I improvise. 'Men. He doesn't trust men.'

'Well, you can trust me, mate. You'll be all right with me. Safe as houses. So long as you're not an illegal. Taking an illegal on to the island. They can put you on the Blood Stone for that.' He laughs.

Hahahaha.

He sets the boy in the boat and I quickly climb in behind. I don't ask about the Blood Stone.

'Mind you,' he continues, 'as your grandmother is currently chair of the InterGen, I guess there'd be mitigating circumstances.'

He slips the rope, pulls the outboard throttle and manoeuvres the boat fast and skilfully away from the jetty. But there's still a slight lurch as the boat turns, as it bumps into its own wash, and that's when the boy begins screaming.

SCREAMING.

63

THE SWALLOWING SEA

The screaming is a lot louder than it was in my dream. And it goes on very much longer. It goes on the whole way across the water to the island.

Peter says: 'Whoa. That's insane. Put that blanket over his head!'

I put the blanket over his head. Not because of the noise, but because I suddenly know with absolute certainty what is in the tower of his Castle. It's a small boat, a tiny crowded boat. A boat with far too many people on it. A boat crossing a bit of sea, any bit of sea, from somewhere known and terrifying to somewhere unknown and just as terrifying. And on that boat are people he loves. His muma, I think. His papa. And they don't make it. Of course, they don't make it. That's why they were missing from the family picture he drew in Skitby Detention Centre, why he was travelling alone with the old man. And maybe he himself fell from the boat. Only he didn't go under because perhaps his muma and papa had made sure he had the only life jacket. Because they wanted him to survive. His muma was sure of that:

You have to survive! That's what she would have told him.

Remember, the world is beautiful. Those would have been his papa's last words as he dipped below the surface a final time. As the boy watched him sinking.

So many people in the water, so much panic and thrashing and so, perhaps, he never actually saw his muma go down. Perhaps the hull of the overturned boat was between him and the orange scarf. Blocking his view, just as the jeep blocked my view in the desert that day. The upturned hull stopping the boy seeing the moment when his muma finally succumbed, went down and didn't come up again. Perhaps that's what's allowed him to hope. Because she might just have survived, mightn't she? Somebody might have rescued her the way they rescued him? Which is why he can't help himself if he sees an orange scarf in a crowd. Because this is what hope does, what the heart does. It refuses to know what the head knows. We understand this, don't we, Papa?

'What on earth's up with him?' shouts Peter.

'The swallowing sea,' I say, hearing the clashing of charcoaled stones. 'The whirling, whorling, sucking, swallowing sea.'

'The what?' says Peter.

That's why I put the blanket over the boy, not to shut him up (because nothing is going to be able to do that) but to stop him having to look at the sea.

64

GRANDMOTHER

Grandmother is standing on the harbour wall at Corrie. She's stands straight and tall like a storybook king searching the seas for incoming ships, looking to see if they have white sails – for life – or black sails – for death.

Peter brings the boat in. Grandmother sees me, she sees Peter, she sees the boy. The boy has stopped screaming. He has screamed himself hoarse. The blanket has fallen from him, he is staring straight ahead. He looks blinded, exhausted, in a trance.

Peter throws the rope to Grandmother, who expertly knots it around the sheep bollard. Grandmother does all this without once taking her eyes from the boy.

I stand up to go to greet her.

She looks past me: 'Who,' she says, eyes on the boy, 'is that?'

And perhaps it's the tone of her voice, or the fact that she's looking straight past me, or perhaps it's just because I've travelled so far and for so long and I'm very tired that I say: 'That, Grandmother, is a human being.'

'Peter?' Grandmother says.

'She told me you knew,' says Peter. 'She told me it was all legit.'

Grandmother looks at me. 'You little liar,' she says.

65

WELCOME

Grandmother marches us down the path to her house. Us in front, her behind. She doesn't have a gun but she might as well have.

The kitchen is as blue as I remember, but smaller. She sits down at the kitchen table with an old-fashioned laptop, indicates for Peter to sit down. The boy and I stay standing, like it's a court.

'She said it was legit,' Peter repeats. 'She said he had papers.'

'And does he have papers?' Grandmother asks.

'No,' I say.

'Oh, my god,' says Peter.

Grandmother looks at Peter. 'I want you to know, Peter, that I will take full responsibility for this. Do you understand?'

'Yes,' says Peter. 'Thank you.'

Grandmother looks at the boy. 'I suppose he has a name?' she says.

I say nothing.

The boy says nothing.

I'm not even sure the boy is in the room. His eyes are absent. His face stunned. I think most of him is still out on the boat.

'What's your name?' she asks him.

No reply.

'Where are you from?'

No reply.

'Originally?' she continues.

No reply.

'Does he even speak English?' Grandmother asks me.

'I don't know.'

'You don't know!'

'He's mute,' I say. Though I don't like saying it. Not in front of him. It seems crass. Unkind. Unnecessary. 'Though he understands English,' I add. 'He understands everything.'

'Does he,' says Grandmother. And then she presses her fingers hard to her temples as if she has a headache there. 'Mhairi – you have no idea how serious this is.'

But she's wrong about that. I see exactly how serious this is. I thought I was coming home. Had the wild but certain idea that this was my final destination, that I was coming to a place where I would be understood. Where someone other than me would have the keys to Castle. Where things could be unlocked and I could still be safe. Where the boy could be safe. Where there would be a different, deeper, kind of truth. Papa's truth. Papa's beauty even. Shining all about me. How absurd.

'Come on,' I say to the boy. 'We're not welcome here. We need to go.' And I take his hand and start off down the corridor to the front door.

'Oh, no you don't,' says Grandmother. She pushes right past us and stands barring the doorway. 'He'll need to be reported.

Registered. Right away. And you too for that matter. Not registering an illegal immediately is aiding and abetting.'

There are two locks on the front door. Grandmother turns the key in both of them. Puts the keys in her right trouser pocket.

Survival, I remember then, is a long game.

'Then you'd better register him under your name,' I say. 'Under Papa's name. Bain.'

'Don't make this any worse,' says Grandmother.

'I'm not making anything worse,' I say. 'That's his name. Mohammed Bain.'

Peter springs into life then. 'That's what she told me,' he verifies. 'She said the family adopted him. In the Sudan.'

'Mhairi,' says Grandmother, 'look at me.'

I look at her.

'Your future,' she continues, 'not to mention Peter's, may depend on your truthful answer to this question. Did your father really adopt this boy?'

'Yes,' I say.

'So how is it that he doesn't have papers?'

'They were stolen.' I hold my grandmother's gaze. She hasn't got a knife, she hasn't got a gun, she is not an Imgrim. 'Along with the money. They took my papers and also his. His papers were stolen too. Because I was carrying them for both of us.'

'Oh,' says Peter. 'Then that's all right, isn't it? We'll be able to prove he's not an illegal. I mean there'll be a record. Somewhere there'll be a record. First port of entry. In England if not in Scotland. It'll be all right. It'll be fine, won't it?'

'Not necessarily,' says Grandmother. 'Since Independence, adoption of itself is no longer a guarantee of residency. So, it's not just about the papers but also about the timing. But the law isn't retrospective.' She looks at me. 'So, if the adoption papers were signed pre-Independence . . .' She pauses. 'Was it more than two years ago, Mhairi?'

'Yes,' I say at once. 'Yes.'

Peter's face is all light and gratitude.

'OK,' says Grandmother. 'Then – for the time being – we just need to file an Interim.'

An Interim apparently means phone calls, statements, online forms. It is a matter of urgency. There are penalties for not filing immediately.

'Peter – you'll have to give all your details, of course.'

'No problem,' says Peter.

'It's not the work of a moment,' Grandmother adds to me. 'Why don't you take a trip to the bathroom? The two of you look like you could use a wash.'

66

BATH

It's eleven months since I had a bath.

'Come,' I say to the boy. He probably hasn't had a bath for eleven months either. If we want to leave via a window we can do so later.

The bathroom is pink. There are towels on the towel rail. Big white towels, almost fluffy. I bolt the door.

'Sit on the floor,' I say to the boy. 'And don't look.'

While the bath runs, I get undressed, drop my clothes in a pile. The clothes smell. Of me and tombs and soil.

The boy has his back to me. I climb into the water. It's hot. Not tepid – hot. I lie back in the warmth. My body looks long and thin. I shut my eyes, just concentrate on the warmth. Feel the water lapping about me.

Then I take the soap.

Soap.

A white round of soap which smells like rose petals.

I wash, still with my eyes shut. Put my hand over the whole landscape of my body. Wash in the cracks and crevices. All the places that haven't seen soap for almost a year.

I take shampoo.

The shampoo smells of pine forests.

I wash my hair. Try to wash out all the knots, though this is not very successful.

Then I lie and wallow in the water, even though the water is filthy.

After about a thousand years, I get out, wrap myself in one of the white, white towels. The white, white towel is warm.

'Your turn,' I say to the boy. And I swish out the bath and run it again. I check the temperature of the water, make sure it's not too hot.

I sit on the floor where he was sitting, put my back to the bath. 'In you get,' I say.

I hear him undress. Feel a tap on my shoulder.

'What?'

He hands me the bar of soap.

'You want me to wash you?'

He moves in front of me, small, naked, not self-conscious. He nods.

'OK.'

I help him climb in the bath. Wash him in the clean water. Flannel his bones. He's even thinner than me. All juts and angles. Only his face is soft, Papa. I wash between his toes and behind his ears. I do not wash his private parts. I make him do that.

Then I take Grandmother's razor.

'Do you want me to do your head?

He nods. I use shampoo because the shampoo smells good. I

slide the razor over the curves of his skull, careful not to nick him.

His head is beautiful, Papa.

The world is beautiful.

67

STARTING OVER

There's a knock on the door.

'I've brought you some clothes,' says Grandmother.

By the time I open the door, the clothes are there but not Grandmother. There's a plain blue shirt for me and a pair of loose grey cotton trousers with an ill-matched leather belt. In case the trousers are too big probably. For the boy, a definitely t°o big striped T-shirt. Under these items are some socks and a pair of women's pants. Everything has been washed, ironed and folded neatly. It smells clean the way the Imgrim woman did.

We put the clothes on. I have to tighten the belt but not by much. Grandmother was always scraggy. I don't forget my knife, tuck it out of sight in the trouser waistband. The T-shirt swamps the boy, way too wide across the shoulders, dangling below his knees. But he looks delighted. Puts on his own pants but not his filthy trousers.

We go out of the bathroom. Now Grandmother is standing on the landing.

'Mhairi,' she says, 'I'm sorry. Do you think we could we start again?' And she comes right over and puts her arms around me. All the way round. An embrace.

I stand like a stone.

'It was just,' she continues over my shoulder, 'not knowing in advance. About Mohammed. It totally threw me. I'm the chair of the InterGen, Mhairi. I have to do things right. By the book. It was my fault though. I should have checked about the papers. Even for you. But if I'd have known – well, it could have taken weeks. You'd have been on the mainland for weeks. You'd have ended up in the camp. Replacement papers – the system isn't exactly streamlined yet. Even for people like you – with every right to be here. But I still shouldn't have sent Peter like that, not straightaway, not without checking but, and . . .'

And she's making a speech and I'm still standing like a stone.

She lets me go.

'But the truth is,' she pauses, 'I wouldn't have been able to wait anyhow. No. I've waited such a long time. I needed to see you. Have you – right here, in front of me. So as to believe it. Do you understand?'

'I understand,' I say.

'You don't understand,' she says. 'You couldn't. I shouldn't expect you to.' Then she drops to her haunches, so she's at the same level as the boy.

'Hello, Mohammed,' she says. 'Shall we be friends?'

He stares at her. His eyes are like cups.

'I expect you'll want something to eat,' she adds. 'Yes?'

We follow her downstairs. Peter is gone. The laptop is closed. Grandmother boils a kettle, opens a bread bin, takes out a loaf.

'I'm not hungry,' I say. The first time in forever I'm not hungry.

'No?'

'What about you?' she asks the boy.

He nods.

So, she cuts him a huge wedge of fresh white bread. Spreads it with creamy yellow butter. Opens a pot of jam which has a label saying 'Strawberry' in her own handwriting. The boy eats. And I am not really hungry, but water still springs in my mouth.

'Now,' says Grandmother. 'I want you to tell me everything.'

That is not possible, so I say nothing.

'Please,' says Grandmother. 'Begin with your father. I have to know, Mhairi.'

'We were – separated,' I say carefully.

I take her to the dusty, desert road out of Khartoum. I tell her about the checkpoints and the soldiers. I do not tell her about the nervous young boy with the predator pack bullets slung about his neck.

'And then,' I tell her, 'Papa got out of the car. With open hands.'

'Open hands?'

'Yes, like this.' I lift my hands towards her as if I was bearing a gift. 'And he talked with the soldiers, negotiated and the soldiers said, OK, we could go. But just Mohammed and me.'

'What happened then?'

'We went. Mohammed and me.'

'And your father?'

'Muma and Papa, they went with the soldiers. But they're all right, Grandmother. Nothing happened.'

'What makes you think that, Mhairi?'

'Because I was there, Grandmother. The soldiers – they weren't bad people. Just kids. Really.'

There's a pause and then Grandmother says: 'Don't you think, Mhairi, that if your muma and papa were still alive they would have found a way to phone by now? Let me know?'

'I didn't phone,' I say.

There's another pause.

'At least not until I was very close,' I add. 'There are many reasons for not phoning. And Papa always wanted to tell you about the boy himself. In person.'

'It's not that I don't want to believe you,' says Grandmother finally.

'I know,' I say.

I want to believe me too.

68

ERRATICS

I take a tour of the house. It's a nervous thing probably. An attempt
to fix the layout back in my head. Though I could probably walk
it all blindfolded. It's also about taking a breath, getting away
from Grandmother.

I want you to tell me everything.

Everything

Everything

Everything

Perhaps I also need to know what's changed in the house. And
what hasn't. Try and map my memories on to reality. The feel of the
house is still the same. And the smell – which is of earthy logs and dry
lavender. As I go from room to room I wonder if what I'm actually
looking for is traces of Muma and Papa. And, perhaps, even of myself.

In the sitting room I find a photograph of the three of us –
Papa, Muma, me. We are standing in front of a glacial erratic. The
photograph is not digital, it's a real thing on paper, in a frame. The
erratic is one of four huge granite boulders that stand on the road
between Grandmother's house here at Corrie and the next village
of Sannox.

Papa said: *The word 'erratic' comes from the Latin 'erarre', to wander. This boulder*, Papa said, *does not belong with all the surrounding rock. It's wandered here. From somewhere else.*

But actually, that's not quite true because I learnt about erratics in geography at school. Erratics don't wander, they are forced to leave their place of origin by ice, by the movement of glaciers. They don't want to move, but they have no choice. They are displaced. Giant boulders twice as tall as Papa, chucked about by glaciers if they were pebbles.

What hope then, I think, for the real pebbles? For the little sucking stones of life?

Mind you, when these giant boulders land, when they finally arrive wherever it is that they arrive, they tend not to move again. The boulder in this photograph has not moved for ten thousand years.

I think about this and I also think how young Papa looks in the photograph. How young Muma looks. How young I look. This is not an accurate photograph. Not any more. This photograph might have been true, but now it isn't. That's another thing about truth and how slidy it is.

Upstairs is a mirror. This is how I know I don't look like the girl in the photograph on the mantelpiece. The girl in the photograph has neat hair brushed up into bunches. She is smiling. It's a long time since I've seen myself reflected in a piece of mirror glass. I've looked in rivers. And I've looked in the mirrors in detention centres. But detention centre mirrors are just squares of metal because mirror glass can always be smashed and used as a weapon.

The mirror is in the spare room, where Grandmother has decided I will sleep tonight. This is the room my parents used to sleep in. My room, the little room along the corridor, she has given to the boy.

The mirror is old-fashioned, an oval of bevelled glass standing on an old-fashioned chest of drawers. This mirror, I think, knew my parents once. Held them. My muma, my papa. Held their faces. Their smiles. And then this mirror let them go.

I look in this treacherous mirror. The girl who looks back isn't a girl any longer and she isn't smiling. But that's about all I can say about her.

In a river, or a piece of metal, you can't see the edges of yourself. You're always in motion, rippled, blurred. This mirror is very clean and the image it reflects is very sharp.

But I still can't see the edges of myself. It's as though I have lost definition.

God, you've changed, Mhairi!

Yes.

But into what?

69

SLEEPING

Night comes.

At least I think it does. It's difficult to be precise because of the light. Not the light outside because there isn't any but the light inside. The light in the kitchen and the sitting room, on the landing, in my room, in the boy's room. Lights which come on with the flick of a switch. I switch my bedroom light on and off, changing dark into light. Just like that.

Grandmother takes the boy to his room. She's made up the single bed.

'You'll sleep here,' she says.

'I slept here when I was your age,' I say. I look at his face. 'I'll only be along the corridor. OK?'

He pads back along the corridor after me, as if checking the distance. 'OK?'

He nods, returns to his room and shuts the door. I'm surprised about that.

I tell Grandmother I'm going to bed too.

'It's early,' says Grandmother. Grandmother wants to talk some more. To ask some more questions.

'I'm tired,' I say.

'OK,' she says. 'Sleep well.'

Grandmother has laid out a nightdress. It's a lacy thing, cream-coloured and made of a slippy material which could be silk. I don't put it on. I just take off my clothes and climb naked between the clean white sheets. The ones that smell of Imgrims. Under the clean white pillow, I put my knife.

I lie there.

The bed is very soft. The duvet falls close and warm around me. It moves as I move. Though I don't move much. Mainly I look at the ceiling. Light from the landing is filtering around the top of the door and making some patterns there.

I shut my eyes. I can still see the patterns on the inside of my eyelids. I press my eyes with my fingers. If you do this, more patterns come. I don't know why. Maybe it's about moving the blood around in your eyeball. I used to do this when I was a child. When I slept in the other room. Or rather when I didn't sleep. I made patterns when I couldn't sleep.

I can't sleep.

I lie awake half-listening for the sound of the boy. I've got used to the snuffling, the sucking, the way his breath evens and lengthens when he falls to sleep. I think these sounds must have calmed me. I didn't know this.

I'm still awake when Grandmother goes to bed. I hear her flush the loo, do her teeth, click off the landing light.

The bed is far too soft. I do not know what to do with this very soft bed.

I sit up.

I lie down.

I turn over.

And over.

It's really very dark when the handle of my door turns and a ghost comes into the room dressed in a pink and white blanket.

The ghost lies down on the mat on the hard floor my side of the double bed. He draws the blanket close around his body and pops a stone in his mouth. Starts sucking. It's not very long until I hear his breath go to sleeping.

I get out of bed then and join him on the floor. If I still had my purple and pink blanket, I'd use it. But I don't, so I just pull down the duvet and cover us both.

I sleep.

70

QUESTIONS

Grandmother continues with the questions. Many, many questions. Mainly about the boy. I keep the answers as simple as I can, so as to be able to remember what I've said. I tell her the boy is the son of my parents' driver. I tell her that his father was killed by a man in a kiosk with a predator pack. I tell her that the boy witnessed this murder and that's why he's mute. Grandmother seems to find this very reasonable. I add that the boy's mother was already dead, I don't know why I tell her that, and that he had no other family, so Papa felt responsible. I tell Grandmother that Papa did all the paperwork and was always going to tell her about the boy but then life intervened. I do not tell her, for obvious reasons, about the other Muhammad and the chiggers. The chiggers don't have any place in this new story. But I think about the chiggers. I think about their jaws and their pus and their itching. When I get in a muddle about the details of the story, and I sometimes do, my head itches.

'Don't scratch,' says Grandmother. 'Why are you scratching? Have you got lice?'

She looks in my hair. I haven't got lice.

Peter does not ask questions. In this he is like Miss Sperry. I go to Peter to get a rest. It's easy to find him. He's almost always in the harbour. I sit on the sheep bollard and watch him move about his business. I listen to him whistle. He whistles many songs but not the grab-my-throat yearning one. He looks purposeful, he looks as if he knows what he's doing. He also looks very solid. I don't mean fat. Not at all. But definitely not thin. Everyone is thin these days but not Peter. Peter seems to exist in some solid way that other people don't. That I don't. Me and my blurry edges and my itchy head.

It doesn't seem to bother Peter that I sit and look. Though sometimes I pretend I'm actually looking at the boy. At low tide the harbour has a little rocky beach. The boy can sit there for hours, putting stones in piles.

Sometime I sit in silence but sometimes it's me asking questions.

'Can you tell me about the InterGen?' I ask.

Peter tells me. InterGen stands for Inter-Generational. Since Independence the InterGen is the island's highest council. It has six members, each representing one decade between the ages of fourteen and seventy-four. To be elected representative you have to be the relevant age. Grandmother is sixty-nine and represents the sixty-four to seventy-four-year-olds. As six is an even number, Peter says, someone has to have a casting vote. At the moment, the sixty-fours to seventy-fours have the casting vote. And that means Grandmother.

'Which makes her about the most powerful person on the island, right now,' Peter says.

'What's the Blood Stone?' I ask.

'Justice in action,' says Peter.

I must look confused because he continues: 'It's where they stand the defendants, in the court at Lamlash.'

'A dock, you mean?'

'Yes. Blood Stone's just a nickname really, what the locals call it. Although it is actually a real stone too. A limestone block, cut from the hills of Arran.'

'So, what's the blood bit?'

Peter stops working for a moment. 'There's a court pistol. Or a revolver. A gun anyway. It sits on the desk in front of the council members. Rotates. Every fifteen minutes a court official moves it. If a defendant is convicted of one of the blood crimes, they can be shot.'

'What – right then and there?'

'Yes. By whichever council member has the gun in front of them at the time.'

'No,' I say. 'That's insane. That's stupid. You're joking.'

'You've been away a long time, Mhairi. Things have changed. You've seen the camps. The island has to protect itself. Or, as Aileen puts it, *Justice doesn't just need to be done but also has to be seen to be done*. That's what she campaigned on. That's what won her the Decade 6 vote.'

Something knocks in my head. Knocks quite hard.

'So, Grandmother,' I say, 'has she done it? Has she pulled the trigger?'

'No,' says Peter. 'No one has yet. It's a thing of last resort. A deterrent really. But it seems to be working pretty well to date.

That, actually, was your grandmother's point. She said that everything had got too remote, too virtual, even on the island. And that we'd all got so used to the idea of taking the needle, and it was all done so clinically behind closed doors that we – or rather the criminals – needed to be reminded of real consequences. *Death you can actually taste*. I think that's how she put it. Something very much not hidden away.' He pauses. 'Anyway, people seemed to agree with her. She didn't get to make High Councillor for nothing. So, I'm sure she'd use that gun if she had to.'

Yes. I'm sure too.

Grandmother and me. Natural killers.

'So what constitutes a blood crime?' I ask.

'Well, the usual stuff. Murder and that. But also crimes which undermine the security of the state.'

'What state?'

'The island, of course. Arran. Stuff like trafficking illegals.' He pauses, leans on the outboard. 'Why do you think she got so het up about the boy?'

'So if I'd, if I'd really brought in an illegal . . .' I trail off.

He puts two fingers to his forehead. 'Boom! Bye, bye, Peter!'

'No! But it wasn't even your fault!'

'Oh, don't worry,' says Peter. 'Boom, boom, Mhairi first.'

71

IF

An official comes from the court.

She knows Grandmother and Grandmother knows her. Her name is Esther and she's in her twenties, bright-eyed and smiling.

'Sorry to be have to be doing this, High Councillor,' she says to Grandmother.

'On the contrary, Esther,' says Grandmother. 'We have processes on this island for a reason. Please – go right ahead.'

Esther doesn't wear a uniform but she carries a large briefcase stamped with the Sleeping Warrior logo. Only this time the hills are not outlined against the Scottish saltire but just sit on a background of blue, as if the only solid thing was the Island, that Scotland herself had just become sky.

In Esther's official Sleeping Warrior bag are various gadgets. She uses these to scan the boy and me. First, she takes digital printouts of our faces, front-on and in profile.

'Which is your best side?' she asks about the profile picture. 'Actors always have a best side. I read that in Hollywood Online.' This reminds me how very far I personally have come from the virtual world. And I think again about the gun in the court of

Lamlash. And how I do not need a gun to know how close death can be.

I tell Esther I do not think I have a best side, but the boy, very solemnly, presents the left side of his face. I think this may be the first joke he's made since we met. It's funnier – and somehow sadder – than Muhammad's donkey jokes.

Next Esther does iris scans and then takes electronic fingerprint whorls.

'It'll just speed up the process of identification,' she says.

'How long,' I ask, fairly casually, 'until we'll get our replacement papers?'

'Oh,' she says, 'depends when you get to the top of anyone's list.' Then she looks at Grandmother's face and adds, 'But of course, I'll try and push it all along as fast as I can. In the circumstances.'

Next, she asks some questions.

'Tedious, I know,' she says, 'but I have to. Just for the record, though I'm sure it's all on the Interims anyway. Would it be all right to start with you, High Councillor?'

'Of course,' says Grandmother.

She asks Grandmother some questions and Grandmother answers. From the discussion I find out that although only two of my grandparents were born on the Isle of Arran this is OK because the other two were born in Scotland Mainland and the Arran residency rules permit this.

'Now, if you don't mind, I have to ask the adoptee some questions,' says Esther.

'Not possible,' says Grandmother.

239

'Oh,' says Esther. 'He's mute. I did read that somewhere. Sorry. Right.' She resets the nanonet record facility. 'Perhaps you'd like to do the honours, Mhairi?'

I do the honours. I spin my story. Our story. It is not correct in all particulars. The boy's face might give us away but he's too smart for that. Besides, the more you repeat something, I find, the more truth seems to attach to it.

Esther finally flips the machine shut.

'Done,' she says. 'You'll still both have to come before the court for formal signing, of course, but,' she nods at Grandmother, 'I'm sure I don't have to explain the legal bit in this company. Otherwise, as I said, it's just a matter of waiting for central base verification. But basically, if everything matches up – bingo.'

If.

Such a small word.

If.

72

WORDS

There are two sorts of words, I find. Ones that slide and ones that don't. Most of the ones that don't slide are to do with suffering. Such as:

Hunger

Thirst

Cold

There is no quibble about this. These things are real. Ask me. Ask the boy. Ask anyone who has ever travelled.

And then there are the words that people pretend are just as real, as fixed. Such as:

Truth

Justice

Trust

But these words slide. Depending on who's in charge, who's making the judgement, and what they have to gain – or lose. So I think these words are all made up, Papa. They are fictions like the borders in Africa. Because, Papa, I do not think my truth is the same as the Imgrim truth and who's to say that the Imgrims are right and I am wrong? Which means, I suppose, I'd have to add

Right and Wrong to my list of slidy words. And possibly also Beauty. I don't want to put Beauty on the slidy list, Papa, because you made that very real to me. But the boy's skull and a bar of Grandmother's soap? Can these things really make the world beautiful, Papa? Is this what you meant?

And then there's that word: *if*. It's a very, very tiny word, Papa. *If everything matches up, then – bingo!*

Tiny but also huge. A word which could end up taking the boy and me to the Blood Stone. The Blood Stone does not sound very likely. The Blood Stone seems pretty made up too, Papa. So, it is possible that it does not exist either.

But I think it does.

73

SICK

I get sick. At first I think I'm only sick in a dream. But I'm not, I'm lying in this bed my parents used to sleep in and it's soaking wet. With my sweat, my fever. In all the times I travelled I was never ill. Not even in the desert after we drank the dirty water the blind girl gave us. Muhammad got sick, he vomited, he had diarrhoea. For days. But my stomach stayed like iron. And the chiggers, the chiggers ate Muhammad's feet but they did not eat mine. Nor did they eat my private parts as they ate his. And now, here in this place which has regular food and plentiful water and freshly washed sheets, I am lying bathed in my own sweat, unable to move.

'Probably just your body letting go,' says Grandmother, 'now that it can.' I hear these words in the ether above me. 'You just stay put here.'

I stay put. My body is so heavy it's welded to the mattress. I have pain in my head and all my limbs ache. Time passes. I do not know how much time or what sort of time. I am in the bed and not in the bed. I hear people coming in and out of the room but I don't see them. Perhaps because I'm asleep or simply delirious. I also hear voices. Or rather I hear one voice.

Grandmother's.

It comes up through the floorboards from the sitting room below. Grandmother is talking to the boy.

Grandmother says:

Say Mohammed.

Say, 'My name is Mohammed'. Mo-ham-med. Can you say that, Mohammed?

Say Grandma. Grand-ma. Can you say Grandma, Mohammed?

When I give you something, Mohammed, you have to say thank you. Thank you. Can you say thank you? Thank you for my drink. This is a drink, Mohammed.

Cup.

Water.

Sandwich.

Can you say sandwich?

She goes on. It goes on. Round and round in my brain. If I could get up, I'd go downstairs and tell her to shut up.

Can you shut up, Grandmother? Can you say *shut up*? Can you spell *shut up*? Can you please just SHUT UP. Can you leave him alone?

But the words keep coming through the cracks in the floorboards.

And then I do dream.

I dream about the Blood Stone. I dream that there's a hollow in this block of Arran limestone. A hollow made by all the feet of all the people who have stood in this place to defend themselves. But in my courtroom, there aren't any people, there are only words. Words coming through the cracks in the walls, words dropping from the ceiling. And the words are falling, all of them falling down on to the Blood Stone. Words like:

Justice

Truth

Right

Wrong

Illegal

Sandwich

Water

Cup

And as they fall the words are just letters, falling letters of black, but when they hit the stone they stop being solid, yes, they liquefy, splash, make red, red splashes as if they were made of blood.

After a time, so many words are murdered on that stone that the hollow is just one huge puddle of gore.

74

BETTER

After some time, I get better. Well enough to open my eyes, go downstairs, eat soup.

Grandmother says: 'All the time you were delirious, Mohammed slept on the floor beside you. Every single night. I worried that he'd catch whatever it was too. But no matter how many times I took him back to his own bed – up he'd get again. Did you know?'

'No,' I say.

Though perhaps I did.

'Oh,' she adds, 'when I was changing your sheets I found this.'

It's my knife.

'It's not a very pleasant item and I hope you won't be needing it any more. Do you mind if I bin it?'

'No.'

And I don't. There are many knives in this house and also an axe.

75

THE LEUCHRAM BURN

As soon as I'm strong enough I take the boy up to the giddy horse that straddles the Leuchram Burn behind Grandmother's house. I walk him through the gate in her back garden, past the row-boat on the trailer (which is still there, though dilapidated now), across the boggy bit of field and up to the beginning of the woodland path. I walk him past the line of small, moss-covered boulders, and I watch as he reaches out a hand to touch that moss, just as I used to do when I was his age. The moss is soft and slightly springy, like curls tight to a head. I lead him through the wood to the point where the burn cascades down off the mountain and let him stand and look. I don't say anything, don't try and teach him anything or explain anything. I just let him experience it for himself, as I did.

I do help him cross the burn, but only because I know where it pools wide and shallow and safe. Then we go on until we reach the tree that has fallen high and giddy above the rushing water. And he sits down. Just like that. There's more moss on this leaning tree now and he fingers it as he sits and listens to the sound of the water, spattering among the stones.

I don't know how long he sits there. Not very long, I think, but long enough perhaps to lay down a memory.

When we first arrived in Khartoum, and I was still small, I used to talk quite a lot about home. Home as in Scotland, and what I missed about it.

Papa said: *Home is not just where you were born. Home is where you lay down memories. In time, you'll lay down memories. Here in the Sudan.*

I said: *No, I won't.*

Then Papa said: *When you talk about home, Mhairi, you almost always talk about Arran, even though your actual home was Glasgow. Why do you think that is?*

I didn't know.

Papa said: *It's because Arran speaks to you, Mhairi, and you are choosing your memories. Laying them down but also choosing them. Never forget the power of your choosing, Mhairi.*

That's why I've brought the boy to the Leuchram Burn. I hope, in the sand and dust of his mind, he will choose to find a place for this giddy tree and this cascading water.

76
MOUND AND WRECK

Grandmother is standing in the back garden.

'Where have you been?' she asks.

'To the burn,' I say.

'If you're well enough to go to the burn,' says Grandmother, 'you're well enough to help in the garden. Do you think food comes free on this island?'

In Before, Grandmother's garden was full of grass and flowers. Not any more. The garden has been dug over and divided into neat lines with logs and canes and sheets of polythene and gauze. Grandmother's garden is now a giant vegetable plot. It is early in the growing season but Grandmother already has (at various stages of growth):

- cabbages
- cauliflowers
- onions
- lettuce
- asparagus
- beetroot
- rhubarb

– raspberries

And also, potatoes.

'You can help me mound the potatoes,' she says, 'and then you can go and get some wreck.'

'Mounding the potatoes' means piling earth up around the stems of the potato plants. This, Grandmother says, stops the potatoes going green. Grandmother, it appears, has learnt many things since we went away.

She crouches down, puts her hands in the soil and shows the boy exactly how to make the most effective mound. The boy is interested, obedient and quick with his hands.

'Yes,' says Grandmother to the boy. 'Well done. Very good.'

The boy beams.

Beams.

And sets about his next mound.

'You're a fast learner, Mohammed,' said Grandmother.

And the little scene reminds me of the time the men showed me how to make an adobe brick. And how I loved making that first brick and how they praised me too. It's a long time, I think, since anyone praised me.

'You'll do well when we get you into school, Mohammed,' Grandmother adds. 'Now come on, Mhairi, time to put your back into it.'

I put my back into it. Soon we have twenty or thirty potato mounds.

'Now for the wreck,' says Grandmother.

Wreck is, apparently, seaweed. You find it on the beach.

'Free fertiliser,' says Grandmother. Grandmother will have

researched this. When Grandmother puts her mind to something, she puts her mind to it.

We go to the beach and collect wreck. When wet this type of seaweed is like reddy-brown ribbons of pasta. Slightly slimy pasta. When dry it's brittle and crushes in your hand with the smell of sea and salt. Grandmother shows us how and where to lay it among the vegetables, how to dig and mulch it in.

'Good boy, Mohammed,' she says. 'Good boy.'

And I can't be jealous. Of course not. Because Grandmother is just doing what I was doing. She's helping the boy to lay down memories.

77

SWEETS

Grandmother has to go to the court at Lamlash.

'Not to do with your case,' she says. 'Just routine business. You'll be all right on your own, yes?'

As if I hadn't travelled ten thousand kilometres from Khartoum.

She's gone for about six hours. She returns bearing gifts. At least for the boy. She brings him a pair of trousers and two right-sized T-shirts. One plain red, the other stripes of green.

'Say, "Thank you, Grandma",' she says.

The boy does not say this but he does put on the red T-shirt.

'Looks good on you,' she says and then she turns to me. 'I thought you'd want to choose your own things,' she says.

This should be true, but it doesn't feel true in the moment. I know this because my stomach clenches.

'Oh, and I also brought these,' she adds.

They're sweets. The bag says 'The Old-Fashioned Sweet Shop' and inside are:

- some peppermint creams
- some fudge
- some toffees wrapped in paper

– some bonbons dusted in cocoa powder

– some honeycomb

She holds out the bag to me.

'No, thank you,' I say.

'What – not even a toffee? You used to love toffees. And fudge – remember the fudge your mother used to make? With her engineer's precision?'

I remember. Of course I remember, the weighing, the measuring and the eating. The sucking of the sugar. All from Before. Water springs in my mouth. But I shake my head. Another denial, though I do not know of what or whom.

The boy takes a toffee, a peppermint cream, a piece of honeycomb. Stuffs them all in his mouth at once.

'Hey, hey,' says Grandmother. 'Steady on, young man.'

But he doesn't.

And she doesn't.

And they laugh together, the pair of them.

I've often heard the boy laugh but not Grandmother.

Hahahahahaha.

As the boy laughs and chews Grandmother points at his mouth and says: 'Too much toffee and you'll get another one of those, you know. A broken tooth.' Then she pauses and adds: 'Lucky that one's just a baby tooth. Otherwise we'd have to get it fixed. Spoils your smile.'

Grandmother does not mention my broken tooth. But perhaps it's because it's hidden behind tight lips. This adult, broken-for-ever tooth.

When I go to bed that night I lie awake.

I'm still awake when Grandmother comes up. Some while after her light goes out, I creep downstairs and get myself a toffee. As if I was a child.

Me – a child!

I stick the toffee to the roof of my mouth, suck and suck as I lie in bed waiting for the boy to come.

But, this night, he doesn't.

78

A VIEW FROM THE HILL

When I travelled, I didn't always know where I was but I always knew where I was going. Now I have arrived, it's the reverse. I know where I am but not where I'm going any more. My brain's gone fuzzy.

I decide to climb to the top of the hill behind Grandmother's house. That's where things always became clear in Before.

'We'll go by the burn,' I say to the boy. 'Stop on the giddy tree.'

The boy shakes his head.

He. Shakes. His. Head.

'He can stop here with me,' Grandmother says. 'Help me bring in the logs. Would you like that, Mohammed?'

The boy nods.

I give the boy a look.

He gives it back. Throws it at me.

So, I go alone. I go fast, I do not stop at the giddy tree over the cascading burn. No, I push straight on up, fight my way through the undergrowth which has grown dense over the years because obviously no one has made the journey I am now making. I arrive at the top with burrs and scratches.

It's a clear day and warm. I can see for miles. Above me there is the huge arc of the sky; behind me the warrior hills of Arran. Nestling among those hills: some villages, some winding roads, no visible soldiers. In front of me: the glittering sea, the Firth of Clyde that divides this safe, functioning place from the mainland.

I breathe a little more freely, but only for a moment because, there, on the mainland, is something else.

The camp.

The dark smudge of it on the opposite shore. A heap of flapping polythene and scurrying ants.

Since I have been on the island I have forgotten this camp. But it has not forgotten me. The camp has been lurking, lying in wait. Which is perhaps what's brought me to the top of this hill. Because I knew it would be there. That I'd see it, have to face it.

And part of me wants to cry out: *Hang on! Not fair! What has this camp got to do with me? Haven't I done my time, done my travelling?*

So I shut my eyes and hope, when I open them, the camp will be gone.

But it isn't.

Although it should be because this camp is based on things which don't exist.

That's when I start to go fuzzy again because maybe it's not just words that slide but reality itself? I look around me, try to get my bearings. Work it out. Check on the solid things:

Sky

Sea

Land

Rocks

Soil

Yes. I think we can agree on these things, Papa. Real things on which a person can depend – things you can actually reach out and touch.

But what about the non-real, the fictions? The things we make up ourselves and then give names to as if they were as real as rocks? Things like:

Rules

Nations

Countries

And also borders.

Always borders.

Borders. Borders. Borders.

Things you can't know, can't touch in the way you can know and touch a rock. Story things, erratic things, things which move about, wander about, won't stay still.

That's why this camp, which is born of the made-up things – the nations and borders – should not exist. But it does exist. The camp is real. I know this because, if you were close enough, you could touch those polythene sheets and those ant-like people.

You might also be able to touch their suffering.

So, no, I can't deny the camp any more. The camp exists, whether I choose to look or not. My brain de-fuzzes. I am going to have to have a conversation with the High Councillor about this camp.

79

PETER EXISTS

Peter also exists, of this I'm certain. He exists because you could touch him (although I haven't) but also because he's always there. There in the harbour at the beginning of the day, sorting his boat or his fishing gear or the crates of things he delivers to other parts of the island. There in the afternoon if you happen to be gathering wreck on the beach. There at the end of the day, unloading, unpacking, coiling ropes. Whistling. He's also there when I get down from the top of the hill.

'Hello, Mhairi,' says Peter.

This is not an unusual thing to say but Peter has said some unusual things since I arrived on the island. These are some of the things he's said:

For instance, the first time he saw me after I was ill: *Glad to see you up and about again, Mhairi. I was getting worried about you.*

Though I do not think it can be of any interest to him whether I live or die.

And: *You need to take care of yourself. Put some flesh on those bones!*

As if a person put flesh on bones the way you put butter on bread. Slather, slather, slather.

And: *Mhairi, stop still a moment. Did anyone ever tell you what beautiful eyes you have?*

Which suggests Peter does not look in the same sort of mirrors as I do.

And: *It's like God gifted you a little piece of sky, a pinch of bright, blue sky either side of your nose.*

Normal people do not say things like this. Especially not people like Peter. This is the sort of thing only people in books say. In my experience. Though I haven't read a book in a long time, so I could be wrong about this.

'Hello, Peter,' I reply in our today. 'Did you know your name means "rock"?'

This information comes suddenly down the years in Papa's voice. I think we must have been talking about Peter in Before. Or perhaps it was Grandmother talking, saying what a strange name Peter was for an island boy, not Scottish at all. And Papa saying: *It comes from the Greek, petros – a stone.* This is probably another reason why Peter exists, why he appears so vivid.

'You exist,' I add. 'Like a rock does.'

'And you,' says Peter, 'exist too. But in a different dimension to the rest of us, I sometimes think.'

And then he laughs, but it's not a horrible laugh.

'Still,' Peter adds, 'it's nice to see you out alone.'

'Alone?'

'Without your little shadow.'

'What shadow?'

'Mo, of course.' Peter smiles. 'Don't get me wrong, he's a great kid but it isn't natural.'

'What isn't natural?'

'The way he follows you about. Aileen even said he slept by your bed, all the time you were ill.'

'He hasn't got much,' I say, quite aggressively.

'True,' Peter says. 'But maybe he needs a friend his own age.' Peter pauses. 'As perhaps,' he adds, 'do you.'

80

THE CONVERSATION

The conversation with Grandmother is not a success. It goes like this:

Me: What is the island doing about the people in the camp?

Her: The camp at Ardrossan? Nothing.

Me: Nothing?

Her: The camp is on Scots soil, not Arran soil. The management of the camp is Scotland Mainland's responsibility.

Me: But, Grandmother, the people in that camp, they want to come here. To the island. And we have more than enough of everything. Plenty to share. Food and land. I mean we have so much food we even have sweets. Not to mention fish. And vegetables. I've seen Peter. He gets fish every day. As for land. I saw it from the top of the hill today. Land stretching in every direction. Empty land. Enough land for everyone in that camp.

Her: Hahahaha. If only it were so simple, Mhairi. Those people there – if we let them all in, don't you think there would be another thousand, another ten thousand, there in a flash? As fast as you'd drain that camp, it would fill again.

Me: Then we'd take them again. And we'd clear more land and they'd mound potatoes and gather wreck from the beach, just like us.

Her: Oh, Mhairi, whatever did your father teach you in those lessons of his? This island isn't infinite. You need to think of it like a raft, or a lifeboat, floating alongside a ship that's going down. There's only a certain number of people that life raft can sustain. If you overload the boat, it sinks, Mhairi. And then everyone dies.

A pause.

Me: So you don't care then? You don't care about the lives of those people in the camps?

Her: Who said I didn't care? Of course I care. But those people cannot be my first responsibility. I'm paid to care for the people of Arran. They have to come first. I have to ensure everyone on the island has proper shelter, enough to eat, medical supplies. That we have law and order. That's my job. My duty. To keep our people safe. Arran functions. You must see that. Still functions. And many places, Mhairi – well, they simply don't any more.

Another pause.

Her (again): Besides, Mhairi, it's a fiction to believe that we can care for everyone in the world as we care for those nearest to us.

Me: A fiction?

Her: Yes. Just imagine for a moment that you felt the same way about each one of those nameless strangers in the camp as you do about your own family. Imagine then the grief you'd feel if one of them died, or two of them or a hundred. Multiply it up – what if you cared about every one of those million sub-Saharans on the move as much you do – well, about Mohammed here? Or your muma? Or your papa? Well – it wouldn't be possible, you'd just burst of grief. Human beings aren't designed like that, Mhairi. We can't be. Our love goes out in concentric circles, getting weaker and weaker the further you go from your family, your friends, your tribe.

Another pause as I try to compute that. Because that idea of concentric love is making me think of the concentric gardens of Castle and what's in that locked, locked, locked tower. I'm also being battered by the word 'love' because it's such a very long time since I heard anyone mention it and I'm not so sure what it means any more, and anyway, isn't Mohammed one of those sub-Saharan Africans I'm not supposed to care for? And I haven't got anywhere near an answer before she adds: 'Or put it like this, Mhairi. How would you feel if your father finally got back to the island and we had to say, "Sorry, we're full up right now with the camp people, you can't come in."?'

I do have an answer to this though.

'That would be all right,' I say.

'All right?' says Grandmother. 'How do you work that out, Mhairi?'

'Because,' I say, 'Papa isn't coming back.'

81

THE DESERT KIOSK

This is what happened. As accurately as I can remember it anyway. My memory does not want to linger on every detail.

As I said a thousand times, Papa got out of the car. The car was actually a jeep, a civilian not a military one. He got out with his 'the world is beautiful' face on and his palms outstretched. He lifted his hands upwards as if he was going to give or receive a gift. He seemed very calm.

The soldiers were not calm. They were very agitated. They were shouting. Perhaps about what had happened in the kiosk. Perhaps about the rest of us getting out of the car.

Muma meanwhile was busy and efficient. Muma got some things out from beneath her clothes. Money, a gold ring with diamonds (I discovered later), plus my plane ticket and papers, which she'd been carrying for me.

'Whatever happens, Mhairi,' she whispered as she handed me these things beneath the level of the car window frame, 'remember, you have to stay alive.'

This was her last instruction to me before she got out of the car. Perhaps she knew it was all up, but I don't think so, I think she was simply doing Just in Case. She was clever like that, Muma. Multitasked quite naturally, keeping any number of possible scenarios in her head at once. I hardly had the packages concealed in my own clothes before she was out standing in front of the men with guns.

'I am a scientist, an engineer,' Muma said dead calm into the shouting. 'I have worked in your country, for your country, for six years. We have clearance to the border. My husband, myself and our daughter, we all have papers.'

'And also the boy,' Papa put in. 'Muhammad – who's travelling with us. He has papers too.'

Yes. It was Papa who mentioned Muhammad. Chatty, chigger Muhammad. Just added him automatically to our family. That is how I know he would have had no hesitation in adopting Mute Mohammed if he had met him on the road as I did. When another old man fell and died. Two very different boys, one he knew and one he didn't. But that wouldn't have mattered to Papa – he would have just have seen children. Human beings in need. And he would have reached out to those children as he would have wished – expected – any other adult to reach out to me if the need had been mine. It would not have been more complicated than that. This is why my story of the adoption is not so untrue. In the slidy world, I notice that only things which are written down are deemed to be true. Things written on nanonets or bits of paper. But I think truth can be spoken and felt and acted as well as written down.

Back in the desert, not even Papa mentioned Muhammad's father. No. No one mentioned him lying ratatatat dead in the kiosk.

The men with the guns began shouting at each other. But in Arabic.

'What are they saying?' I asked Muhammad.

Muhammad did not reply. I think his mind was still in the kiosk.

Quietly I unlatched the back door of the car the opposite side from where Muma and Papa and the men were, but held it to, so it didn't look like it was open.

'If I say run,' I whispered to Muhammad, 'then you run. OK?' If I had known then what I know now I would have added: 'And don't look back.'

'This has gone on quite long enough,' said Muma. 'Who's in charge here? I want to speak to your superior.'

Papa always laughed about Muma's desire for superiors. 'It's just a way of cutting out the middleman,' said Muma, 'getting straight to the top.'

Only it wasn't that day. That day, it was fast-track to a bullet. Or any number of bullets.

Ratatatatatat.

And there was Muma – face down in the dust.

'Run,' I shouted to Muhammad and I pushed him out the back of that car and into the desert. He ran like the wind and, actually, I do not think he looked back.

I did look back.

Which was a mistake.

I couldn't see Muma any more because she was on the ground and the jeep was between us and her. But Papa – I saw Papa. Heard the noise, the second ratatatatat, and saw him fall. But he didn't fall in the way the noise suggested. Didn't judder with the bullets like you see in films. No, he fell like a flower, slowly and rather beautifully as if blown by the wind. Or maybe he fell very fast, as fast as gravity and the bullets took him, only I watched him in Arrested Time, didn't want him to fall, so held him falling. Falling, falling, falling. But never fallen.

He never hit the ground.

Never finally disappeared into the dust behind that jeep. Not that I saw anyway. That's how I know about the boy and the orange scarf. About how – if you want to – you can keep people alive with the power of your mind. How you can continue to stand them upright or hear their voices or spot them in crowds even though you know perfectly well that they are dead.

82

WHAT I TELL GRANDMOTHER

After the Never-Fall, I ran too. I was right behind Muhammad.

Of course, I wondered why the soldiers didn't run after us. But then they had the car and Papa's money and whatever was packed in the suitcases, and they probably thought, what's the point of breaking a sweat and wasting bullets? It was almost too hot to run even if you didn't have a hundred bullets round your neck. Besides, they could rely on the desert killing us soon enough.

I do not, however, share this bit of the story with Grandmother. How I ran away and left my parents there. No. I don't say anything about this. I don't like this part of the story. So, I just tell her what happened before the running away. But I make it quicker, shorter. I make it a bit like this:

Well, you needn't worry about the camp on Papa's behalf, Grandmother. Because Papa's not coming back. He's not coming back because he's dead. Dead. Dead. DEAD!

When I say the word 'dead' aloud all the locks in Castle go *Boom!* All but one that is.

He got out of the car with his hands all meek in front of him and they just shot him. Bang Bang Bang Bang Bang Bang BANG! And they

*shot Muma too. Shot her first actually. And then him. Bang bang bang.
So she isn't coming back either. She's not coming back and he's not
coming back. No. Not now. Not ever. So you can take in as many people
from the camp as you like and it won't make any difference at all. Do
you understand?*

And Grandmother could say:

Oh, oh oh.

Or:

Poor Papa.

Poor Muma.

Poor you.

Or even:

Oh, poor me.

But she doesn't do this, she just gets up and walks across the
room and hits me full in the face.

Bam.

Hits me so hard I fall down.

Punishes me for coming back when Papa didn't. Which is OK
by me because it's pretty much the way I feel too.

83

BEES

That night I dream of bees. There are three bees in the dream and they have heads, thoraxes, wings and legs but no abdomens, so they are spinning their own. They are making the most beautiful coils of colour about their lower regions. The coils have the brightness and translucency of boiled sweets. The bee coils are not striped but single-coloured: one orange, one yellow, one lime green. I have never seen such beautiful, industrious, strange creatures.

I am sorry to wake up and find the creatures gone.

I don't know why I have dreamt this dream. I don't think it belongs to anything in my life right now. But I could try and make it so.

I could say:

— *These three bees are me and Grandmother and the boy – each constructing our own bright defences in our own particular colours. I think I would be the orange and the boy yellow and Grandmother the green.*

Or I could say:

— *These bees are beautiful and that's enough. Oh Papa, what a beautiful world!*

Or:

– *The sting of all three bees is wound about with vibrant sweetness.*
And I could remember what you told me about joy and pain,
Papa, how they're all wound about together and how you can't
have one without the other. That it's only if you love someone
that you cry when they are taken from you.

In this way, I could pretend the bees have meaning. I could make meaning out of them. There isn't anyone on earth who doesn't look for meaning. But sometimes, I think, things don't have meaning. They just happen. Like the bees. Like Muma and Papa being shot.

So maybe the truth is that not everything has to have meaning and that's OK.

But it doesn't feel OK.

84

ZOOMING

After the hitting, Grandmother does not come to hold me. She does not ask if we can start over. Perhaps, this time, she's waiting for me to come to her. Perhaps she wants an apology. Or just someone to hold her. How can you ever tell what another person wants? It's difficult enough to tell what you want yourself. Sometimes it's easier to know what you don't want. One of the things I don't really want at the moment is for my heart to race. But it does race, sometimes three or four or five times a day. There are many reasons why your heart might race. These are some of them:

- when you're suddenly aware of footsteps behind you
- when you're about to jump from a window or a moving vehicle
- when you climb a riverbank only to meet the boot of a soldier
- when the person in front of you has a knife – or a gun

I did not know you could feel this same sensation looking at the arm of a man. Most particularly Peter's arm, or rather his arms plural and also his shoulders. Although maybe it's not exactly the same sensation as the fear one. The racing that comes from fear quickens your breath and dries your mouth. This new sensation seems to quicken my breath but wet my mouth.

It started when Peter began to look at me a certain way. It's difficult to describe the look, it hasn't happened to me before. It's a bit like his eyes are pins and they're all prickling into me. It is not an unpleasant sensation, just a little unusual. It makes things happen on the back of my neck, makes my skin feel like a wind is blowing over it. I don't really have a word for this feeling, but it does have a soft racing quality so I shall call it zooming.

It occurs to me that I am sometimes quite clever and sometimes quite stupid. I have been particularly stupid about the zooming. Things have only come into focus since I realised that the zooming goes two ways – when he looks at me but also when I look at him.

It's happening right now. As I look at him working in the sunshine.

Because of the warmth, he's working in a pair of shorts and a T-shirt. The T-shirt is actually more of a singlet, so you can see his arms and the beginning of his shoulder blades. He has those strong, easy muscles you get from daily physical labour and his skin is bronzed from working outside summer and winter alike. I like Peter's arms, I like his broad, bronze island shoulders. I like his solidity, the way he moves slowly, unselfconsciously about his boat. But these are not things, you'd think, which would make a person zoom.

I also like his head – though it's slightly too big for his body. Big and solid and woven about with rough, straw-coloured hair. He's let this hair grow too long, has to push it out of his eyes as he works, slick it back with his own sweat. I'm sitting on the sheep bollard so I can't see his eyes but I know what colour they are. They're grey, but around the pupil itself are little gasps of yellow.

Peter has not said anything unusual recently. Possibly because I didn't much react to what he said the last few times. I just looked straight through and around him. But I find myself on the alert now – just in case. I find myself listening out for these things. Waiting. That could be part of the zooming too, I suppose.

When Peter finishes, in his own time, whatever it is he's been doing with the last of the crates, he turns to me. Knows I've been watching.

'Do you want to come out,' he says, 'in the boat?'

Zoom.

'No,' I say.

'Why? You'd like it. It's a beautiful evening. I could take you for a spin round the Holy Isle.'

Zoom, zoom, zoom.

'I might like it,' I say, 'but he wouldn't.' I point at the boy, who's on the rocky beach, piling stones. He piles stones most days. When the sea washes away his piles he just begins all over again. 'You know what he's like with the sea.'

'I wasn't asking him,' says Peter. 'I was asking you.'

85

THE HOLY ISLE

We go out in the boat. There's the sky, the sea, Peter and me. All these things are real. The boat is blue with a plain wooden wheelhouse. I sit on the white-slatted side seat while Peter stands, guiding the wheel with a single hand. Almost a single finger. There's the noise of the engine, the slosh of waves, the occasional cry of a seagull.

Neither of us say anything. We don't have to. We just look at each other occasionally and there's a bit of zooming. He steers the boat south, skirting the coast until we see the island. It rises out of the water like some huge emerald basking seal just east of the bay of Lamlash. As we approach, a cloud scuds off the sun to bathe its sleeping back in sudden, soft, yellow light. My mind goes drifty as I hear Papa's voice: *Inis Shroin*.

'Inis Shroin,' I find myself repeating aloud.

'What?' says Peter.

'That's what Papa said the island used to be called thousands of years ago. In Old Gaelic. Inis Shroin, Island of the Water Spirit.'

'Ha,' says Peter. 'Nearly became Island of the Condemned a couple of years back.'

'Hm?' I say but I'm not really listening.

'It all got tangled up in the Independence negotiations,' Peter continues. 'The InterGen realised if we were going to have our own legal systems we weren't just going to have to have a court again, we were also going to have to have a prison. There was talk of commandeering the island.' The words are floating high above my head. I can see them in the air. 'Save having to build on Arran. Cheaper and more effective anyway, an island prison.'

There's a short pause and then he adds: 'But that's before the idea of the Blood Stone and the revolving gun came up. That was even cheaper.'

'I don't want to talk about the Blood Stone, Peter.'

'Good.' Peter cuts the engine. 'Nor do I.'

We are in the island's shallows. Close enough for Peter to heave over the silver anchor. I watch the following rusted chain links clatter over the side of the boat.

'The sun will set behind the island,' Peter says. 'I've been watching the sky all day. At this time of year, when it's this clear with this sort of puff of cloud – well, it could be one of those really beautiful evenings. All red and gold.' And he comes to sit on the white-slatted bench my side of the boat. The bench you'd have to sit on if you wanted to watch the sun set behind the island. He leaves a gap between us. At least fifteen centimetres.

There's a silence, but a companionable one. The boat rocks, gently, and real wind lifts the hairs on my forearm.

'I didn't know that about the original name for the island,' Peter says after a while. 'Though I suppose it figures. What with the island being used for burials.'

'Hm?' I say again. My mind is on Peter and also the fifteen-centimetre space.

'Originally the Arran islanders buried their dead on the Holy Isle because spirits weren't supposed to be able to cross the water. It was to stop the dead haunting the living.'

'I don't want to talk about the dead, Peter.'

'Mhairi,' says Peter, 'what do you want to talk about?'

That is not an easy question. 'Maybe I don't want to talk about anything.'

'OK.'

There's a pause.

'Maybe I just want to sing.'

'Sing?'

'Or hear you sing.'

'Me!' Peter exclaims.

'That song you always whistle. Or used to whistle. When we were children. The one about travelling and homeland. Mists. Returning.'

'My dad's song, you mean?' he says. '"Where'er I Roam?"'

'Yes!' How could I have forgotten? His father's song. And my father's too. The playing of a fiddle at a window opened on the night. Papa's voice soft among his sacred hills.

'Whistling isn't the same as singing, Mhairi,' Peter continues. 'I don't really do singing.'

'Please, Peter.'

So he begins. Hums. Tries. And then the words come and I don't know if they're the right words in the right order but they cradle me anyway. *Where'er I roam, may this be my coming home.* So I find myself joining in. And it's not about whether we are tuneful. I'm sure we aren't tuneful. But the pull of the music, which is the pull of the past and of longing, travels through us.

And when it's finished – though it will never really be finished – he looks into my eyes. And I don't know what my eyes tell his but he closes the gap between us. Makes those fifteen centimetres into zero centimetres, lies his naked leg alongside my leg, and even though I have long trousers on (just as I did in the desert) I can feel his leg there. And also his mouth, moving towards my mouth. And I like his mouth. Actually, he has a really beautiful mouth, more beautiful, in fact, than his arms or his shoulders. But when it comes towards me it stops being Peter's mouth and begins to be the dark hole of the man's mouth in the tomb at Meroe, the one that smelt of tobacco and madness.

So I scream.

SCREAM.

'Hey, hey,' says Peter and he leaps backwards. Quite a long way backwards. 'What's up? What's the matter!'

I scream some more. Even though the noise is hateful.

'Stop it!' he adds then. 'For god's sake, Mhairi, STOP IT! What is it with you and Mohammed? Do you want me to get *you* a blanket now?'

And when the hateful noise doesn't stop he bangs about the boat until he finds a large tarpaulin, which he throws over my head.

'There,' he shouts. 'Better now?'

And it is better. I'm grateful for the heaviness and the darkness and the just me inside.

I go quiet.

86

THE CHARGE SHEET

When we get back to the harbour Grandmother is standing on the quayside. She does not look happy. In fact, she looks even more thunderous than she did when the boy and I first arrived on the island. She takes the rope Peter throws her and knots it around the sheep bollard. The tarp has fallen off my head just as the blanket fell from the boy. I don't know what I look like but Peter, who has steered back here in silence, looks grim. His mouth set in a line. But there is some sadness in that line, I think. Though I have not always been good at judging other people's emotions. Grandmother, however, is not concerned about what our faces do or don't say.

'Into the house, Mhairi,' Grandmother says. 'Now!'

At first I think Grandmother may be angry at me for leaving the boy but she marches me straight past him and his (slightly larger) piles of stones without so much as a glance.

On the kitchen table, her laptop is open on a message from court official, Esther. It's marked *Ret1787 Interim Report Trafficking Illegal Alien – Confidential*.

'Read it,' says Grandmother.

So I do.

It's a list of what the officials know about my movements over the last year and a bit. Ret1787 was, apparently:

1. Registered in Khartoum. Cleared for travel to the border.

2. No record of transit through the Sudanese/Egyptian border.

3. Detained at Cairo Airport for Violation Code 634H.

4. Deported to London, England.

5. Detained at Heathrow Detention Centre 6. Verified as juvenile and but not formally released in care of authorities due to detention centre riot escape.

6. Detained at English/Scottish border Skitby School Detention Centre. Suspected of not being a juvenile and formally charged with trafficking an illegal alien – known as 'Mo'. Unauthorised escape with said alien.

7. No record of transit from Scotland Mainland to the Isle of Arran.

8. Interim registry Isle of Arran. Registered as travelling with Mohammed Bain. Search enquiries on Mohammed Bain return no information. No Mohammed Bain listed on either individual country data banks or Global North data banks. Finger and iris scan enquiries ongoing.

Grandmother is good at questions. These are some questions she might ask me about this charge sheet:

1. *How did you manage to turn invisible at the Sudanese border, Mhairi?*

It wasn't easy. I paid with Muma's diamond ring. And

virtually all the rest of her money. This was a small price. The smugglers weren't asking just for money. Nor were they, it turned out, taking any chances. The lorry dropped us the Sudanese side of the border, drove safely and emptily through passport control, only to pick us up again eight kilometres north into Egypt. We did this same journey on foot. Walked alone through the night and the sand.

2. *What is a Code 634H, Mhairi?*

It's what you get when you don't get your papers inked at a border. When your supposedly Global Passport doesn't also contain an official 'entitlement to travel' stamp.

3. *Why, if you were verified as a juvenile at Heathrow, weren't you released into Authority Care?*

Because, Grandmother, there was a riot in the centre, quite a serious riot and I had to take my chances. Managed to escape with my life and a fire flint. The first thanks to a bulletless gun, and the second thanks to a man called Phil.

But Grandmother doesn't ask any of these questions. She is not interested in the journey, only in the destination. Where I've landed up.

'It's all a fiction,' she says. 'Isn't it?'

'Yes,' I say. It's quite a relief that word: 'yes'.

'No one stole your papers,' Grandmother continues. 'You lied about that as you have lied about everything else. Including the adoption. Your father never adopted this boy. In fact, your father never even met Mohammed. Supposing his name is Mohammed. You met him. But he wasn't on the plane with you to Heathrow. No. He didn't come into the country with you.

282

You can only have met since you travelled north. You've risked everything, Mhairi, for a boy you can only have known for a matter of weeks.'

This last part is not true but I do not challenge Grandmother because she has never travelled. It's only when you've travelled that you begin to understand about Time and how it shifts. How it's not the length of time – the minutes or hours or days or years – you spend with a person that matters, but what happens in that time. How time expands with all the things (big and small) you experience together. Things which, even if you could find a way to speak about them, no one else would ever be able to fully understand. Not in the way your fellow traveller understands anyway.

'What will happen to him?' I ask.

'Mohammed?' says Grandmother. 'He'll be deported, of course.'

'Deported?'

'That's what I said.'

'Where to?'

'To wherever he came from, Mhairi.'

'No. Not possible. And anyway, he's alone. He's a child!'

'He still has a country of origin.'

'No, he doesn't. At least, he may have a country. But he doesn't have any people. He doesn't have anyone to go back to!'

'He told you that, did he?' says Grandmother.

'No. But they're dead. His people are dead. I know it.'

'You can't know that, Mhairi. And, in any case, it's none of

283

your concern now. So, may I suggest you spend a little time thinking about yourself. And also Peter.' She pauses, but not for long, before she adds: 'Now go away, Mhairi – I can't bear to look at you.'

87

ANOTHER CONVERSATION

But I'm still standing in the kitchen when there's a knock on the door.

It's Peter.

'Is everything all right?' he asks. His face is still grim but a different sort of grim. He enters the door – and the conversation – as if he's heard raised voices, as if he's Grandmother's equal and has the right to know. Perhaps he just didn't like the way Grandmother marched me away, without so much as a word.

'No,' says Grandmother. 'Everything is not all right. You obviously haven't been home yet. Or you'd have seen a copy of this. Look.' She points him at her laptop screen.

While he scans the document she says to me: 'I asked you to go, Mhairi.' And when I don't move, she adds: 'Peter is also a defendant in the case. Tomorrow you'll both have to be taser-tagged. To stop you talking together until the case is heard. So you might as well start now. Go, I said!'

I go, not because of whatever the taser-tagging means, but because I'm not sure I will be able to bear Peter's face when he lifts it from the screen. Though I will be able to hear if he cries out because my bedroom is right above the kitchen.

I go upstairs and hear nothing. So I lie on the floor of my room and listen through the cracks in the floorboards.

There's more silence and then the sound of someone sitting down very heavily in a chair. I imagine Peter at the table, his straw-coloured head in his hands.

'As I said right at the outset, Peter,' says Grandmother's voice. 'I will stand surety for you. Not in my role as High Councillor, of course. In the circumstances, I couldn't join the panel when the main defendant is my own granddaughter. But I know how the council operates and with just five members there won't have to be a chair anyway, a three to two vote will be good enough.'

'A vote,' says Peter's voice, deathly quiet, 'on what?'

'The sentence.'

A creak of the chair as Peter moves perhaps, can't help himself. Or maybe it's Grandmother, sitting down beside him.

'But it won't be the Stone, Peter. The boy's obviously a child and Mhairi's also still a juvenile. Just. So, it'll be Life Years.'

'I'm not a juvenile,' says Peter. 'I'm eighteen.'

Now I wish I could see his face. Because this isn't deathly quiet, this is just quiet. A broad, bronze quiet.

'True,' says Grandmother. 'But I'd argue – and I'm pretty sure they'll argue – that you are an accessory rather than an instigator under the terms of the Trafficking Act. Given the mitigating circumstances, you'd then get a number of Life Years which the court would actually award against Mhairi.'

'Award my years? Against Mhairi?'

286

'Yes,' says Grandmother.

'No,' says Peter.

'It's the way it works, Peter. It's not your fault.'

'It is my fault,' says Peter. 'I mean – I did it. I just took the boy. On her say-so. Didn't ask to see his papers. I could have asked to see his papers! Why didn't I do that!'

Because I've travelled a lot, Peter, and you have hardly travelled at all. And I'm sharper than you. I'm good at manipulation and you aren't, Peter.

'Or I could have phoned you for confirmation,' Peter continues. 'Why didn't I do that, Aileen? I could have done that!'

Because you're like Papa, Peter. Trusting. You look for the good and you find it.

'She would have lied to you as she lied to me. In fact, she did lie to you. That's why she will get the years.'

'How many years, Aileen?'

Grandmother pauses. 'Technically fifty, but with mitigation, it'll probably come down to about thirty.'

'Thirty?' says Peter. There's a pause while he does the maths. While he works out that I'll be forty-four when required to go to the needle. That I now have a scant thirty years left to live. 'That can't happen,' says Peter. 'I won't let that happen.'

At least I think that's what he says.

I won't let that happen.

Does Peter say this? Does Peter say it through the floorboards about this girl he's only just re-met, whom he hasn't seen for years? This girl who screamed when he came near her?

Time.

Time and Peter.

Peter who has never travelled, Peter the rock, does Peter know about Time?

'It will be out of your hands,' says Grandmother.

'What about Mohammed?' Peter asks then.

'He'll be deported.'

'No,' says Peter again. 'No. That'll kill her.'

88

TASER-TAGGING

The following morning court official Esther returns with a man in a white coat.

'I'm so sorry, High Commissioner,' she says.

'Don't be,' says Grandmother.

'This is Dr Connell,' Esther adds. The man is small and dark but he has unnaturally large hands, with long, thin fingers. In those fingers he's carrying a shiny metal box which he flips open to reveal swabs, needles and an assortment of different-sized tagging-chips.

'This won't hurt,' he says. 'But you'll need to take off your top.'

I look at Grandmother.

'Do as he says,' she says.

So I do. I take off my shirt and stand half-naked in front of the man.

He gets out a piece of paper. Reads it. It's some sort of legal declaration, something that apparently entitles him to insert an electronic tag under my skin. I think two things simultaneously: he could have read this when I was still fully dressed and also that, in Before, we only used to do this to dogs.

He attaches a clean needle to a syringe.

'Turn around,' he instructs. I wonder then if he also does End of Life Clinics? If he pushes needles like this into people who are seventy-four? People who are going to die. People he is going to kill. People like me, in thirty years' time.

Time.

'Just a scratch,' he says. 'Bit of local anaesthetic, that's all. Keep still now.'

I do keep still because he's aiming somewhere near the top of my spine. And I can't see him now. Can't see what he's doing. And that's the point, Grandmother told me last night. They put the tag between your shoulder blades, at that place on your back that you can't reach. That you'd need to have someone else to help you if you wanted to gouge it out. The chip relays an account of your position, your movements, twenty-four hours a day. Helping someone to gouge out a legally inserted tagging-chip is, Grandmother says, a very serious crime.

The needle goes in and I feel the plunge and push of the anaesthetic being forced into my bloodstream. I wonder then what they put in the End of Life Clinic syringes? I wonder how much fatter those death needles are and whether the poison is colourless or not? Stupid thoughts. He swabs my back.

'Can you still feel that?' he asks.

'Yes.' Strangely yes. Me, who has often felt nothing, feeling the light touch of a wet swab.

'What about now?' He tries again.

'No.'

'OK, I'm going to do the insert now.'

He takes an instrument from some see-through packaging. I think it's going to be a scalpel, but actually it's more like a tiny shovel, the blade a shallow, inverted 'V' shape. He makes no attempt to shield me from what he's doing. But I would look anyway. It's in my interests for that blade to be sharp. They have to use a blade, Grandmother says, because the tag I need is not just a microscopic tracking and identity chip which can be inserted by injection. No. I am getting a bigger sort of chip, the one you can programme to give taser-shocks. The taser-shock will activate every time I come within a certain distance of Peter. The genius of the system is, apparently, that Peter will also get a shock – even if it's me doing the moving. The closer we get to each other, the higher the level of shock.

Dr Connell inserts the tag. There is no pain, no physical pain anyway, but I feel the push of it as he slides it under my skin. I feel glad about this. I feel it's my body resisting, making a statement on my behalf.

'There. All done,' the doctor says, sticking something over the wound. 'Very clean. Should heal up nicely. Preferable not to bath though, for a few days at least, if that's OK?' He directs this remark not to me, perhaps because I still have my back to him, but to Grandmother. He says it as if bathing is an important consideration when you have just had an electronic taser-tag inserted in your back. This tag which, Grandmother says, will now be with me for life.

'Put on your shirt,' Grandmother says.

Esther hands it to me. 'The setting is for twenty metres,' she says. 'I should pace it out, if I were you. Get used to the distance you need to keep between you. I know Peter lives close and you don't want to make a mistake. People who make a mistake once don't normally do it again,' she adds. 'If you see what I mean.'

I see what she means. If I get close to Peter, it's going to hurt.

'Of course,' Esther adds, 'as the chip is to prevent conversation of any sort, it is also responsive to any attempt by you to use a mobile device. I don't suggest you try that either. Otherwise, of course, you have total freedom to move wherever you like on the island until the court date is set when you must present yourself in Lamlash. Do you want to ask anything?'

No. I don't.

'Good,' says Esther. 'Peter next.'

Peter's beautiful bronze back sliced open with a knife.

It's always the same when people get too close to me. They don't do well. They don't do well at all.

89

GLOBE

Grandmother has a globe. It's made of tin and belonged, she says, to her own grandmother. It's so old that it shows white for ice at the Arctic and white for ice at the Antarctic. So old that it doesn't even have Equator Central marked, let alone Equator North. I don't know why Grandmother has kept this globe. Perhaps because Papa played with it when he was a child. I imagine Papa spinning and spinning this beautiful world.

When Esther and the doctor leave, Grandmother gets it out for the boy. It's about a third as big as he is and it still spins on its stand.

'Mohammed,' she says, 'can you show me where you live?'

She asks him this question because the authorities have, it appears, drawn a blank. None of their searches have revealed a single thing about the boy. It's as though he doesn't exist. Has slipped through the net of life. Or rather through the web of man-made rules and regulations.

He is a magician after all. Just as Miss Sperry is a witch. People who stand outside of things.

'This is where we are now,' says Grandmother and she turns the globe with her fingertips until she gets to the pink triangle of the old United Kingdom. She points at Scotland. Only three cities are marked: Edinburgh, Glasgow and Wick. The Isle of Arran isn't marked. In fact, it's not big enough to warrant even a tiny pink dot. On this map, the Isle of Arran does not exist. But Grandmother puts down her pink finger anyway. 'Here,' she says, 'this is us.'

Us.

Then she traces that finger south and east, stops at the Sudan. 'This is where Mhairi started. In Khartoum.' Khartoum is marked. It even has a little star, for capital city, I suppose. 'Where did you start from, Mohammed?'

She moves her finger about Africa, reciting the countries as she touches them: 'Chad? Niger? Mali? Morocco? Algeria? Libya? Egypt? Can you show me?' She scrutinises him, looking for a reaction, trying to spring his secrets.

The boy stares straight ahead. His eyes like cups.

'Your people,' presses Grandmother. 'Where do your people come from, Mohammed?'

I see the flick of something in the boy's neck. Just a tiny twitch, but I see it. The tension. The beat of his blood.

'Could be anywhere,' I say. 'Anywhere at all.' And I put my hand on the top of the globe, on the place where the Arctic ice once was. And I begin to spin. Make my fingers like a giant spider over the top of the world and I spin and spin.

'Stop it,' says Grandmother.

But I don't. I keep it spinning, spinning and spinning, to stop the boy having to answer, stop him being pinned down, pressed down.

'I said stop it, Mhairi!'

But it's the boy who stops it. Suddenly reaches out his tiny hand and clamps it hard on to the globe. And I think the globe will continue to spin because of the momentum I've built up. But it doesn't. It stops dead.

With his hand in the sea.

We all look at the blue for a moment and then the boy gathers his hand into a fist with a pointing finger.

'No one lives in the sea, Mohammed,' says Grandmother.

'No,' I say. 'But they do die there, don't they?'

The boy takes a moment, runs his tongue over the sharp edge of his broken tooth. And then he nods.

'See?' I say to Grandmother.

But it is not a victory.

That night the boy is back sleeping on my floor.

90

THE DISTANCE

I pace the distance. It's the length of Grandmother's garden. Twice this length comes to about the middle of the harbour, where Peter's boat is. This means I cannot sit on the sheep bollard and watch Peter work. I cannot even safely be near the bottom of the garden when Peter is working. But I want to watch him work. So I go up to my room and open my window.

Now I can see him.

But not the tag under his skin of his back. This is because the day is overcast and he's wearing a light sweater. So I can't see his naked arms and I can't see his back. Can't see that place between his shoulder blades from where, if he was an angel, his wings would grow. The place where they have inserted an electronic tag. *Not many people believe in angels*, Papa said, *but I do*. Magicians, witches and angels. Papa believed in them all.

I look at the angel in the harbour. He goes about his business in his usual slow, deliberate way. I feel something strange. It is not zooming exactly, more an urge to touch. I want to go down to the harbour, wade out to that boat, and take off Peter's sweater. And his singlet, if he's wearing one. I want to look at his naked back, reach out and touch the wound with my own hand. Feel it. Trace it. Stroke it. I want to touch his arms and his face. I want to lie down in the boat with him, the sky all arced above us. I want to feel his leg against mine.

Skin to skin.

I even want to touch his mouth. Maybe have his mouth alongside my mouth, his lips on mine. I want his beautiful mouth so close that I smell it, taste it. Know what the breath of Peter is.

It's surprising what you want when you know you can't have it.

91

FREEDOM OF MOVEMENT

The boy is not tagged. I'm not sure whether this is because he's under ten, or because he's mute (and therefore unlikely to interfere with the cause of justice), or simply because, if he makes a run for it, he'll be doing the Arran authorities a favour. But he doesn't make a run for it. In fact the more I stay indoors, the more he does.

He brings his beach with him.

Fills flowerpot after flowerpot with sea-washed stones and brings them to wherever I am. Sits on the floor and piles them. I sit on the floor with him, helping him with the pyramids.

Sometimes he mounds the stones in size order, the largest ones first. Sometimes his constructions are colour-coordinated: a pile of shale greys, a pile red-brown old Corrie sandstone. Sometimes he interleaves the stones, a layer of round stones balanced on a layer of flat ones. I try to spot his patterns, copy them, honour them.

Grandmother says piling stones is a nonsense. Grandmother says doing tasks with no purpose is a Waste of Time.

But this is because Grandmother does not understand Time.

And she does not understand control.

When your life is mainly controlled by forces beyond you, you take charge of the things you can. No matter how small.

Or that's what I've found anyway.

92

SOMETHING BIGGER THAN OURSELVES

'It's bedtime,' says Grandmother to the boy after supper. 'Off you go now.'

When we first arrived on Arran, she would take him upstairs herself. Read to him sometimes from Papa's old storybooks. I know this because I sat on the landing to listen. Now she sends him to bed by himself. No more stories. No more happy-ever-after.

And why should I care about that?

It's not much more than I told him myself in the shack where he smashed his stones.

'Your own bedroom, mind,' Grandmother adds to his departing back. 'I don't want to be finding you on Mhairi's floor again. Understand?'

The boy does not turn but I see a slight pause, a flinch which makes me think he will not sleep in his own bed tonight.

'Why do you mind him sleeping on my floor,' I say when he's gone, 'when you don't mind him being deported?'

'Don't be stupid,' says Grandmother and she gets up and clatters with dishes.

I leave the stupid bit alone. Just reply: 'Well, they won't be able to deport him anyway. Not if they don't know where he comes from.'

'That,' says Grandmother, 'will just mean him having to stay in detention longer.'

'Detention?' She's taken me by surprise. 'Why does he need to be in detention? Why can't he just stay on here?'

'Because he can't,' says Grandmother. 'Not after the court case.'

'Why?'

'Because, Mhairi. Because of the rules. Because of the laws of this country. And also Scotland Mainland. Trafficking comes under Federal Law. He'll be sent back to Skitby, where he was first detained as an illegal. And that's the good news. If he was older, if he was of majority, they'd send him to an Expulsion Centre.'

I also get up and clatter with the dishes. Just to have something to do with my hands. To stop me twitching.

'Last time he was in detention,' I say, 'he went on hunger strike. He'll do it again. I know he will. He won't last in detention. He'll die.'

'No need for the melodrama, Mhairi.' She hands me a dishcloth. 'Anyway, they'll force-feed him if they have to.'

Force-feed.

I dry a fork, I dry a knife.

'He'll also get proper psychiatric care,' Grandmother adds. 'Therapies to help him regain his speech.'

'Didn't help him last time,' I say.

'Maybe you took him away just a little bit too early for that,' says Grandmother.

Beneath the cloth I feel for the knife blade. It's serrated. 'When you thought he was your grandson, you brought him sweets. Clothes. You taught him things. Thought about how he'd get on at school. You even,' I pause, because I hear myself beginning to shout, 'you even,' I repeat, 'made him want you, want to be with you. Like you! And now you can't even be bothered to take him to bed!'

Grandmother wipes her hands. 'And why do you think that is, Mhairi?'

I have no idea so I stay silent.

'To help him detach,' she continues. 'Him from me. Me from him, for that matter. Help both of us. Try not to make it any worse. When they take him away.'

'Take him away?' I repeat and then I do shout. Properly shout. 'Why don't you fight! Papa always fought. Papa fought for everything he believed in. Papa would never let this happen. Never just stand by and let a child – any child – just be taken away. Put out of sight. Disposed of like a piece of garbage in some detention centre. Some prison. Because that's what they are really. I know, I've been there. They're prisons!'

'How dare you bring your father into this?' says Grandmother. 'You know nothing, Mhairi. Nothing at all.'

And that's it. I chuck down the dishcloth. And with it the knife. I have to throw the knife down because I don't trust myself. Even if she is my own grandmother. I just don't trust myself.

'Sit down, Mhairi,' she says and when I don't, she pushes me into a chair. 'Sit down and listen for once.'

Grandmother does not sit. She stands above me, arms folded, eyes ablaze.

'I am sixty-nine years old, Mhairi,' she says. 'In slightly less than five years' time I will be taking the needle. I'm healthy. I have a great deal to live for. So, if I am going to submit willingly to the needle, I have to believe in the reason for it. And I do believe in the reason. Which is the greater good. That's why we do it – all of us here on Arran. Why we make the promise. Like every other person in every other Equator North country that's signed up to the Life Term Charter. We say, this island can sustain only so many people. So, we agree that it is better for all of us here on the island to have enough food to live healthy, happy lives, even if those lives are briefer than we would wish. Because you see, Mhairi, this isn't just about me, it's about all of us. About the community. About how many vegetables this island can grow if we all cultivate the land, all put our backs into it. And the soil still remain fertile. About how many fish we can take from the sea and there still be fish left for our children and our children's children. But this doesn't come without sacrifices. When Arran ratified the cut-off age of seventy-four, we were saying, all of us on Arran were saying, we believe in something bigger than ourselves. Bigger than our individual lives, bigger than the lives of our own children, or, Mhairi, our grandchildren. But it's a fragile balance. And we have to guard against things – or people – who want, for whatever reason, to destabilise the system.

'So yes, I'm sorry about Mohammed. And about everyone in the camp. And even about everyone in Equator Central who is forcibly on the move. It isn't their fault, I understand that. But nor is it our fault. And we are doing our best to protect as many people as this land can sustain. But there can't be exceptions. Not for Mohammed. And not, Mhairi, for you. Because these aren't just rules and regulations as you'd like to think. No. They are the fabric that holds the community together. Makes the life – the life we chose and sacrifice for – possible.

'Now do you understand?'

And maybe I do. At least I do until I go upstairs.

93

THE PROMISE

The boy is lying on my bedroom floor. But not comfortably, not snuggling down with his pillow and a blanket. No. He's spread-eagled, his head on one side, his left ear stuck to a crack in the floorboards. He's crying. But silently, as if he can't lift his head. As if whatever he's heard from the kitchen has crushed him flat.

The deportation. The being sent away, chucked away. Like a piece of garbage.

Trash.

That's where we put trash in this country.

'I'm sorry,' I say. 'I'm so sorry.'

But sorry doesn't move him. Not a bit. And it doesn't move me either. Sorry – what use is *sorry*?

'Look at me.'

But he doesn't. Just lies there in his flattened misery.

'Well, listen then. Listen very carefully. The deportation. It's not going to happen. I won't let it happen.'

I won't let it happen.

As if I'm Peter. As if I had some form of control. As if I believed things could be different.

The boy doesn't stop crying but he does twist then, turns on to his back, puts his fists in his eyes, and grinds at his tears. Stares blinded at the ceiling.

'Mo?'

I don't know why I call him Mo. Mo is not his name.

'Mo?'

He pulls his top lip over his broken tooth, chews at himself. Still doesn't look at me.

'You're going to stay. Here. Here, on Arran. No one's going to send you away.' And, of course, I want that. Want my Leuchram Burn to be his Leuchram Burn.

But it isn't.

'If you want to stay, that is.' I pause. 'Do you want to stay?' I think of his golden lands. His family. His past. All the things balled up in that tiny body. All the things which might pull him another way.

'I mean, I know it's not home. Won't ever be home. I know . . .'

What do I know?

After all this time – what do I know!

Not even his name.

'But if you want to stay – you only have to say.'

As if it was that simple. As if the world was beautiful, Papa.

But the world is beautiful.

It has to be. And – if it isn't – then we must make it so. Isn't that right, Papa?

Which is why I sit and wait.

And wait.

What is Time anyway?

Finally, after whatever passes, passes, the boy sits up. Looks at me.

And nods.

'Right,' I say, 'right!' As if I've won some sort of battle. As if my elation is justified. 'Over my dead body do you get deported!' I smile and I touch my broken tooth. 'You and me together. I promise.'

Slowly his hand goes to his mouth and he touches his own broken tooth. But he does not smile.

Perhaps he doesn't believe my promise. Perhaps he thinks it's a lie. A *fiction*, as Grandmother would say.

Just the random promise of some random queen in a storybook from Before.

94

PAGE NINE

Skitby Detention Centre has sent through my Global Passport. Grandmother picks it up at the Lamlash court, brings it home and opens it at page nine.

'You need to start filling this in,' she says.

This is because, apparently, the law allows fourteen-year-old defendants to log 'Provisional Credits'. Provisional Credits, Grandmother says, will be used in mitigation, to decide my final tally of Life Years. What I put here, Grandmother says, could reduce my sentence substantially. In addition, that is, to the statutory discount of seven years to which I'm entitled because I am still under-age.

I sit in my room and look at the blank sheet of paper. I look at it for quite a long time. Long enough for Peter to take his boat out of the harbour, run some errand and bring the boat back again. As I watch him secure the boat and wade towards the shore I wonder what is written on his Global Credit pages. I expect it's things like:

– Peter can drive a boat
– Peter can mend an engine

- Peter can fish
- Peter runs an island delivery system

Things which can be verified, things which are useful for Grandmother's island community. I don't expect the piece of paper says:

- Peter has broad, bronze shoulders
- Peter has zooming grey eyes with gasps of yellow
- Peter watches the skies for sunsets of red and gold
- Peter understands Time
- Peter is a bit like Papa – good and trusting

I am not an Imgrim, not a judge at the court of Lamlash, and I never will be. But, if I was, I think I would do things differently. I would give people stones and ask if they could explain things with just a piece of charcoal. I would lie them under an umbrella of stars and ask if they still felt the same about things. And, when they'd finally come to a judgement, I'd ask them to walk a thousand kilometres, just to be sure they didn't need to change their mind about that judgement. I would value things that can't be stamped and verified. In fact, I'd outlaw anything which could be stamped and verified, anything that could be scored too easily, given a grade. I'd throw away the ink and the stamps and the rules and the regulations and then I've have to hope – oh yes, I'd have to hope – that there were more people on the planet like Papa and Peter and the boy than people like

Me.

Yes. That would be the problem. I can see that.

'How are you getting on?' says Grandmother coming into the room.

'I'm thinking,' I say.

When she leaves, I think about the boy. What I'd put on his pages. I could fill sheets and sheets about the boy. Not rules and regs but real things. I could talk about:

- His intelligence and determination. How he tracked me that day when I tried to leave him behind.
- His ability to forgive, to forget. How he never once blamed me. Not for the leaving. Not for the shouting and hitting. The hitting him around the head.
- His tenacity. His refusal to give up, ever. No matter the distance to be covered or the bleeding of his feet.
- His hopes for the future, his dreams – the stars and flowers which he gifted me on the stones in the shack.
- His resourcefulness, his courage. How he starved himself and drew that broken tooth picture to bring us together in the detention centre.
- His thoughtfulness, his kindness. How he gave his blanket back to Miss Sperry in case someone needed it more than he did.
- And his spirited cheeriness, his laughter in rivers. His laughter even with Grandmother. His beautiful, beautiful chipped-tooth smile.

These are some of the things I would write on the boy's Global Passport. I'd probably fill all the pages available and have to stick in some extra ones too. I'd leave space at the very end to write:

These are the sort of qualities I think we need in the citizens of our country. Don't you?

'Still nothing?' says Grandmother at dusk.

Still nothing.

95

BURNING

That night I dream of Peter.

I dream I want to see him so much I don't care about the taser-tag. In fact, it excites me to think of getting close enough to him to trigger an electric shock. In him. In me. We feel it anyway, don't we? That spark and fizz. What can the authorities make us feel that we haven't already felt?

So I go outside. It is not night in my dream, it's the middle of the day. Peter is in his boat but he's busy and he doesn't see me at first. And I'm pleased about this, I want to see how close I can get before we're triggered. Before the blood begins to boil in our veins.

I open Grandmother's garden gate and cross the road towards the harbour. Feel my excitement rising. But it is my excitement and not the taser-tag. Maybe I've miscalculated the distance? Or maybe the boat's a little further out than normal?

Thirty metres.

Twenty metres.

I keep walking. It must be less than twenty metres now. But I still feel nothing. And he obviously feels nothing either as he continues head down about his business in the wheelhouse. I pass the sheep bollard.

Fifteen metres.

Less.

The boat is in the middle of the harbour, but it's moored to the bollard so I can pull on the rope, pull the boat and Peter towards me. So I do.

Now, with the jerk on the boat, he does see me. Turns around and smiles.

With that beautiful mouth.

And I pull him towards me. Wait for the boil and fizz. Perhaps they just have the setting wrong? Two metres not twenty after all. Peter is still smiling, standing in the boat being drawn towards me, smiling, smiling, smiling.

And so close now I can touch him. So I do. Reach out my hand and

Boom!

Peter explodes. Peter is a ball of fire. Peter melts and burns. His face slides off his skull.

But I'm all right. Nothing happens to me at all.

I just stand there solid as the sheep bollard, the frayed end of a rope in my hand watching him

Burn.

96

AXE

I don't sleep much after that.

I understand that there is probably no more meaning to Peter burning in my dream than there was to the bees with boiled sweet abdomens. But it doesn't feel like that. It feels like there is meaning only I don't like that meaning.

I try to take my mind off things with Concentration.

I concentrate on the soft sucking sounds of the boy on the floor. But that just makes me think of something else I don't like.

The promise.

Papa always said: *You should never make a promise you can't keep, Mhairi.*

Yes, Papa.

Or, as Muma always said: *Our family aren't quitters, Mhairi. If you don't see your way around a problem at first, you just have to think a bit harder.*

Yes, Muma. I know that too, but it doesn't help because I've been thinking and thinking and not getting anywhere at all.

When the first rays of light come through my bedroom curtains and I'm still awake, I decide to get up. I dress and very quietly, so as not to wake Grandmother, go downstairs and out the back door and up to the gate that leads through the field to the hill where the Leuchram Burn is. It's by this gate that Grandmother has the little wooden lean-to where she keeps her logs.

And also her axe.

I pick up the axe. It's extremely heavy but not very sharp. I know this because I run my finger along the blade, which is thick and slightly rusty from being kept outside. But it's the right sort of axe for splitting logs and that's what I'm going to do.

If you want to think, Papa always said, *do something physical. If your conscious brain is engaged in a task, it gives your unconscious mind a little more freedom. I always do this*, Papa added, *when I have a problem to which I think there is no solution.*

I roll Grandmother's chopping stump out of the lean-to and position it on the piece of level ground where she positions it. I know it's the right place because of the lie of the earth and the scattering of wood chips. I take the first of the logs to be split from beneath the tarpaulin that Grandmother wraps them in to keep them dry. Splitting logs is one of the many jobs to be done around the house that Grandmother has not offered to me. Perhaps she thinks I'd be dangerous with an axe. I position the log in the centre of the stump and then I lift this axe.

It's so heavy that I feel the muscles in my upper right arm strain as I try to keep my right hand (which is near the axe head) steady in order to begin the swing, to bring the axe up from behind my back so I can get a good, long downward stroke. As soon as the axe passes over my head I feel gravity take charge, I feel the axe head falling like a stone, thunk into the wood. But I haven't got the blow quite right and the blade sticks in the wood and I have to pull it free and begin again.

So I do.

Again and again I lift that axe and let it fall. Perfect my technique, go for the edge of the log, follow the lines of any existing cracks, get my eye in, swing the axe blade higher and higher, bringing my hands together more swiftly on the handle, sliding them down with the force of gravity, so when I finally hit, I hit true.

And the log splits.

Our family aren't quitters, Mhairi.

It cleaves in two.

Think!

And I take the two pieces and I hit again

Never make a promise you can't keep, Mhairi.

And again.

Think!

And again.

I'm a rhythm, a production line. I'm a machine.

Think. Think. Think!

I feel sweat pouring down my face but I don't stop to wipe it away.

Harder. Think harder!

I keep going, smashing those logs, splitting them, one after another. I'm working so hard I don't hear Grandmother come out of the house and I don't see her until she's stood right in front of me. Grandmother isn't one of those people stopped by a little log-chopping. If Grandmother wants to say something she says it.

'They've set the court date,' she says. 'Three weeks on Thursday.'

The axe is up, nothing can stop it falling.

So it falls.

Crack!

'Two days after your fifteenth birthday,' Grandmother adds, watching the wood split clean in two. 'But don't worry. As I said, the law isn't retrospective, so it doesn't change anything.'

Wrong. Wrong about this as about so many other things.

Fifteen.

This fifteenth birthday changes everything.

I lay down the weapon. I wipe my brow. My thinking is done.

I finally know what I am going to do.

97

MY BIRTHDAY

On this birthday-which-changes-everything Grandmother bakes a cake. Grandmother is not particularly interested in cakes so I take it as a peace offering. My refusal, over the last few weeks, to fill in those blank pages in my Global Passport has not made her happy.

Grandmother says: *It'll count against you if you write nothing.*

But my decision means there is no need for me to fill in these pages. Besides, when I look at these pages they don't look blank to me at all. I've finally admitted to myself what I've known all along. That I was never going to be able to write on these pages because, in my mind, there is no room. These pages are full, crammed already. They are soaked with pus and crawling with chiggers.

Grandmother says: *If you don't help yourself, how can you expect anyone else to help you?*

And yet she is trying to help me. She's drafting – and redrafting – a statement on her laptop. It's about my life since I left the Sudan – what she knows about it anyway. It's about my age and how I lost my parents and the miles I've travelled since. It's about why I might have done something so completely-out-of-character as falling in with an illegal alien. Grandmother is also writing about Peter. For these things I have to be grateful. Just as I am grateful for the cake.

The cake is vanilla with a layer of cream and jam she made last year from the strawberries in her own garden. She lays the cake on a wooden board and then searches in the kitchen cupboard for some candles.

'Thought so,' she says, extracting a little plastic container.

The candles in the box are all blue, or shades of blue, and almost all of them have been used at least once before. Perhaps they were ones she used in Before. When Papa was young. Grandmother is good at conserving things.

'You can help her blow them out, Mohammed,' says Grandmother, as she arranges the candles in a ring on the cake. 'After we sing "Happy Birthday".' She lights the different-lengthed stubs of wax. 'Do you know "Happy Birthday", Mohammed?'

The boy is not listening to Grandmother, he's just staring at all the tiny little flames as if they were the most captivating thing he'd seen in all of his life.

Grandmother clears her throat and begins. 'Happy . . .'

'Wait,' I say then, 'wait,' and I drop to my knees. My eyes are now on the same level as the boy's, the same level as the candles. 'What about you?' I say. 'When's your birthday?'

He doesn't reply of course, but then he's lost in the flames anyway. And I wonder if they have such birthday candle lighting rituals wherever he comes from and, if they do, whether he's also imagining a woman in an orange scarf with a smile on her face as well as a match in her hand?

'You must have had a birthday,' I say, 'since you've been travelling. Yes? Had a birthday, but no chance to celebrate it, maybe?'

Still nothing. No reaction of any kind. So I blow the candles out in one breath, just to get his attention.

'Hey!' says Grandmother.

But it does the job. He looks at me.

'So exactly how old are you? Five? Six? Seven?'

Very slowly, he raises his left hand and spreads his thumb and fingers wide.

'Five then,' says Grandmother.

But he's not finished. He adds a rather uncertain thumb from his other hand.

'Six,' I say. 'Six?'

He nods, or maybe it's a shrug. I pull the fifteen candles out of the cake anyway, rearrange them in the shape of the number six.

'There. Now it's our cake. Yours and mine. Do you want to light the candles yourself, now you're so grown-up?'

And he does. And Grandmother doesn't interfere, doesn't try to help or guide him. Just lets him get on with it.

Then, in a strong, tuneful voice, Grandmother sings and the boy and I both blow (simultaneously), and if anyone had taken a picture at exactly that moment you might have thought we were all just one big happy family.

98

THE JOURNEY TO LAMLASH

The court day dawns very blue. I thought I would be afraid but I'm not. I elect to sit in the back of the car and the boy comes to join me which leaves Grandmother driving alone in the front with only the boy's suitcase for company.

It takes nineteen minutes to get to Lamlash and most of the journey is along the coast. I look out of the window at the sunlight on the sea. A light breeze is lifting a million golden scallop-shells on the surface of the water. I think about this sea and how it wraps around the island, wraps around the world, lapping at places which otherwise would be separate. A vast, stretching, embracing sea of sunshine blue. Oh Papa, how beautiful the world is this morning!

The boy is not looking out the window. The boy is staring at his hands in his lap. Of course, I haven't told him exactly what I'm going to do. So maybe he is nervous. In fact, I know he's nervous. I know this because when Grandmother packed him this small suitcase of clothes and wash things last night he added some stones. Not his sucking stone (which he has as always in his pocket) but a selection of grey shale pebbles and red-brown old

Corrie sandstones. As if he believed he wasn't coming back tonight. Not to Corrie, not to the harbour, not to Grandmother. As if he believed he and his suitcase were going to go straight from the court to Skitby School Detention Centre. Which is what Grandmother has told him.

After Brodick, the road turns inland for a few kilometres, which makes it all the more spectacular when you round the final bend and see Lamlash Bay laid out like a blue lagoon in front of you, the low-lying mound of the Holy Isle shimmering just across the water. The Holy Isle makes me think of Peter, of course, and how we nearly kissed that day. But didn't. How I ended up under a tarpaulin.

At the northern end of the bay, Grandmother takes a sharp left, doesn't follow the road round now, but tracks the shore eastwards for a couple of minutes until she reaches the court. There is no notice on this building to announce it as a court. If you didn't know it was the court you'd think it was a slightly oversized bungalow; low-lying, grey, unremarkable. Not the sort of place where there might be violence. Grandmother parks up.

We get out and walk to the entrance. I have a sudden inclination to take the boy's hand. But I don't. Court official Esther is waiting for us by the steps. Peter has apparently arrived already.

'Just to be clear,' says Esther, 'the taser-tags are both in sleep mode. Of course, should there be any attempt to escape . . .'

'Don't worry,' interrupts Grandmother, 'there won't be.'

And, today, she's right. Because there is no escape. Not from this building and not from the past. That's what I've decided.

Which is why today I have come armed with nothing but the final key to Castle.

99

PETER, THE STONE AND THE GUN

The courtroom itself is also unremarkable. Just a rectangular meeting space with a polished oval table on a dais one end and seating for about fifty people the other. Before it was requisitioned for a court, it was a marriage hall apparently and that's what it still looks like. The chairs painted gold with red plush seats.

There are about ten people in these seats and, of course, they stare at us as we come in. Officials, journalists, members of the public, I don't know and I don't care. My eyes are taken by Peter, the Stone and the gun.

The Stone lies between the oval table and the public seating. It's not as it was in my dream, not a smallish, hollowed-out, one-person stone. No. It's large and flat. A heavy, brutal block of grey limestone about ten centimetres high and at least two metres wide. Directly behind it are three chairs. In one of the chairs is Peter.

Peter is staring straight ahead – across the Stone – to the oval table on the dais where, I suppose, the councillors will eventually sit. Esther has brought us through the side door, so that's how I first see him, from the side. In profile, he does not look like the

323

Peter I know. But this may also be because he is wearing a suit which is slightly too small for him and he has brushed his hair and it falls unusually straight about his face. I'm used to seeing him working, so his stillness is also odd, I realise. Instead of being broad and bronze and mobile, he looks constrained and white. Unlike everyone else in the room, he does not turn towards us as we enter.

The man behind him does look though. It's Peter's father. At least he looks how I remember Peter's father, only older and greyer. I think of him as a kindly man, a man with a fiddle and a smile, but his glance is not kindly. He looks at me quickly and then turns away like a shutter going down. Perhaps this is why Peter is staring straight ahead, held by the burn of his father's gaze in his back. I wonder where Peter's mother is then because the chairs either side of his father are empty. This makes me realise that I haven't really asked Peter anything about his life since I left the island. People who are not self-absorbed, normal people, they ask about such things.

Esther indicates that the boy and I should take the two remaining chairs behind the Stone – the boy in the middle. This means I cannot touch Peter and Peter cannot touch me. It also means that, if I look at him, or he looks at me, everyone in this courtroom will see. And, for some reason, I do not want to give them this pleasure, so I look at my feet.

Which means looking at the Stone.

Like the brick in the desert the Stone, when you get close to it, is rather beautiful. Rugged, gritted, pocked. But not red. Not yet anyway. No, it's grey, or flecked grey. Tinged with green, shot through with veins of white. Porous too, I think. As the brick was porous. Porous things soak up liquids..Fresh red blood, for instance. Which dries, in time, to a stain of brown.

Peter is still looking at the oval table. Which means, I realise, he's actually looking at the gun. The gun he told me that they move every fifteen minutes during a case so, if it comes to shooting someone, every member of the council is equally likely to have to pull the trigger. I look at the gun too. It's not a small, portable weapon like my bulletless one, the sort that slips easily into a pocket. No. It's a large, ugly, institutional plastic pistol made by a 3-D printer. It's meant to be large because it's meant to be seen.

Then I remember how Peter described Grandmother's island justice. Real consequences, things not hidden away.

Death you can actually taste.

100

THE COUNCIL

It's only a moment before Esther says, 'All stand please,' and the InterGenerational Council file in and take their seats at the oval table. Because Grandmother cannot be part of the council today there are just the five of them and they sit age order left to right. I know this because the triangular identity badges in front of each of them do not bear their names but the decade they represent. Council members 25–34, 35–44 and 55–64 are all men in dark suits. 45–54 is a woman in a bright scarlet jacket wearing bright scarlet lipstick. These are the elected members. The final member, 15–24, is randomly allocated, as I remember Peter telling me, on a case-by-case basis to cope with conflicts arising from those still in full-time education.

Today the final member is small and wiry and she's picking at her wrist.

It's Finola.

101

THE PLEAS

I have no time to consider the whys and wherefores of Finola's release from Skitby Detention Centre or the nature of what is – or is not – random, because Scarlet Jacket is already calling the court to order. The gun is sitting in front of her which seems to entitle her to open proceedings, which she does by introducing Mr Robert Binnie. Mr Binnie is a thin, crabbed man who sits hunched over a three-screen nanonet at a desk just below the dais.

'Any points of law on which the council needs advice,' says Scarlet Jacket, 'will be dealt with by our legal expert, Mr Robert Binnie. Though I do not foresee any particular complications in the matters before us today,' she checks her schedule, 'that of the State versus Bain and McKensie and the attendant Deportation Order. Will you stand please, Mr McKensie?'

For a moment, I have no idea who Mr McKensie is and then Peter stands up.

'Step up to the Stone, if you please, Mr McKensie.'

Mr McKensie steps up on to the Stone. And of course, it makes him taller, eight or ten centimetres taller. It also makes him look very exposed.

'Are you Peter Cleland McKensie of Corrie Bay?' asks Scarlet Jacket.

'Yes,' replies Peter in the softest voice I've ever heard.

'Peter McKensie, you are accused of aiding and abetting the trafficking of an unknown illegal alien into Arran on the 4th May this year in contravention of the Scotland Mainland and Federated Territories Immigration Act. How do you plead?'

'Guilty,' says Peter.

'Thank you, you may sit.'

Peter sits and then it's my turn to be called. I step up to the Stone where I dreamt all the words of gore.

'Are you Mhairi Anne Bain of Corrie Bay?' asks Scarlet Jacket.

'Yes,' I say and, in this strange rather Slow Time moment of acknowledging myself, I allow myself the luxury of wondering about randomness after all. I wonder exactly how random this woman's choice of a red, red jacket is. I wonder about the random choice of a random person aged 15–24 for the court of Lamlash turning out to be Finola, whose knife I stole. Finola, who has every reason to hate me. But then, life, I suppose, is a series of such random moments. Such as the one that brought us all here to today. The crack of a small twig on a hillside, the noise that made me turn to see a dying man holding the hand of a child.

'Mhairi Anne Bain, you are accused of wilfully trafficking an unknown illegal alien into Arran on the 4th May this year in contravention of the Scotland Mainland and Federated Territories Immigration Act. How do you plead?'

'Guilty,' I say. Of course guilty. If it's a crime not to abandon a child. Guilty of the other crime too, the opposite one. The one which is locked behind the final door in the tower of Castle.

'Stand down,' says Scarlet Jacket.

I stand down.

How quick these things are. How apparently simple.

'Before sentence is passed,' Scarlet Jacket adds, 'the council will now take a moment or two to revisit the written submissions in mitigation.'

The members confer, they push Global paperwork between them, reference documents on their nanoscreens. They read, presumably, what Grandmother has written on my behalf. On Peter's. They talk long enough for Esther to move the gun from Scarlet Jacket to Dark Suit *35–44*. So it's Dark Suit who finally asks me to stand again and says: 'The council notes that you have chosen not to append any Provisional Credits to your Global Passport. Is that correct, Ms Bain?'

'Yes,' I say. 'That's correct.'

'And why is that, may I ask, Ms Bain? And before you answer, I should warn you that the court is minded to allocate Mr McKensie's years against you.'

'I have not supplied any Provisional Credits,' I say, 'because I don't expect to be leaving this court alive.'

And all the people who have been half-asleep in the plush red public seats wake up. They gasp.

'Kindly explain yourself,' says Dark Suit.

So I do.

'I am fifteen years old,' I say. 'The age of majority for gifting Life Years. When the court has deducted whatever number of years are appropriate for my trafficking offence, I intend to donate all my remaining years to my brother here.' And I point at the boy.

There is more hubbub, a current of excitement. It becomes clear which are the journalists in the public seating area. These men and women, who probably only came to the court because it was the High Councillor's granddaughter in the dock, go on to high alert. I imagine them typing their headlines: *First Blood to the Stone! Justice in Action! Death You Can Actually Taste!* There are exclamations, urgent whispers. But, for me, it's still just background noise to the two voices that count.

One voice is Grandmother's. She's on her feet, she can't help herself, even though she's sworn not to take part in proceedings today. 'That can't be legal,' she announces in a strident voice from the front of the court, trying to take some sort of control. 'A convicted trafficker gifting Life Years to the very alien she tried to traffic? Ridiculous.'

The second voice is Peter's and it's very soft. It barely makes its way to me across the boy's head.

'No,' says Peter. 'Please, Mhairi. No.'

102

THE RULES AND REGS

Mr Binnie makes short work of the legal niceties. The law, says Mr Binnie, (offering to list the particular statutes if the council so require) states quite clearly that discharged felons may indeed gift Life Years.

'Ms Bain being a "discharged felon", Mr Binnie adds, 'the minute she signs the formal court *Taking the Needle Agreement to Sentence* document.'

'So long, of course,' Mr Binnie is pleased to clarify, 'that the aforementioned discharged felon has full and certain right to residency under the terms of the Scotland Mainland and Federated Territories Residency Act.

'A criterion which,' says Mr Binnie, 'Ms Bain appears to fulfil.'

Moreover, any such validated resident may – it turns out – indeed gift Life Years to whomsoever they choose, irrespective of whether the recipient belongs to Equator North, Equator South or even Equator Central.

'This is a long-held precedent,' states Mr Binnie, 'predicated on the case of White v. Assiz, where it was asserted that there was no accreted disbenefit to global population numbers . . .'

'Yes, yes,' interrupts Dark Suit 35–44. 'And?'

'And,' continues Mr Binnie, making it clear he would have preferred in the interests of accuracy to have cited the full case, 'and, and except, it is normal practice in any such case when a gifter wishes to gift the entirety of their remaining years, to suggest a "cooling off" period of at least ten days before signature, in case the gifter changes their mind.'

'I won't change my mind,' I say.

'In which case,' says Mr Binnie, 'it is merely a matter of establishing whether the gifter is of sound mind. Or,' he adds, looking at me over the top of his glasses, 'not.'

Esther moves the gun from Dark Suit 35–44 to Dark Suit 25–34.

103

MY RIGHT MIND

There are many things I could present to the court to prove that I am in my right mind.

I could tell them, for instance, what I learnt from Muma. Muma said: *Whatever happens, Mhairi, you have to stay alive*. Well, I've stayed alive. I've stayed alive while others have died and I know now that staying alive is not enough. Not the only thing that matters. It's how you stay alive. What you do – or do not do – to stay alive. What you risk and what you sacrifice. That's what matters and I have sometimes, Muma, made the wrong choices.

I'm so sorry, Muma.

Or I could talk about the camp. I could say, Grandmother's right. I can't care about all those strangers in the camp. Probably couldn't even accurately count the numbers huddled under those tarpaulins. Their lives – they are all out of my control. And yes, I have certainly learnt, with some bitterness, Grandmother, that there are things in life which you cannot control. Things you must let go of. But that, I think, makes the things you can control even more important. And one of the things I can control, Grandmother, is what I choose to do with my own life. So no, I can't save all those unknown people in the camp. But I can save the boy, Grandmother, and I intend to.

Which brings me to Papa, to what I finally realised he was trying to teach me all that time. About being who you are. Or more precisely, who I am. Me. Mhairi Bain. Of course, there have been times on this long, long journey where I've lost sight of myself, become all blurry in the mirror, unable to see the edges of myself. But times also when there's been some definition. Like the time when I spun my gun in front of the Imgrim in the detention centre even though I knew I had no bullets. A little gesture to remind me of myself, my defiance, my refusal to give in. Just as you were yourself in the desert, Papa, when you got out of that jeep with your open, open hands. Which spoke of your open, open, ever-hopeful heart. And now I want to do what you would do, Papa. You who taught me a kindness I seem sometimes to have forgotten. Because, Papa, you would save the boy. You would put him first. Say: *Look at this child, this innocent child, he deserves everything I can give, doesn't he?* And anyway, Papa, my own life means nothing, if you can't be proud of me.

And finally, there's Time. I've thought so much about Time. And what if I hold in this moment, this moment on the Blood Stone, all that is precious to me? Not just the boy and you, Papa, but all the goodness of the world as I've seen it. Large or small. The kindness of Miss Sperry, the decency of Dr Naik, the solid, trusting dependability of Peter. What if I roll this goodness up with some desert stars and a sea spun with golden sun-shells and the cascading water of the Leuchram Burn? What if I hold all these things around me in a bright cloak of Now Time as I wait for the bullet?

It will be enough, surely.

104

WHAT I ACTUALLY TELL THEM

I do not think, however, that the court will understand these things. Understand about Muma and Papa and Control and Beauty and Time, so I don't say any of that. Instead, I get out of my chair, step on to the Blood Stone and put the final key in the final lock of the final door in the tower of Castle.

'A long time ago,' I say, 'in another land, there was another boy called Muhammed. He was older than the boy you see here beside me, but not much older. About ten. The son of my parents' driver in the Sudan where we lived for seven years. I didn't know him well. Not at first. But I got to know him. He was a funny, chatty child. He collected cigarette packets and jokes about donkeys. He could tell you a surprising amount about the hijleej tree. And he held, so he told me, the world record for spitting water melon pips. Now, I'm sure I don't need to repeat what you must have already read in my Grandmother's submissions about what happened in that desert kiosk, a year and a lifetime away. All you need to know is that Muhammad lost his father there. And I lost both my mother and my father. We escaped though, Muhammad and I.

Escaped together into the desert. There were times, when the vultures sat on the sand ahead of us, I thought we wouldn't make it. But we did make it. At least to the border with Egypt. Muhammad's grandfather lived in a village the Sudanese side of that border. That's actually why he'd been travelling with us that day, to make a visit with his father to his grandparents' house. I knew – roughly – where that village was located. It would have been barely out of my way for me to take him there, see him to safety. But I didn't do that. Because I needed Muhammad to stay with me. Because he spoke Arabic and I didn't. Because, with Muhammad, through Muhammad, I could negotiate with the smugglers, get safely across the border, head to Cairo, where I had a ticket for a plane to England. So I lied to Muhammad. I said we were nowhere near his village. I said, with the way the border ran, it would be better for him if we crossed and then he tracked backwards. I said he'd be safer with me. With me to look after him. And of course, he was still in shock, traumatised by the death of his father, so he believed me. Or if he didn't believe me, he came with me anyway, perhaps because he was young and used to having people telling him what to do.

'After we crossed the border, we rejoined the smugglers' lorry. Drove a hundred and sixty kilometres north before being dropped to walk again. It wasn't what I was expecting, I told Muhammad, and now it was too far for him to walk back alone. He had Equator Central papers, it would be no problem, I told him, when we got to Cairo, for me to get someone to accompany him the whole way back. I'd even use my last bit of money to pay for it, I said. I said that without ever expecting to have to pay, because he was ill. He'd been ill for miles. Since Sudan, in fact. Had had diarrhoea since drinking the water a blind girl gave him near the pyramids at Meroe. He also had chiggers. Chiggers are tiny spider-like things that burrow into your skin and then they itch. And if you scratch them, and Muhammad scratched them all the time, the wounds get infected. They fill with pus. Muhammad's ankles got infected and then his feet. Soon he couldn't walk. He was slowing me down. I was worried I wouldn't make it to Cairo before the date on my plane ticket expired. Ironic, considering how I never made that plane anyway. How I got picked up, put in detention – deported. But I didn't know about that when I walked away from Muhammad that final time. Just left him on the side of the road. Walked on without him and didn't look back.'

This last bit is the only untruth in the story. I did look back and that's when I saw that look in his eyes, the look that said so clearly: 'You're leaving me here because I'm going to die, aren't I?' Said it with his eyes because he was too weak to talk by then.

And I still turned around and walked away.

'So you see,' I tell the court, 'it only seems fair that I give to this boy what I failed to give to the other.'

There's a kind of silence then. At least there is in the courtroom. In my mind, there's an almighty crashing. A smashing and screaming as each block of stone in the tower at the centre of Castle comes crashing down around me. But, despite the noise, the stones don't all come down all at once. No. They come down individually and very slowly. They come down in Arrested Time so I can see each one falling. See them as they hit me. One by one. But I don't move to get out of the way. Of course not.

I just stand until there is nothing left but rubble and blood.

105

WHO LOVES WHOM

The council take a vote. Four to one they decide I am in my right mind. The one is Finola. I do not know why Finola thinks I am not in my right mind. I expect she has a game plan, though I do not know what it is. Unless it is simply to refuse whatever it is that I want. This can be revenge of a sort.

Grandmother stands up again. 'Surely any decision concerning sanity needs to be made by a psychiatrist?' she says. 'Verified. Verified by a psychiatrist. Or a doctor, at least!'

'May I remind you, High Councillor,' says Younger Dark Suit, 'that, with respect, proceedings today are out of your jurisdiction. If you make any further interruptions, I will have to count it as contempt and insist on your removal from the court.'

Grandmother likes Rules and Regs so she has to sit down. Mr Binnie is, however, entitled to speak.

'I'm afraid I've found an impediment,' Mr Binnie says as though he's rather pleased with this fact. 'Gifts of Life Years in these circumstances do not, of course, serve to extend a recipient's life, merely to entitle that recipient to full residency for the period to which the gifter would otherwise been entitled.'

'And your meaning?' inquires Younger Dark Suit.

'Only that if the intended recipient is a child, as in this case, the Life Year Deed Agreement may not be signed unless a competent adult agrees to sponsor the child. In effect, agrees to be responsible for that child at least until they obtain the age of majority.'

There's a silence.

And I wait

And wait

For Grandmother to step into that silence, contempt of court notwithstanding. To speak up. To declare that she'll be there for the boy, that she'll stand with him, sponsor him, take him home to Corrie and start helping him unpack that tiny suitcase.

'Mrs Bain?' says Younger Dark Suit, finally, giving her the invitation.

Grandmother stays sitting, her mouth quite shut.

It's Peter who gets to his feet.

Peter who steps on to the Stone.

'I'll take him,' says Peter.

Peter – who never seemed to care much for the boy. You never know, I think then, how people really are – who they are – until you see them at a cliff edge. See how they behave when it's just them – and the drop.

'I'll sponsor him. Look after him,' Peter adds. 'For as long as it takes. I swear.'

Oh Papa, you would like the man that this Peter is becoming.

'I just ask one thing in return,' continues Peter, 'if I might, I mean, with the court's permission, please – please don't allocate any Life Years due to me to Mh— to Ms Bain. I will serve those years myself.'

No, mouths Peter's father. No!

But Peter's not looking at his father. Peter is a grown man now and he's looking at me. He's a good man. A man who has heard the story of Muhammad and who continues, even so, to believe the best of me. Wants to give me a second chance. But I cannot afford take this chance. Because I know something Peter doesn't know. About the burning. About how it's not just Muhammad. It's Muma and Papa. It's everyone that ever gets close to me and to whom I get close.

'If you gift me those years, Peter,' I say then, 'I will simply add them to what I can give the boy.'

This is not a gentle thing to say to Peter. His face tells me this. But it is better to see the hurt in his eyes now than the burning and sliding later. Because this is what Peter doesn't know. How everyone I love suffers. How they get bullets in their chests or chiggers in their feet or their back dug out for taser-tags. How they burn and burn and burn and I just stand there looking.

'Enough,' says Younger Dark Suit. 'While the court appreciates your offer to sponsor the boy, Mr McKensie, it is not for you, and certainly not for you, Ms Bain, to attempt to allocate or reallocate any part of the sentencing. It is for the council to make judgement; it is on that matter that we will now confer.'

They confer, Peter sits, I sit. The boy sits.

'Do you understand?' I whisper to the boy.

It's been complicated. He's only six. He stares. Waits. Like a held breath.

'Peter's agreed to take you. So you can't be deported. You'll go back to Corrie. Go back tonight. He'll take good care of you.' I'm whispering but I'm sure Peter can hear. And I want him to hear. 'He'll even pile stones with you. As tall as you like!'

And then I lean down and say something I never thought I'd hear myself say to anyone.

'I love you,' I say to the boy.

And then I repeat it to see if it stays true.

I love you.

It stays true. It doesn't slide at all.

106

WHO STAYS AND WHO GOES

The court has made a decision. There's a lot of speech-making and legal jargon so I only listen to the important things. Peter's years are suspended in recognition of his agreement to sponsor the boy. I am to be deducted (with mitigation) a total of twenty-five years. This leaves me free to gift the boy my remaining thirty-four years. The only thing that stands between me and the Blood Stone now is my own signature. And they have given me a pen.

'I don't understand you!' shouts Peter at me. 'It isn't right!'

But it is right.

'It shouldn't be the Stone,' says Grandmother. 'We have moved beyond the blood crime to the legitimate gifting of Life Years. Anyone gifting Life Years is entitled to the needle!'

She's trying to buy me time. It takes time to get to an End of Life Clinic. Time to change your mind.

'*Justice needs not just to be done but be seen to be done* – isn't that what you always said, Aileen?' Younger Dark Suit says, as the journalists tap and scribble, adding, 'Meanwhile, I believe I asked you to refrain from interrupting and you have not refrained. Esther – can you please remove Mrs Bain from the court?'

It seems unlikely to me that Grandmother will go. But she does go. I don't think it's because Esther has two burly court officials to help her, I think it's probably because Grandmother does not wish to see what is going to happen next. Perhaps Grandmother cares for me more than it sometimes seems.

I sign the piece of paper.

'You're insane,' shouts Peter. 'Insane! It doesn't have to be this way.' He says it as if I'm making a sacrifice. But there is no sacrifice in doing something for someone you love.

'And you can take Mr McKensie away too,' says Younger Dark Suit.

'No,' says Peter.

'Yes,' says his father and begins to steer his son towards the exit.

'Has everyone gone mad?' says Peter.

Peter's father looks back over his shoulder. 'I'm so sorry, Mhairi,' Peter's father says. It sounds quite genuine. And of course those looks like shutters coming down were only what any parent would feel about someone threatening their child, I suppose. So many things I'm still learning.

I keep my mind focused on the learning so as not to see Peter go. Or rather to not hear him. Although, of course, I can hear him. Those sudden huge choking sobs. Peter is raging and crying out loud and he doesn't care who knows about it. But it will pass for Peter. He deserves someone else and he will, no doubt, find that person. A good person, a kind person. Someone who will not stand by while he burns.

Soon only the council and a couple of expectant journalists with cameras remain.

And also the boy.

He hasn't moved an inch.

And part of me wants to ask him to go myself. But then I remember it will not be the worst thing he's ever seen and sometimes, finality can be helpful. It can help you believe. Stop walking those dead people about as though they are still alive.

So I say nothing and nobody else does either.

When all things are finally ready, the gun is in front of Finola.

107

WHAT FINOLA DOES

If you believe in eating meat, Papa always said, *you should be prepared to kill the animal yourself.*

I wonder if this is the same with human beings and justice? That, in this case, to pull the trigger, you have to actually believe in the justice, believe in the Blood Stone? Finola is not an elected member of the council. Finola has been randomly assigned to the council. Randomly assigned to be the one who pulls the trigger.

And she's dithering.

The court has been cleared, the decision made, the papers signed. Everything is in order.

I am standing on the Blood Stone. Elevated ten centimetres taller than myself: high and exposed. She is less than two metres away from me and she could not miss. She is aiming at my heart. She is probably doing this because my chest area is larger than my head area and she wants to be sure. When she fires.

If she fires.

The 3-D printed gun looks bulky in her hands. It would look bulky in anyone's hands, but she has those tiny, tiny wrists and those twitchy, nervous fingers. If she's not careful, she'll pull that trigger by mistake. She's shaking enough to. Puts a second hand on the plastic grip plate to steady herself. Now she has two hands on the gun. How long does it take a person to fire a gun? How long did it take that nervous young soldier with the predator pack in the desert kiosk?

No time at all.

No Time.

'For god's sake,' I shout, 'shoot!'

Because all this delay, all this dithering, is pulling at the bright cloak of Now Time. It's allowing me to glimpse a place where I can't go. A place I am forbidden. Because of the burning. Yes. This tearing of the cloak is allowing me a final look at the future. And not just one future either, but all my possible futures. There they are standing just ahead of me, almost within touching distance, these bright, bright places of possibilities. Papa's world! Where you could take the hand of a child and walk him to a place you love and the people there would recognise him, stretch out their upturned hands and cry: *Oh, welcome! You are welcome here!* A land where longings could be real, where there could be someone waiting, someone that I could love and them not burn. Where kisses might not end beneath tarpaulins. Where kisses might end on sweet mouths beneath open skies. Where I could say those words: *I love you.* And someone – someone – could actually say them back.

And I'd believe them.

Believe them

Believe I wasn't bad after all.

And Finola's another person I've damaged. Finola has every reason to hate to me. Finola would be right to hate me. But this is the cruellest thing she could ever do, this dithering.

'Please,' I beg and I have never begged.

But I'm burning now.

Finally I'm burning. Only I'm burning to live. Oh Muma! Oh Papa! This whole beautiful world!

'Can't you just do it!' I scream at Finola.

'No,' she says. 'I can't.'

'It's me,' I scream. 'Ret1787.' Though she must have read the papers. 'The one that took your knife. In Skitby. That got you searched and stripped and sent to the Management Unit. Where they shut you alone in the dark. Where they only fed you water. Don't you recognise me?'

'Yes,' Finola says. 'Of course I recognise you. That's why I can't do it.' Her hands have stopped shaking now. And, all of a sudden, she doesn't seem so small any more either. She rises big, bigger than Grandmother, bigger than the courtroom itself as she says: 'Because of that place. Because of knowing some of the things you know. And because,' she says finally, laying down the gun, 'I always thought, in another life, the life perhaps we both should have led, you and I might have been friends.'

108

THE LAST TWO MINUTES

Many things happen at once then. They pile on top of each other. The first is Mr Binnie.

Mr Binnie says to Finola: 'This is most irregular. If you knew the defendant you should have said so. No one can sit on the council if they know the defendant. It's a serious offence not to declare such a thing. Why do you think the High Councillor stood down?'

And he starts reaching for the gun.

At the same time, through the side door, I see Peter. He's not sobbing now, not at all. Perhaps Peter, being Peter, needed just a little bit of extra time to catch up with himself. I remember that time he came to knock on Grandmother's door the afternoon she received the Interim Report, how he knocked and came in as if he didn't need anyone's permission any more. That's what he does now. He just comes back into court through the side door. As though he's suddenly seen the light, Papa's light, Papa's world, our right world, and he will make it happen. He will write a different future. Though it might just be that he needs to know why there's been no shot.

Esther meanwhile is saying: 'I think, in any case, Member 15–24's time with the gun is up. I think the gun should be with Member 55–64 now.' Member 55–64 is an Older Dark Suit, who has not said anything to date but now says: 'Give me the gun.'

From the look on Finola's face, I think she would be quite happy to relinquish the gun but it's difficult for her to do so when Esther and Mr Binnie and Older Dark Suit are all reaching for it simultaneously.

I can't stop the thought that none of this indecision and fumbling would have happened if Grandmother was in charge. Which is when I see her appear beside Peter in the doorway.

And then I think I know what the ending will be after all. That Grandmother will walk through that door and take the gun and fire it on behalf of her community. Fire it for the greater good. For all things bigger than ourselves. And I wouldn't blame her because everyone can only finally be who they are.

But actually Grandmother is barely over the threshold when she says: 'What on earth is going on!'

And that alone is enough to trigger things. It certainly triggers the gun.

109

THE ROUND HOLE

I do not hear the gunshot. I do not see the bullet. Of course not. Few things travel faster than a bullet. Except love perhaps. Which is why I see the boy.

I see him in Slow Time.

Very, very slow time.

He starts moving just before the struggle on the dais, makes his decision right in the middle of the endless fumbling. As if he's finally lost patience with the adults. As if, quite suddenly, he knows that it's all down to him. He's just had enough. And if he had a voice to speak, he'd speak. Stop this nonsense once and for all. But he doesn't have a voice, not after what they've all done to him. Or, if not them, others like them. So all he can do is act. So he acts.

He steps right up. On to the stone.

How he gets in front of me, that I don't know. But his head is at about the level of my heart. Which is where the gun is pointing. And he just stands there. Right in front of my heart. Which is when I realise it's not about them at all. It's about us. Him and me. About the thing between us that is stronger than all of them.

For there he stands.

And stands.

This little titan.

Stands there for about a thousand years.

Saying *I love you* without any words at all.

And I hear myself scream: 'No, no, NO!'

But screaming has never been of any use. And it's no use now with the bullet coming.

Smack it comes. Straight into his forehead.

And, of course, I immediately put him into Arrested Time. Try to stop him falling, just like I did with Papa. Falling but never fallen. And I do keep him there for a moment, but he's only very little and so close to the ground anyway, that it's just a breath before he's laid right out on his back at my feet.

The hole in his head is round and surprisingly neat. And there isn't a lot of blood. Just a splash really. I watch it soak red into the grey limestone.

110

WALKING OUT

I lift the boy up. I take him in my arms. This is only the second time I have ever held him. The first time was when I caught him as he jumped from the detention centre window at Skitby. He felt dense then, heavy. He does not seem heavy now. He seems light as a bird.

His deep-as-cups eyes are still open. I always wondered what was right at the bottom of those deep, deep eyes. But, whatever it was, I will never know, because it's gone. Like a candle going out. I slide his eyelids shut as if that would give him peace. Although I know he is beyond peace now. Peace is something people pretend a lot about.

Now I'm holding him closely I see a little singe around the hole in his forehead. A tiny ring of burning. I bend over him, kiss him. Kiss that wound. The scorching is rough against my lips and the blood tastes, as blood always does, of iron.

I carry him towards the door of the court, towards the outside world.

Behind me there is noise. Recriminations. Whose hand was on that gun? Whose hand was finally on the gun!

As if it mattered.

They all murdered him and none of them did. What else is there to know?

But at least it stops them from caring about me and the boy. So I keep walking.

Grandmother, who would not speak up for the boy, would not take him back into her home and heart, puts a hand out to me as I get to the door. Tries to take my arm.

But my arms are full.

And Peter, Peter says: 'Oh Mhairi.' But he doesn't try to touch me and he doesn't try to touch the boy. One day, Papa, I will thank Peter for his understanding, his goodness, thank him for offering himself as father to this boy. I will also tell him what this boy has just taught me. That home isn't just a place after all. It's people. The people you love. The people you refuse to lose.

I keep walking.

I walk through the car park and down to the shore. Stand under the arc of heaven. Stand on grass and grey pebbles, looking across the bay to Inis Shroin, the Holy Isle. The sun is lower now, but it still throws tiny golden coins on the surface of the water.

Our family aren't quitters, Mhairi.

So I begin again.

I am alive, Muma!

And Papa.

Papa, the world is

The world

Oh, Papa

ACKNOWLEDGEMENTS

Much of my thinking about the environment has been shaped in discussion with Tom Burke. I first knew Tom when I was in my early twenties and he was Director of Friends of the Earth. He now heads up the independent climate change think-tank – E3G. All environmental opinions, inferences and projections in this book are clearly mine – but any weight or wisdom they have, that I lay at his feet. One day I hope the world will be the better place for which you have always worked, Tom.

Librarians are always important. Huge thanks to Jeanette Brooker, librarian at Khartoum International Community School, who first invited me to visit the Sudan. And to the visionary educationalist, Samia Omar, who set up KICS and generously facilitated my post-visit trip into the desert to sit beneath that umbrella of stars.

I also took trips in the UK – walked where I knew Mhairi was going to walk. Particular thanks to Elaine Cooper and Robert Dawson-Scott in Glasgow, not least for the introduction to Ruth Johnston and her marvellous book *Glasgow Necropolis: Afterlives – Tales of Interments*. Robert was also gentlemanly enough to offer to accompany me on my midnight ramble around the tombs.

Gratitude to those B&B owners who hosted me on Arran and answered my endless questions with such patience and grace. Particularly Sherie in Lamlash and Frances in Corrie. It was Sherie who directed me to an administrative building whose civil marriage room just happened to be labelled 'Old Court' and Frances who brought me the gorse which smelt of coconuts and loaned me Wellington boots so I could walk in the little burn that runs behind her harbour-side house. The Leuchram Burn . . . Sorry about Grandmother commandeering your house, Frances. She can be like that.

Back in London – the enthusiasm of the team at Hachette has been extraordinary. Thank you all so much. It's not always like this and it's buoyed me. Special mention for the sharp intelligence of Anne McNeil.

Then, as always, there is my agent, Clare Conville. Sine qua non.

And finally, there's the small boy I met at the edge of the desert in Morocco. A boy who said absolutely nothing – but whose laugh will remain with me for ever.

Nicky Singer's writing career kicked off at school, when she won a bar of chocolate for a story she'd written. This is easy money, she thought, I'll do this again …

Nicky is now an author of many books for children and adults across fiction and non-fiction. She has also written plays. Her first children's book *Feather Boy* won the Blue Peter 'Book of the Year' Award and was adapted for TV (winning a BAFTA for Best Children's Drama) and commissioned by the National Theatre as a musical. In 2012 her play *Island* (about ice-bears and the nature of reality) premiered at the National Theatre and toured 40 London schools. She subsequently re-wrote *Island* as a novel with illustrations by former Children's Laureate, Chris Riddell. Nicky lives in Brighton but always feels like she is coming home when she crosses the border into Scotland, the land of her grandparents.

Sadly, these days she is rarely paid in bars of chocolate.